THAT GIRL

ρ

JUDY MAY MURPHY is a Dubliner by birth and has a background as colourful as the characters in her novel. Her early childhood was spent in London, before her family moved back to Dublin, spending summers in Westboro, Massachusetts. On leaving school, she trained as a dancer in New York, while returning to Dublin with enough regularity to earn a BA in Drama and History of Art and a Masters in Literature with her thesis on the Micropolitics of Post-Modern Theatre (both from Trinity College). Her plays have been produced in Dublin and New York, and her adaptation of Samuel Beckett's *Embers* won her the ISDA award for Best Director.

She gave up theatre to work on *That Girl from Happy* and paid the rent by working as a casting assistant and chaperone on major Hollywood films, and writing comedy for radio. During this period she decamped to Kathmandu for six months, and more recently she spent a year in Paris, teaching acting and writing lyrics for French composers.

Judy May Murphy is currently living between Dublin and LA and is working on her second novel.

To Heston Friends

that girl from happy

Judy May Murphy

WOLFHOUND PRESS

Published in 2000 by
Wolfhound Press Ltd
68 Mountjoy Square
Dublin 1, Ireland
Tel: (353-1) 874 0354
Fax: (353-1) 872 0207

 Wolfhound Press receives financial assistance from The
Arts Council/An Chomhairle Ealaíon, Dublin, Ireland.

British Library Cataloguing in Publication Data
A catalogue record for this book is available from the British Library.

ISBN 0-86327-820-5

10 9 8 7 6 5 4 3 2 1

Cover Image: Slide File
Cover Design: Mark O'Neill
Typesetting: Wolfhound Press
Printed in the UK by Cox & Wyman Ltd., Reading, Berks.

Janie

Somewhere along the south coast of Ireland, there's a beach, a stretch of sand enclosed by small rock-caves at one end and a cluster of houses on a gentle hill at the other. Most people don't stop there, either because they are local and assume it to be worthless, being so familiar, or because they are tourists driving to a resort town four or so miles along the road. Even the stalwart amateur explorer of the 'true Celtic way' (and such innocuous romantics do exist) would miss it on account of its occurring just after a bend in the road and just before the small hill. Most only notice what lies beyond, where the landscape empties itself out in rolls of unbaked clumsy turf and sand, and enormous blue sky space, massive and majestic behind the salt-pickled wooden houses. This leaves the savage little beach in younger-sister mode, ignored and left to run wild.

In order to appreciate this beach you have to erase from your mind every popular-romance bookcover you have ever seen, every souvenir shop, every amateur painting competition, every difficult jigsaw, because this is a typical beach, and we have learned to shun the typical or only to appreciate it when it is resold to us as high kitsch. We forget that such a place sounds, animal and water and wind sounds, on its own without us. It feels crunchy under foot and under hoof, with large-grained, gravelly sand and smooth pebbles. No one put those there, they just arrived uninvited, a bit like the girl who is standing there now, watching the water.

It is a furious hold of sea water, churning and angry. The girl looks powerless against it. Breakable as driftwood. A serious mouth on her, a grown-up mouth shut tight against secrets even this soon in her story, balanced out by baby eyes, soft and liquid and large against the size of her face. She has eyes of a colour to confuse later lovers, changing grey to blue to green each time you see them, and skin as pale as real white, not skin-white or cloud-white but white like milk, bloodless and clear. Although she is tiny her arms and legs are too long for her, being only thirteen, not unlike the brittle driftwood branch she trails behind her as she makes off nearer to the caves. Her mid-length light brown hair is curled and whipped by the sea wind, becoming its own animal.

She has been here for hours now and doesn't seem to be doing much, sometimes inspecting the shoreline for perhaps a washed-up message, sometimes looking out to sea, like a fisherman's widow, eyes hunting through the waves. She watches the water smash against the rocks, always with blows as hard as hammers, such a brutal, vicious place for someone of her understanding. Unrelenting, nothing laps, or blooms, or wafts, or trickles here. There is a wind which could lift you and throw you to the rocks, except you would be nothing to it and so it blows right through. Occasionally, only from a distance, she looks to the wooden houses and the high wooden wharf, never going up that far, sticking to the rocky end of the beach. And such glances. Tender and obscure, the reason for them hidden.

At times she seems to disappear entirely, usually at low tide, and if you took your eyes off her for a moment you might be forgiven for thinking she had ebbed back out with the sea. In fact, you would find her sitting in the larger cave, on a shelf of rock sticking out a foot and a half from the cave wall, waist height up from the ground. When Sunday children play here it is their treasure cave with pebbles piled high on the shelf like gold, the shelf then becomes their table where cups and plates made from shells are placed. She often finds them there when she arrives and sweeps them away, having no time or thought for childlike deceptions, for playful elaboration. It is a shelf of rock and she is a girl who sits there, no fairy princess in her palace, no gypsy girl scared by the storm, no mermaid, no one else, just her as the world sees her when the world doesn't care, Janie Kelly in black jeans and a jumper.

Eventually, only after she has watched the air grow darker, the smudge of yellow-orange which should have been the sun sink low in the distance, only then will she walk back up the road. Perhaps now she lets herself think of the tea that waits for her, hoping that the others will have finished so she can hold fast to isolation for a short time longer. Some old women are sad when they see her, thinking, 'If I were back that way, I would be running and laughing and talking to boys, and nothing would worry me, not a thing.' And they sometimes stop her and say, 'And have you no boyfriend, a lovely girl like you?' And she simply says, 'No,' and keeps on her way. On up the two miles of road to the little farmhouse where her parents insist

8

on spending the whole summer, believing that they are real friends with the farmer's family and with the locals that they wave at on their scheduled walks.

This is their seventh summer here.

The couple smile on their daughter's sobriety, they have been expecting this phase. Every four days they bring her into the town and try to buy her things which she doesn't want or need, because otherwise it wouldn't be a proper holiday. They hope that the families in the village are as understanding as they are about her current reserve. Still, she spends all her days with the other kids, so maybe she brightens in their company. They keep away from the beach entirely; their daughter needs space to grow, to interact on her own terms. They are her parents, they understand these things.

She has her usual small bedroom, the cold segmented chipboard progeny of the one her parents sleep in, the dividing wall so thin it could be tunnelled through in seconds with a rusty spoon. She has to cry mutely at night in case they hear her and make her choose more things when they next go into town. Yes, she can hear them having sex, but it doesn't bother her, they are the same dispassionate well-meaning people in bed as when they are out walking or discussing types of trees over breakfast. They never disturb her in her room, assuming she is writing in her diary the events of the day. The mother will sometimes sneak a look for the diary during the afternoon, but can never find it. It is so well hidden, being full of such adolescent adventures. It's all rather exciting. In fact, it doesn't exist.

Judy May Murphy

When she is down at the sea or when she is walking the road or when she is in the tiny room, she is remembering. In her mind there is her real-life family, parents, aunts, a grandmother, and also her better-life family, the one she was really made for.

This other family were from one of the houses at the top of the hill and she has known them since she started coming here. The father was always alone, the mother, though not dead, was never spoken about. The father, his son and daughter who were twins a year older than Janie, and their slow friend, Dowie, from next door, who Janie had thought for years was a boy but turned out to be a girl after all, and a white mongrel dog whom she never made friends with, this made up her better family. She made sense here with these people. No one made special time to have a conversation with her, to ask her how things were going, instead all of them talked and listened all the time, all toppling over each other, and it all got said and it all got heard.

On the first day of this summer she went up the beach to the house and rang the doorbell. She did this only on the first day every summer, entering unannounced by the side door after that until September took her back again. They would be expecting her, with special biscuits and orange squash and photographs of Christmas and who had or hadn't grown much since the last time, and all of this had her smiling a great smile wider than her face as she jigged up and down a little on the granite-slab doorstep.

The father never left the house but worked in the study all day, so the outdoors belonged to the children entirely. Any other adults were away in the fields working other people's land or serving in shops. Most days Janie would eat two breakfasts, one with each family, but half-sized, sparking comments from all. She would never admit to either host about her secret other toasts and marmalades. The children would all potter about in the den or the garden and sometimes in the conservatory where the spiders were, finding bits of string, or hollow biros which they would pack with matches, squashed paper clips or sugar, depending on the emergency they were planning that day.

The day they thought the tide might catch them in the cave, they armed themselves with drinking straws to breathe through. Once, when a broken leg each seemed a distinct possibility, rations of cornflakes and shoelaces for making splints made up the necessary kit.

Added to the daily tackle were more long-term items. Since he was seven the boy had had a compass, and this is what first decided Janie's respect. She was not the type to bow down in adoration, however, always striving to equal those she admired. So, two years later, she produced the single-blade penknife she had cried for and begged for, out of earshot of the summer, and which her parents had eventually bought for her on the condition that she practise using it in front of them first. The year she got the penknife she was nearly nine and was instantly promoted from third to second in rank by an unspoken understanding — not that they ever decided to have ranks — so the girl-twin cast herself in the mode of helpful Indian and the group was tight and complete.

The three sat for hours in the cave when the rain came down, writing letters to each other in a secret code so complex that they needed pages of notes to encode and decode them. They kept these notes in sandwich bags tied around their necks with garden twine, and hidden beneath jumpers. Janie kept some jellybeans in there too and they all admired her fore-sight, especially as a jellybean emergency did inevitably happen every day before they were even an hour out from breakfast.

She never knew what to make of Dowie and was glad that the ration was only for three sweets per day, and that Dowie was an obvious cut-off point. Dowie never joined in with these sessions, only being summoned to help when a boat needed hauling from one end of the beach to the other for some smuggler reason, or when the twins' father heavily reminded them not to leave her out.

The dog was a guard dog so they never called it by its name, and after a couple of years they couldn't even remember what it had been. Anyway it wasn't really their dog, it just sort of hung out in the village and ate crisps and biscuits and the odd discarded dinner. Although it was a dog it was mostly a wolf during the summer — a guard wolf, naturally.

So Janie stood on the doorstep of all this, that morning. She had made a more permanent pouch out of a small pencil case and neck-chain, and was dying to be admired for it, it could even hold the knife. She rang the bell again, and waited. And then again, and waited, and she gradually realised that they must be in town for the day. She would run back to the farm-house and insist on a journey there that very morning. And then she noticed that the chair was missing from the porch.

Please be kind to her, she is only so young, and children cannot organise their lives the way that older people can. They have been weaned off saying, 'I want', and rely on

That Girl from Happy

being offered things. To go to her parents and say, 'I want my other family back' was out of the question. It seemed cruel now that they had sent each other letters from across the cave but had never phoned or written when they were apart for so many months. Why did her parents not keep in contact with the father? They should have known and told her and fixed it, they really should have.

For weeks she just wanted, just ached like anyone who doesn't know to grieve, just waited for God or older people to give back what she had before. Because Dowie couldn't talk and was more helpless than even she was at changing anything, Janie left her be. When she appeared on the wharf Janie did not invite her down, so she stayed away. There was no comfort anywhere, Dowie and the wolf-dog were as stale pepper to a hungry child.

If even once her mother had come down to the beach and put her arms around Janie and asked what was wrong, where were the friends, then Janie could have cried out loud, and cried and cried, and maybe her mother could have fixed it or taken her away to a place where it didn't hurt so badly. But this did not happen. Her resonant memory-dream, for all its being hopeless, was the nucleus around which all other thoughts and actions now revolved. This total idea of what had been so precious became caught in her mind, like a germ in a warm bottle. And the impasse, where the wound was the same every day, retarded her sap-filled heart. Trapped now in limbo, where the germ could only grow instead of Janie, she would always be thirteen.

It was worse that it happened this year, this year her

anticipation had not been of the usual general excitement of days and days of anything happening. This year her hope had been scripted into particular possibilities, things that might happen, if-onlys and whens. Her expectations and aspirations had been rehearsed and revised through the autumn, dreamed on through the winter and refined and rejuvenated right through spring. And now these same hopes were punishing her for feeling so much. This was no gentle chastisement but a relentless, tortuous beating, mocking her pain. We are older, we are too cynical for pain. She is only young, but edging closer to us with every day spent on that beach.

One day in the middle of this solitary summer you can see Janie sitting with a dying seagull, as it struggles for breath and flinches from its barbed-wire wounds. The three of them together would have rescued it, a proper real emergency, but on her own she can only think to tell it a story. She tells it about how a girl called Janie and a boy went together into the smaller cave and tied plastic Coke bottles together with beached string and made a sort of raft. She tells it how the girl and boy did not answer the other girl, the boy's sister, as she shouted for them, of how they stayed in the cave all afternoon, writing notes to America, to Peru, to China and to Greenland, and put one in each bottle. She tells it how they returned that night at midnight, cloaked under fear of death-by-grounding, to launch the raft which would save them from their island. And the bird seems to be listening.

Anyone passing might think it was the gentle rain but she is crying because the bird is dead, and again it had nothing to do with her. She buries it far back in the large cave and covers it with ugly stones which would not be collected by anyone.

Every day she uncovers the dead bird and places it on a tiny bed of seaweed to tell it more stories. On this day in the late summer she is telling it about the way the girl called Janie and the boy would sit together, not looking at each other, usually absorbed in something else, and talk. If children think time endless, and adults think it short, she certainly stepped over that line, and hated the evenings for arriving. The talk was always about travelling and climbing mountains, saving the people in Africa, owning camels and speaking twenty different languages, even of building an aeroplane.

One day, when the sister was sick upstairs and the weather too awful to escape to, they sat in the den with a KEEP OUT sign hanging on the door (against the curious hoards) and drew how they could build the aeroplane from what they had around them: the cucumber frame, the one-wheeled bicycle, the shutters off the empty cottage across the way. The next day it rained again as she had prayed it would and the two sat and designed the insignia for the wings and tail.

After that day they would slip out of the house, just the two of them, leaving the sister slowly to realise that she was on her own, until in her boredom she went off to Irish College for the rest of the summer with a schoolfriend, and they all knew that something had changed. After that they never again charged noisily across the wharf, all three with their plans and provisions. Still, these were days of a different perfection, and Janie and the boy-twin spent their hours seeing how heavy were the frames and shutters, collecting wooden crates in the shed, checking that the superglue was still where they had hidden it. Then they would leave off for a while to go down to the beach and play through the more usual activities. As they threw stones at the sea to kill the sharks or collected enough white rocks to be able to write SOS on the shore, millions of moments were brightened as the name of the plane, the right day to start to build it, where they could get fuel, where they could test it and launch it, were discussed between the two.

One day she goes to dig up the bird and it has gone. Janie sits and smiles all day because this is just how she had hoped it would be. Yesterday she had told the bird the most important story of all, and now its spirit has flown across to another land to tell him she is here, to remind him of everything which he had been made to forget. And before the end of the summer, he will come back.

Janie freezes now at night, having taken her blankets down to the beach where they lie buried in a black bin-bag under the marram grass above the tideline. She'd had to get up at four in the morning and walk that road in the semi-darkness, but on her return she met many locals who smiled at a city girl being up with the cows. 'For a walk,' she told her mother, knowing how a murderer must feel when meeting his mother, shovel in hand.

Janie woke up late on the last day and her mother packed her things as Janie ate breakfast. She didn't get to go down to the beach. He was there, she knew he was. Her neck strained to see the two miles down to the sea as the car turned the other way. There had been no time to collect the knife from the back of the cave or the many tins of food which they had assumed she was cooking in the other house for lunch.

For the next six years Janie's parents would study their daughter's summer melancholies in a villa in the south of Portugal.

But as they drove back home in four hours of total silence, she was glad she had told the bird the last story before it flew away.

In the same way as he had often said to go into the kitchen or the cave and he would follow right behind, the boy had said to meet on the wharf at midnight. When they met there, knowing they had no reason they could put sense to for having this night-time excursion, he said that they had to talk about putting off the actual building of the plane until the next summer. A couple romancing on the beach, and his family inside the house, and the possibility of someone passing on the road, left the reeds behind the caves their only place to go. It was a warm clear night, the moonlight breaking the black darkness which is night-time outside the cities. They talked there on the dunes for an hour or more. Once they had planned what each would do during the winter — he would collect more materials, she would read up on how to fly — they both fell silent and just lay there about six feet apart. Just as she was falling asleep he jumped up and grabbed her hand, running with her down to the far side of the rocks where they never went, warning her to tell no one. As they got to a small wooden rowing boat he dropped her hand and they each took hold of a piece of rope and pulled it to the water. She asked him if they were stealing it and when he said nothing she knew that they were. No discussion needed. The only time ever he made a protective gesture towards her was now as he took her hand and helped her inside the boat. Hundreds of times over the years she had been precariously hanging or falling onto or off something dangerous and he had only stood by, waiting for her to continue. Now she let him steady her awkwardness and something had changed. Wet to the waist from wading out with the boat, she didn't care. There was no wind so they drifted. He sat at the opposite end and held on to the rope in some claim of authority, one which she didn't challenge. It was perfect. The moment was so full of perfect, leaving no room for her to realise what type of moment it was. So she did not say to herself, 'This is the happiest I will ever be,' but it was.

Dear Boat-Boy,

I am writing to you from the kitchen again, what's new?! Senior school isn't much different from junior school except you have a different teacher for each subject. It's so boring around here and no one understands the first thing about me, and certainly not about our plans and the adventures — they think it only happens in books. I think even if I tried to explain it to someone they wouldn't understand. They might believe me when I said how horrible it is not to be able to have it back like it was before, if it was someone really nice, and they'd listen to all the details and so on, but they wouldn't get how enormous and important it is — that's why I can't risk sending this to you by sea in a bottle — it might get into the wrong hands. So I'll hold onto it until I see you. No one understands how alive the adventures make you or anything about the situation. They wouldn't understand about the aeroplane. It is a hopeless case.

That Girl from Happy

It's the same way that you can't explain a smell to someone if they have never smelt anything like it, or if you had to tell someone who was born blind what a thing looked like. You could get close, you could explain that a lemon smells acidy and fresh and sharp or you could describe a thing the blind person has touched and say if it is or isn't like that. But there would be no telling what they'd be imagining unless they had experienced it first hand for themselves. That's why there is no point in me telling anyone. If I did tell someone it would be like a story and I feel like it isn't just a story like some of the other things that happened to me when I was little or at school or a friend's house. It would be a betrayal of the first order, so I haven't opened my mouth about it once and that's how it's going to stay. They just wouldn't get it.

I.M.Y.L

Janie Kelly

P.S. I am practising a new signature.

Aimee

'Aimee, over here.'

Janie had been dead a couple of days now and somehow we had to drink coffee in groups on account of this. Lucy called me four times this morning so I surrendered to her late brunch, in spite of a five-star hangover. Luckily, a girl called Fat Molly was there, too, so I didn't have to talk. Between them they filled the scrambled-egg-on-toast and cappuccino part of the ordeal, chunked it up with talk about the unreality rap.

'I keep saying "is" instead of "was",' Fat Molly flaked, 'I can't get used to it.' Sure thing girlie-girl, it's all about you and your grammar. Like we give a shit, like no one else giggled ineptly when they heard.

Laugh like a bad thing, your friend is freshly dead, a slice of the action has fallen to the floor, butter and honey side down, licked clean by the undertaker and the god of the day. Here you are on your hands and knees lapping at the crumbs like a desperate pack of little doggie freaks. Me included. Me especially, I've got my own secret licking place.

Fat Molly seemed to think it was all about her, not Janie, and Lucy wasn't doing much to kill that notion. Fat Molly was claiming she was off her food, although by the skinny-speck look of her I doubt she ever does more than gargle juice.

A media couple I'd never seen before walked by.

'We were so sorry to hear about Janie, will she be buried here or in Ireland?'

'In Ireland,' said Lucy, 'but there's a service for her at the funeral parlour today at five.'

They couldn't make it so they were sorry all over again.

Janie Jay Kelly is dead, the word flew. It called to mind the early layers in a pass-the-parcel game, no one wanted to hold onto the news for themselves, quick to pass it on, not knowing how to react when it landed in their lap, realising all that lay beneath was probably another useless layer. They'd quickly lift the phone to tell the next invitee.

'How awful … she can't be … no, I don't believe it … her parents must be so....' Conversation by numbers, shit-scared of getting it wrong again like with that first nervous laugh.

Josh joined us in time to eat the leftovers and so not pay, along with two others who I've been introduced to and forgotten their names so many times they are starting to feel like that recurring trick math problem you can never luck into.

Sucking and blowing on cigarettes like demons, no one said much outside of, 'Is there another ashtray?' Couldn't stick this all day. I wanted to go shoe shopping but I knew this would look bad. I need the shoes to go with all the new clothes, which I'll explain soon.

New York can make you feel guilty for not relinquishing enough of your day to caffeine so they stuck around looking pale until suddenly the lack of purpose caught up with them *en masse*, and they all left the café to go iron things and sleep and play hot potatoes with the phone. Lucy said she'd call me later, must be she's tied together with phone lines.

At last I can breathe again, the crowd clogs up the air more than their smoke could. I say yes to a coffee refill. I take out a black marker pen, start to scribble things into perspective on the paper table-cover.

Ah yes, this feels familiar, even without forming words on paper it always seems as if I'm writing my life, as if its purpose is not found in the moment to moment, but lies in its being read back later as a total form, as if I won't exist until the very end. I am one black letter after the next, sticking out like very badness on the nicely white page.

It's as if I don't exist without a reader.

Beyond all this, in the backwards direction, I am certainly a nothing, in a nothing place, a sub-suburbia, unformed, hidden from words. The am that was is a dry empty girl on a dirt road in the South, in a town no one's heard of even if they live only ten or so miles away. Coming from nothing, what a danger it is to give me this much being, so I'll not be saying much about what I was before.

Maybe this goes further, perhaps I write other people too, and you, because you read this and are nothing to my world until you do.

If you talk really fast like in a competition, aged seven, you can get stuff said in half the time or less. Technically, that means you can live two lifetimes, so read faster than you normally would please, that way I won't be responsible. Me, I talk so fast you'd swear I was in need of a Lithium jab, but this is a strategy rather than a disorder; people can't get through a blizzard, can't get close, can't push through the iron word wall. But today I am writing slowly like oil, and with a stability which I haven't felt since Kennedy died. That he just had to go and get killed way before I put in an earthly appearance is more the pity.

A simple picture, the shape of it, that's what you need. If I do now, out of the kindness of my boredom, show you the world according to Aimee, or a fractured piece of it, will you only say you've been there, or somewhere very like it? Are my people so very much the same as yours? If yes, can you not for once celebrate the comfort of similarity? At least understand that my existence is original to me if not to your sophisticated mind, and please don't expect to understand fully, some loops are uncompleted, the circles of my mind are more like worms, I'm a difficult person, head-sore, brained beyond reclaim. I think I must have multiple personalities, just haven't got it together to separate them properly.

Here are my bits of it anyway, I'll leave it up to someone else to fill in the pieces I don't know. I could go for the soft option, tell a joke or two, but I can never remember any so here is an unfunny story instead, anything amusing is probably lies.

Wind back a day or two so you can follow my trail.

I'd just spent the night with the lover of the dead girl.

I knew she was dead, but he hadn't yet found out by the time I'd left. She wasn't lying blue in the basement in a bloody pool of gore or anything like that, in fact she was halfway across town, which would have been ideal if she were still alive, but wasn't really significant under the circumstances.

The whole thing would make for an excellent film except for the fact that he's an Italian named Tony and she was

Irish, beautiful, and destined to die a tragic death, and everyone has seen that. Fuck her anyway, she's ruined my week.

Her lover is a darkly greasy man, nothing irresistible to excuse what I did. By very early that morning, when the sun was the only thing rising, he started to not exactly regret what had happened between us, but to wish he didn't have to play out the second half of it. If men had their way, we would melt under sheets, becoming just one more laundry stain. He had to let me stay though, it's only manners after you've fucked someone to let them sleep off their excesses wherever they land. So the poor tan bastard was realising that he'd have to speak to me in the morning and eat breakfast with me, even kiss me a mouthy goodbye before starting to sow the seed of my discouragement with a carefully chosen phrase. We women are too many candy bars — they can't bear to look at us when their fill is full.

I started playing a game as I lay there, predicting his possible final phrase, wondering (without too much wonder) whether he'd come up with anything original that I could recycle myself someday, or if his stallion looks and gold chain would run to the full cliché; 'It's a pity I haven't time to meet you like this more often,' a possibility, or, 'I really enjoyed last night, you're going to make the right man really happy.' No, no one would be that obvious, would they?

And what would I say to him in return? Did my blue eyes, goy button nose and scrag of long blond hair necessitate their own script? My end-of-party trick, my stamp, was always to slip quietly out, stealing the vodka on my way, leaving some fumbled note to commemorate the mess and put an end to it, but this time I wanted to play the scene, to act it to a climax. So what would I say? (the wonder came stronger now) something to really stump the little shit: 'Well, can I see you tonight, Tony?' or perhaps, 'Do you like children?' or would I just slam out my trump card, 'Thanks for the fuck, and did you know your girlfriend's dead?'

The possibilities came dripping silently out of me into his still and crumpled room, sitting ready like dull knives should the battle require them. We women live whole lives as men sleep. This one slept with his limbs twitching as if he was dancing in his dreams (with a new woman no doubt), and I started to think how the dead girl had often been there, how she had seen him dance like that, how she may even be watching right then, standing at the foot of the bed looking on in that knowing way that the dead have about them. Did she pity me as I did, or hate me for the monster I was proving to be? Did she wish she'd travelled on with us living folk a little further down the yellowed road?

The dead don't frighten me, I can't afford to let them — after all, there are many more of them than there are of us, and most of them have been around for a lot longer, too, so it would be an arrogance — don't you think? — to get all territorial about the world, insist that ghosts all take off into the heavens or the woods or the floorboards. I don't know. It was good that she might be there with me, company against the sleeper, better still that I couldn't see the look on her face.

As the room grew brighter I scanned around for a glimpse of anything which might have been hers, a deodorant, a T-shirt, pills, a magazine, so I could hold it, have it, use it, and further fuck with the remains of the girl called Janie Jay.

Janie Jay the newly flown. Home now, I guess.

I'd got to learn how she'd been loving for the past few months by way of Italian Tony's habits and strong preferences, he'd do well to write a manual for his maintenance. Through those traces that we all leave on our lovers, the imprints of tone and smell and cadence which can take an age to fade, I'd felt her, felt I was her when I lost myself to it, and I knew that this was as close as could be got to Janie now, the closest I could get to being her. But even this was not enough to make me cry. Had she cried on these pillows? I wondered. People cry, you know, I've seen it.

The grease-stud woke from his dream harem just before seven and, to get away from me for a while, made us both some coffee which we drank in the bed, hiding our places. He looked too large for the room, his arms huge from lifting things, pulling ropes, moving screens, biceps like trees, like you wouldn't believe, sinews enough for several men, but strong men are always the weaker; energy needs distribution, you see. So his brain is as soft as his nose, with the help of some considerable snow. Very businesslike, when working on *Riders to the Sea* he'd kept them snowed under nicely for months; they miss him now they're off on their different trips around the Tri-State small-town theatre circuit. And to imagine I thought he was the playwright the first time I was there, but he's Irish and dead too. Ages dead, can't pin that one anywhere near my ass.

Apologising every two minutes that there was no food in the house, Tony overexplained that he had to be off to work soon but he'd walk me to the subway, and some hundred other things that I half-heard, not taking in the meaning of the words or even the gist, just knowing the tune well enough

That Girl from Happy

already, understanding perfectly what was getting said. When they start calling you 'darling' or 'lovely', you know the time to leave has passed already. It's not that they've forgotten your name, it's just that the good stuff isn't coming naturally and they have to resort to the show. Such behaviour from Italians is to be expected, but coffee this bad was not, so I reckoned the bad taste must have come from inside my own mouth, a spillage from my large vat of guilt and anger. That my sickness could taste of amaretto was a little too much to expect.

With him studiously not watching I dragged my grey velvet sheath-dress on over my head and eased my blistered swollen feet into the expensive mules I had bought the weekend before, which I now realised were to be one very short-term investment, foster shoes. My feet, Janie's neck, I thought, opposites and equal, bruised, roughed and fricted, sisters in discomfort are we. I next pulled on my blue hand-knit sweater and quickly threw my underwear into my bag, too embarrassed to put them back on remembering the speed and enthusiasm with which they had left me the night before.

Italian Tony soon enough patted me off to the door — 'Party's over, girl' — where I stood, a framed picture of his infidelity, still smarting from a lip kiss that Judas would disown. He delivered the inevitable parting blow: 'I know a friend of mine who you'd just love. Here, let me give you his number.' Sick little piggy-man, a friend for your friend. Throughout my milky shaky teenage years and beyond, the various Samaritans I've found myself knowing have proven extremely eager to guide me numerically. Main problem being, at least from where I lie, that the recommendations and the numbers are too often accompanied by words like 'special' and 'funny'.

Still, I took the stupid number to be polite, hugged him (again a decorum thing), and, once outside, told him I'd make my own way to the station so he wouldn't be late for work. As he threw me a Disney wave and a smile, I thought what a pity it was that it was such a fake smile, as it would probably be his last in a while. I rounded the corner, then turned back around again, wondering if I should take the pleasure of breaking the news to him myself after all. As expected, he was re-entering the building, perhaps to eat all the bagels and pancakes and cereal I had seen in the cupboards the night before, conjured up to existence once again now I was gone.

I headed roughly in the direction of home.

Well, the only way to go down is to go down quickly, and I had hit bedrock at my very first dive. Unchecked and fool-rusted, empty as a kicker-can. My motley random life swings always on without my really trying, and before I know I'm playing, I'm fouling the ball.

Cold as it was, I submerged both my hands into grit-specked icy water which had collected in the bottom of a drinking fountain. Dirty girl.

Standing there in my two-days-ago dirty-girl dress, looking to the park and to the whole sickup street as if just about ripe to heave, I left my hands immersed until the pain started to play with me, seemed like heat, felt like an answer, then I pulled them back into the heavy air. An old bum came by. 'Go on in,' I said in my famous drawl. 'The water's good.' And I surrendered my water to this man who looked in need of a little introduction to the art of the wash.

I had reached the park, not a picture-book park, no mothers and babies and sweet childhood anything there; it's built like a prison-yard for asshole people like me and the bum, decrepit but somehow comfortable with it. His hands and my waters, grubby as pigs. On leaving, I nodded at the men still gathered at the gate, our local pushers, cute too, 'the lollipop league' we call them.

The water cooled on my hands in the seven o'clock early air, crusting the edges of my mohair cuffs into bubbles of almost frost, which I put to my mouth to ice it after the things it had said and not said. I dragged myself down 7th to the steps of my home, stopping first at the corner store to buy me a glutful of cake, at least one of each item in the Hostess range to show I'm non-discerning in my choice of destructive pleasures, and a few more cookies besides on account of the deepness of the pit needing filling. In the bag it went, knowing in my sinning that a Twinkie or a Devil-dog had limited thera-peutic applications. Yeah, like that was going to stop me. This national snack-food rite is an accepted substitute for real emo-tional progress and it won't get me pregnant or give me AIDS.

All this time, all down the streets and along the aisles of the store (barely one step up from a drugs front) this bigger, better, sharper being had been sitting in my ear like a Jimminy thing, commentating my every minute move, warning in a faggy little voice that a crash was on the way. Well, fuck it, I'd be crashing with my mouth full.

I brought the cake junk into the shower with me, cleaning up the outside while polluting the in. Keeping my feeding arm stuck outside the stall, I ducked my head out every half minute or so to shovel in one more calorie bomb. The telephone rang about a hundred times, like a mother calling, and I was not even curious, not even bothered by the sound. The voice-mail was off so for then I didn't exist, the little life on hold until I got this sorted, in my head at least.

What in the good devil's name had I done? I'm a dirty little jeepster chick, I'm a mmmmm, a mucky tart with a mouth like a gaping toilet and a life like a sucking black hole, worse, I'm slipping. Was that out of character, what I did? Or once you do a thing, does that then become your character? I tried to avoid washing between my legs more than is necessary, convincing myself that I had enjoyed the whole thing, in a physical as well as a twisted way.

What was he doing by now? Wishing he had kept me around for the morning to make good with the hardness that greeted him in the shower, or had he already phoned to try and make contact with the dead? Was he eating breakfast? Fuck him, I bought my own breakfast, thank you. Admittedly it was the type of breakfast you would buy if you had only been allowed have oatmeal for your entire life, but no one was here judging me since I rinsed out my ears, so I didn't feel bad. Well, not about the food anyway, the other stuff I knew I was almost obliged to feel guilty about.

I rent an unfurnished apartment in the East Village which has largely stayed that way, with the notable exception of a long wooden dining table which I turn upside down to make a bed by night, and right-side-up by day to be an ironing-board, stepladder, chair or whatever. Nowadays even furniture can't be what it was born to be; my table writes home that it's hugely successful — table number five in the Russian Tea Rooms. I write that I am a writer.

There's a small caving passageway leading from the paper-thin door with its decorative locks to this single sore-open space, a plastic shower unit in one corner, and a cupboard-like affair off to one side where the toilet lives. The toilet doesn't smell bad but the floors do, and the walls dribble with water, summer and winter, tiny rivulets ooze their way down the yellowing paint with its fuzz of black spores. I'm used to better but isn't everyone these days? My pride and joy and worst enemy is a late-1960s television which will no doubt junkout just before that model becomes hopelessly fashionable. Watching this TV is a dangerous sport as to get sound and picture together you have to kneel like some special kind of whore — it's the only way to get the angle good on the aerial. I feel like the only cursed soul in the city without cable, but no doubt there are a couple of hundred more who feel the same way and will present the same symptoms as me at the chiropractor in a couple of years.

If my memory serves me well, the carpet is a brown-and-beige flecked affair, but it's been coated with liberal layers of magazines and clothes and bags since the middle of my first week here. Many, very many, cake wrappers were now being added to this over-carpet of my own creation. The cream in the middle is the best bit so I sucked this out of the remaining cakes and ditched the spongy shells with the wrappers.

Now towel-dried roughly and having thrown on an oversized T-shirt, I was squeaky clean and shining, if a little stiff. I sat with my back straight to the wall against a bag of laundry, with an old coat for a cushion and another stuffed laundry bag supporting my crooked knees. From experience

I knew that this was the absolutely most comfortable it was possible to be in this demijohn, this bladder full of Aimee.

I sized up the apartment as I planned my next evasion, scanned it lazily with my brain, half-opened my critical eye, vowing once more to do something with it. The size is the bastard of it, too big to be cosy yet too small to make a bold statement, too enormously huge to keep tidy yet too small to have people stay over (even short ones), too big to decorate on my own, too small to be paying this much rent. I often feel this way about myself, too big yet too tiny, like a last meal. It is administered by the devil, the windows barely let in enough sun to read by during the day yet just about hurl the light from the street into my face when night comes, laughing at my cheap curtains. It's not exactly my dream.

I always wanted a space with a ceiling that ended higher than the roof even, and strong enough beams to hold a swing, cut from redwoods that had already died of natural bureaucratic causes. And I often picture myself swinging forward and back and in neat circles, all day, with the sun streaming in on top of me, then at night changing the large wooden seat for a hammock and swinging again softly until morning. However, now when I looked to the ceiling of this stumpy apartment to imagine my swing, to escape to my innocence, there was no seat or hammock or sunshine, but there was instead a too-clear image of a woman swinging on the end of one rope, with the other one left for me. Her limbs and head hung loose as the rope grew ever tighter around her neck. And she was winking at me with her dead eye. This corpse was my new playmate, Janie Jay. I fell asleep where I sat, dreaming of swinging alongside her, neck caught and mouth open, swinging in the darkness but no longer alone.

I woke up to the phone and caught it before remembering that I didn't exist right then.

Gradually over the next few days I would have the sad and shocking news broken to me by at least a dozen people, and I correctly predicted that it would prove to be the most nomadic of stories ever to have started out rooted in fact, performed, rather than told, by people more eager to paint over the lines than to read between them, as hard evidence and actual truth hovered in the background like uninvited guests. It is always this way with a drama. The story will be cut and shuffled (pick a card, any card, and I'll tell you it's the right one), zapped around like everyone's watching it on a different station. To get Lucy off the line I tripped and suggested we meet for a late lunch, but sadly she just remembered something she had to do, just as I was about to remember the same.

I shouldn't have picked up without a strategy, caught off guard, not good. It was too early in the game to be sleepwalking; now it would be impossible to admit that I already knew. Stupid fucking mistake, another. I'm riddled with them, big wormholes in my psyche. Are we still allowed to have a psyche, or has it been replaced by something less ethereal? The new-age psychology jargon is totally beyond me, my inner child slipped out unnoticed. I would probably be deported from California if I ever tried to visit, thrown out for being too literal.

I did indeed have something urgent to do elsewhere but had a small skirmish to brave first before attempting to

Judy May Murphy

challenge the wider world. I reached out to face once more the battle of Heap Hill, a forested mound in my space, an ever-growing complex of clothes, shoes and hats. It's more than a junk-nest, it's the unknown, like cancer when you're clean of it, or the dark for the unblind. The evil expanse has begun to bond with the wall as it creeps upward in self-worship, reaching with lace and leather tentacles toward the damp line beyond which it will certainly be unable to breathe. I don't normally name inanimate objects — that's milky, princess shit, as if cars and coats function better for being called Betsy or Maisy (it doesn't make you cute, lady), and is only marginally more acceptable than pet-naming erotic body parts while high. But Heap Hill is like a person, living, breathing, spewing up, so excuse me just this once, especially seeing as I don't have a cat or anything.

The Heap oftentimes does the choosing for me, usually coughing up some particularly mediocre rag, but it's never let me down on the big stuff — occasions — always handing me something deliciously inappropriate, so I leave it grow. Once I've worn an outfit outside, or eaten in it, it goes straight into a laundry bag, seeing as how mixing semi-clean and grubby clothes with the clean but bored ones would be an environmental risk not worth taking. The day any rascal micro-organisms join that pile, a whole new eco-system will come into being, and I'm having enough trouble, thanks, dealing with my life and the odd unfortunate death without having to take responsibility for an entire new race of fabric-fetished invertebrates. My desultory housekeeping would quickly be famous if I ever invited anyone back, but I don't, so the problem is solved in an aberrant kind of way.

I looked around as I left, closing the window, flushing the toilet (in case a burglar needed to go), checking if anything was out of place, though admittedly anything would want to be dangerously awry to get noticed in this ready-mix menagerie. This confusion I live in, it disturbs me something grim; if I owned a CD collection or had a feel for symmetry, I'd probably have had to be committed long ago. It is without doubt the most perturbed little room ever to have evolved, and I match it mess for mess.

I shut the door gently, wary in this avalanche terrain, and went to pay my respects.

Earlier I'd thought I might need a little dose to soak my tongue, just one miserly short mouthful to get me there on the burn, but the feeling had left me at that point, probably fucked off to double Italian Tony's need presuming he'd heard by then. I sped down the road, skip tripping on over myself. I wanted to dance with dead folk, I was dressed for it, wearing my cheery clothes: red fake-lizard Cuban-heel boots (two years old and only just softening up), tan cigarette-leg pants, cream crew-neck, red beanie and a stingy-cut three-quarter-length tan suede coat. When you dress for an occasion I find it's best not to try to correspond with it — far better to counteract your life with your look. It's a control thing for sure: slut-skirt to your in-laws', evening dress to the park, especially useful when you can't be sure the emotions are yours, whether they are natural or learnt. Between 12th and 11th I started singing, but needing to keep that distinction between me and the crazy people, for a while at least, I stopped, and just stayed grinning.

I realise I must sound callous, perhaps hysterical, certainly inappropriate for someone of my middling sanity, but it must be understood that I had so thoroughly grafted Janie on to me over the months before her death that it felt as if, with all the talk about her, all the attention, the intensity with which everyone would now be focused on her, she was soon to be more alive than she ever was. They say that to leave is to die a little, but it seems to me that to die is to leave a little, and only a little. People only really happen in other people's heads, and Janie would be on most people's minds by that night. Besides, she was so much less threatening this way; I might touch her now without her standing in my way.

Her apartment building is a few blocks up from mine; I held back from running the last block — again, had to keep that distinction.

Our type (young, cashed-up, ready for whatever doesn't exist), we're phone-based, café-bar-based, based in each other's party faces, so I could confidently assume there'd be no one gathered at her home. Home is where we go to recover from our make-up, rest our faces from the smiling, rest our sex bones from the action, recover a sense of what we were when we started out that morning or early afternoon. The friends would congregate at the Happy Lounge that night, our church substitute, Garth-the-bar standing in as curate, desperately trying to remember which one of his customers was Janie (The little fat kid? No, she was sitting over there), and producing a little word or two for those who look like they might be persuaded to drown their sorrows *in situ*.

I'd never been to her place before that day, but I had the address and, simple, no name beside bell number six —

isolation had been her thing for the last while. I stood with my ear to the door for a while, freaking out some creeper-by old lady by pretending, as she ran past like a broken beetle, to plead to be let back in for the sake of the kids. Then, as someone approached the door from inside, I made ready to scratch around my pockets for my lost keys that never were.

That afternoon's shining knight was a clean-cut Fordham student, or some wet with an unhealthy love of spiral-bound notebooks. He was cute though with his freckles, blond curls and big brown eyes and ... fuck me for a sad bitch, I was scoping college sophomores. Jesus, move your little ass along there, Aimee, you're in trouble deep enough for a day.

'Listen, if you've lost your keys, the landlord is upstairs inspecting the pipes, I'm sure he'd lend you a spare set.'

Kid still had braces.

'Thanks, I'll ask him.' What was I thinking? Freak, in your freak clothes, and your spare pen. I don't hate that type — that would take a caring I can rarely muster — they just make me feel like I've caught some kind of rash, the kind that needs amputating.

The landlord was right where the student placed him, listening along with the plumber as if he really understood the wheezing music in the pipes, like a strictly R & B man at the opera.

'Yeah, you're right, does sound a little backed up.'

The man himself sounded this way, his head stuffed with a semi-solid mucus substance, his throat a sticky shaft, nasty, very. Wearing those nondescript pants they advertise in the Sunday papers, which can be green or grey, a beige office-shirt with the cuffs and collar-button unfastened, and a pair of black-and-white sneakers, he wasn't winning any kind of competitions here. While he was not vastly over-weight, you could tell that in five years' time he would be. I wondered if he'd one day make the link between the egg and gravy stains on his shirt and his romantic shortcomings; when it comes to women, this man's anticipation to gratification ratio must be very high indeed.

He mashed his chubby hands together before wiping their sweat onto the belly of his shirt, in preparation for another chance to fail. A man like this is too thrilled at having a young woman smile in his vicinity for it to occur to him that she might be the wrong woman. Poor fuck didn't know what he was hit with, a Baptist-sized smile, then, taking a breath deep enough to keep me on the same phrase for the rest of the day —

'Janie Kelly number six hi so sorry to bother you I can see you're really busy my mother had been staying for a couple of days and when she left this morning I think she took the keys would there be any way that I could I mean I know how busy you are and...'

'No problem, just get a new set cut.' He jangled at a large belted ring of keys and handed over two of them, holding onto my hand for a moment, then sliding his little-dick-fingers over mine as I pulled away. I thought of how I'd spend the next day washing that hand.

'Oh thank you so much I really appreciate it really thank you...' and so on with the verbal suck-off as I bounced down a couple of flights to number six. Bouncing, I don't do that, I never ate the right vitamins for that, must have rubbed up against a touch of student.

In.

Janie's room was expert perfect, complete in its every ordered line. A photographer could come from one of those house-and-home magazines and not even have to wipe a duster over the place, or add a bowl of lemons, or whatever it is they do.

She must have been a savage in a worker way, cleaning every visible surface and the invisible ones she knew would send out signals. Years ago I used to stuff the entire contents of my room under the bed before friends came around, months ago even, but this here apartment was a project rather than a chore; perfection like this has to be cultivated. I could see that this wasn't just a tidy room — it was systematic aesthetic, evidence of a mind with a method. Tidy makes me feel criticised, perfection attacks me, pisses me off.

The floor was varnished pine boards, the walls a clean white, studded here and there with framed prints which I'd never seen on any other apartment walls. If you have been into more than five people's apartments in this city you will understand what a feat that is. The light switch operated the main ceiling light and two side lamps, each with pink light-bulbs in them, washed over by the yellow sunlight through the one tiny window they gave a warm glow to what might otherwise have seemed harsh or barren. Me they made grey.

The story is supposed to go that the struggling Irish actress lives in a meaner type of holding pen than the American trust-fund baby and her kiss of fortune. However, as my inheritance is more subsidising than wildly autono-mising, once my rent and bills go through I can't be sure I'll be eating, so it's a mistrust I'm funded with, that's what keeps me poor. It's both safety net and trap, the worry of the street never hits me, so I never leave the small plenties of the orchard to work the hardlands, except for sufficiently long to write about it maybe. I never get desperate enough to try for the big prizes like this luscious little nest.

I sat on the brass queen-size bed with its white linen bedcovers; my ass was too untidy for it so I sat there for longer just to show. There was a huge mahogany wardrobe which I riffled through next; stuffed to the hinges with clothes, a sea of shoes and boots in rows underneath, it was an orderly, carefully layered scrummage, arranged by colour and type, and heaving with promise rather than menace. The wardrobe itself would, under any other circumstances, make you play *The Lion, the Witch and the Wardrobe* in your head for a while, but it's no fun knowing you have an Ice Queen of your own lying in an uptown tomb. Besides, I couldn't take any chances with time, a person might call by, a legitimate one, maybe to retrieve something they had lent to Janie before they got embroiled in a proof-of-ownership battle, or maybe just to scavenge like I was. No, I was different. I was the last of the great hunter-gatherers, my credentials impeccable, my intentions relatively pure. Or maybe I'd just come to smear my life on top of hers, to bloody her white face before it made a mockery of all us oily dirty-girl travellers still stuck on the journey.

I swear I would jerk off the entire board of 'Bed and Bath City' for a shot at a bathroom like hers. It was a whole proper bathroom with a bath and shower, and matching things, toothbrush holders and towel rails and shower-curtain hooks in the shape of fish. I took a piss in the toilet, — it felt better than pissing in mine, more productive.

There was a partitioned section in the main room with a sort of mini-kitchen neatly slotted in. I opened the ice-box to check out whether she'd predicted her exit, but I got the feeling that anything could be lurking in there, like Janie had faced her demons and put them in the cheese compartment, so I opened it a crack and saw a yellow birthday cake, ouch. I closed it quickly. Lovely covered stove too, all flush with everything else. It was most definitely the sort of place that required a wealthy boyfriend or some breed of friendly friend or two in the wings. The *Riders to the Sea* money must have been running out, over a year in one production and then back to cattle calls for soda commercials, must have hurt. Not that she wouldn't have coped, Janie had a way, an entourage of Wall Streeters traipsing around, sitting on her skirts, and cash-fat gay men, hetero-hags and the odd up-town married dyke. Least that's what they say. Italian Tony might have been a help if the sidelines were flowing. I wondered what the landlord did with all his money, didn't spend it at the tailor's, that's for sure, must just have been the real owner's sad cousin who the family had a conference about.

Back in the bathroom there was a shelf lifted straight from a duty-free perfume poster and I thought how she must have been smelling slightly rank by then. I took a bottle of Chanel eau de toilette and some Chloé body lotion, slipped them into my pockets — useful for later.

Jesus, she had all this to alleviate her smarting soul and yet she still got her ultimate wish, consolation prize and winner's gold, some people had it all.

Judy May Murphy

Before I went, I nudged and poked my hand under the bed, hoping to find a mess to placate me. Instead I found a tidy box with all her letters and notebooks in it, in a way I thought they only did in family films. I decided to take it, and some of the clothes too, I loved her stuff.

So I was standing there, laden as a pack-mule. Christ, what if I'd got it all wrong? What if she was still alive and about to walk in on me? What would I say, standing there with her most private possessions? 'Hi, my name's Aimee, I want to be your friend'?

The thought made the wood creak and I turned toward the door to see Mr Landlord standing in front of me, silent but for a moist lapping sound he made with his mouth, hands patting his chest.

'I think you owe me an explanation, yes?'

I froze like an ice-monkey, some aphonic fool, as he continued.

'You know you can't have other people live here without my say so.'

Things occurred, great things to say, but I bit back and offered, 'She wasn't living here, she was visiting. I couldn't let my own mother stay in a cheap hotel.' (My own mother I'd let stay in a cardboard box in the rain, with or without a lid, but I was being Janie.) Please God let him be referring to that, I thought, I was in no fucking mood for digging myself out from under a self-made quarry of shit.

'Well, even so, Miss....'

'You're right, I am so sorry.'

'Why don't I call around here again tomorrow and we'll ... discuss it?'

That pause between 'we'll' and 'discuss it' could have fit a whole innuendo army. His flabby mitts went straight to the shirt-front and he backed away, nodding at my assumed agreement, out of the room, wiping invisible drool from the side of his mouth as he went. He'll probably keep going for years on the story of the tenant who returned from the dead just to visit her apartment one more time and ride him like the bucking stallion he is.

As the clothes and I collapsed onto the bed I could hear a slight rustling, and, sensitive as I am to the sound of un-chaperoned banknotes I slid my hand under the pillows where, to my mild disappointment, I found a folded sheet of writing paper. A love letter of some sort, no doubt. Into the box. Deciding not to risk falling asleep or moving in, I bundled everything into my arms and left the room, the building, the street, staggering under the size and weight and general enormity of the load. I didn't feel much like singing by then.

Once inside my own building, I still ran, kicking open my unlockable door, crashing down in the middle of the room, back in my own damp hole which now mocked me with that seedy, shitty little way it has. God it was dark.

In my usual free-form approach to organisation, I threw Janie's clothes onto the top of Heap Hill, where they sat like sugar frosting, the new girls in town always looking prettier than the ones you know.

Three forty-five, hadn't eaten since that morning, didn't even get to snack on a student. I noticed that my hands were quivering, either because I didn't eat lunch or because breakfast was so damn junky, or maybe I was shaking to distance myself from the stillness of certain dead people.

Slumped over the box of letters, my head hanging between my stretched-out arms, I hugged the box to me, suddenly weaker and heavier than I'd ever been. I could feel my face twisting up all ugly as the pain in my head dug so deep that I started to grunt in time with each flash.

It was as if I were only half there. I could see this other me, standing calmly beside Janie on top of the Heap, watching me as I felt a stab between my eyes from deep in behind the surface. Grasping for some piece of softness to hold against my face, I nuzzled up against Heap Hill, which slowly fell a little, burying us.

Just as gravity means you don't actually have to concentrate to stay stuck on the world, you don't have to concentrate to live life either — convention does it for you. This is why I sometimes go out drinking with the others. Some say that there is no such thing as gravity, that the earth sucks. This is why I stayed in that night with a bottle, loosing out my over-tight joints and rivets.

I thought about Janie, about how I loved her so much and how I would have her for ever, how I would become her, wear her clothes, touch her men, walk her ways, how she would be so mine that I would hold her entire just under my skin. How unfortunate she had to leave us and go to the homecoming party, all dressed up in ribbons and ropes. She ought to have stayed to shorten the road, to teach me to laugh like it meant something, to show me how to cry. I would have her heart in spite of her, of this I was sure. It was an Absolut certainty.

Janie's heart was a special, a once-off, it held more tears than the volume of itself, and each one spilled was

That Girl from Happy

replenished from the ocean she kept there. I wondered whether she was born that way like Superman, or if it was a Spiderman kind of a thing — did she malform in an accident one momentous day?

Just in time, this pen is running dry.

You could make your own cut-and-paste Janie in your head, with a breakable twig, a pair of cartoon boots, a big-eyed look, and set it in this same ridiculously hip café. The customers picking over their regular dishes today must be thinking the surfaces have altered in hue, but the difference lies in the fact that the chair two tables down from me is wearing the wrong person. Janie used to sit there alone. I could swear on a spit that today was the first time the others had visited this café, knowing it to be half a holy place now. I know why Janie would sit in that particular chair; it was on account of the picture that would meet her at eye level over tea, an image of herself played by another and framed in silver. That's why it's my favourite too. The woman in it is lifeless and rotting and the whole earth looks blue as if a great hand shook the globe, and the earth and the sea became one. The café walls and each space that might other-wise be relaxed into, are covered with such pieces by famous artists, but Janie always made the artwork look painfully real, being so soft petal herself, as if spun from fine breaths.

I try to imagine her within the body of the man who is sitting there, replacing her, but in my imagining I acci-dentally make him stand and lift the picture off the wall. Before I realise he is doing it of his own accord, he has placed the picture in one of his bags, zipped it closed and is off down the street having left an okay tip.

And my next step is set on its way.

If there were prizes for freaky, my life would win one. What a day.

I wasn't allowed go to my own mother's funeral, but I don't care about that — I mean, it's just like a bad family party without food, it doesn't mean anything.

As expected, Janie's service was a bitch, an instability-fest of the first order. It confirmed it for me, I'd sooner opt for an alluvium colonic than attend a funeral do any day.

All those people, Jesus, tormenting themselves like that, worse than in the play, worse than a wedding even, writing little goodbye messages in the condolence book and whispering tiny treats to the casket, don't even get me started. Those that kept their teary seepages held back for the duration, they were just as bad, like parents who care before the prom, all those kisses and handshakes. I was waiting for the sandwiches to pass before me on the collection plate, or at least to be squashed against some smiling man to keep an instamatic flashing on, grooving to the sound of dead folk. It was lank.

'Seeing Janie off' was the phrase of the hour, that was our objective, that was our end. As we granted her this final big favour it struck me that, in real terms, as our skinny little prom queen didn't even attend, except in body, we were one pathetic mob, an audience without a show. I wanted to scrawl it up large, to storm the altar, to shout loud to those dumb faces that there is no holding a dead person's hand, just clutching at blue fingers, that's all there is. Death steals on up in a second, the core of a life nicked by some devil in a blink, no time for long lingering goodbyes. Don't freak me with your crying. Sing if you must but understand you simply cannot walk them to the gates; it's not pre-school, my friend, it's some place way beyond the finish line, the exclusion zone, no-go except for the over-qualified. Please, be my guest (I wanted to say), walk each other in some shoddy little stroll down the memory of her, just realise you're a little too late to really say goodbye. And for God's sake, use a hanky.

I'd rather be sent off without a crowd. When my time's up, perhaps I'll go with just a round of applause from my evil fifth-grade teacher and a deaf girl playing 'Copacabana' on a Moog, and spare everyone else.

The religion side of it doesn't bother me much, though I'm not a great fan, too much of it impeded my growing years. I did stubborn teenage battle with a litany of elders who knew better than to enjoy themselves, who conspired to wrench me every Sunday from my recovery, cramping my emerging splendour with their moral stratagems, confusing me with behaviours totally against their lessons preached. Extremely unctuous old folk, hit on the head by a chancy creed on the stray, only reason for it. Hell's fire always seemed to me a nice warm place to rub my cold little ass against, but I will always have a soft spot in my head for religion. This will probably grow larger the closer I get to final curtain.

The rotten nut of it is that you can't be around to enjoy the freedom. Other than that, death's not such a bad idea. So I'm not anti-death or anything. In fact, dying gets to be sort of a kindness to the rest of the world, especially when the person winds up aged about a million, decrepit as a green skanky toe, fucked on a cellular level, beyond money or repair. Like a four-safety-pins pair of panties giving at the crotch — ditch them, they're disgusting, buy a brand new pair with a support-gusset front and a thong back, less likely to set off the security alarm at the airport.

Nostalgia? Get over it.

It's good that old people die — while they live they are screwing up the myth that says 'forever'. You can see the mechanisms slowing through their translucent liver-spot skin, see the weak draining of the sluggish thinning blood, see the hole in their years, when so rickety-brittle, so slow and fogged-up, they stop travelling toward death and instead it travels back to meet them, to pick them up, scoop them (bags, pills of confusion, diapers and all) into the great hole, which with great practicality and blessed little ceremony, closes around them. The funeral celebrates the end of the nursing bills.

When the young die, it's a slap in the sentiment; they career toward the chasm with energy and rush, they insist the hole wraps around them. They are buried alive in death.

I sometimes think I want it both ways: to have my death and beat it, to dart over the line and pull myself back in time to catch breath. Some might call it 'death wish', but that part is a given these days; my problem is I also want life. I may not be good at living but I'd make for excellent field research.

The glasses were a nice touch, huge oval, black '60s things, and people presumed I was crying underneath so no one encouraged me to 'let it out'. I had to admire Italian Tony, he wasn't buying into any shit, just showed up like he should, didn't really look at anyone and was out the door at the end before you could crank out a second Amen. I'm glad we didn't catch each other's eye, I know we'd probably have laughed.

The Friends

Seeing her again when he had just learned he never would, wishing he could walk away with this image of her under blue, be the only one to look at it, touch it, was as much of a jolt as the news had been. Within that moment, at that start of recognition, Sammy realised that the café was practically empty and the staff out back collecting orders or filching a small rest from the clatter. Opportunity felt like permission to a mind weakened by regret. The two of them completely unescorted, Sammy and what was left of Janie. He felt as if he was already in the middle of the theft before it had begun. Pulling the picture away from the wall and walking out with it in his bag seemed like an act of completion — it was too easy a task for it to be wrong.

He didn't look back, so didn't see the tangled beautiful blonde tripping after him in his getaway path. He half-hoped to feel a hand on his shoulder, a stern body to call him to account; he really needed authority to step up and make of him a child.

Aimee pursued as easily as a mother might follow a toddler as it faltered, not sure if now was the time to confiscate the toy. She hadn't even a thumb-sketch plan of what to do, so there seemed no point in accosting him for the sake of it. Still, she wasn't about to let this apparition keep what was hers, no more than if he'd walked off with her own face. Through her very association with it, Aimee had earned the Janie picture — as a false, second-hand Janie herself, she and the picture were twinned. Would he stash it somewhere astute? Or maybe he had a seller waiting — she'd read somewhere that most robbers stole to order these days. He must have been a pro, such composure.

Sammy's other celebrated thefts (excluding rubbers freed from restrooms, ketchup from diners, glass tumblers from clubs, all that legitimate illegality) had begun a score of summers ago in a fishing town to the east of somewhere more substantial in Michigan. The Village fête was bigger than Christmas, longer anyway, and full to puking, with beer, beef and handicrafts. It took the people's minds off the nothing that filled their days. Every year since he could shout for them to wait up, he and his buddies had stolen candy-apples, corn dogs and badly-made stuffed toys, which they would present to some highly unimpressed local girl, fuelled by the naïve presumption that girls liked that sort of thing. These girls could not afford indifference, but they would stand resolute in disdain throughout their unimpressive lives, even while being buried in the least-expensive-but-one casket to lie forever under an inferior angel-dredged headstone with the wrong Bible quotation on it.

Their reaction was not a judgement against the immorality of the act, only against the worth of the prize and, by association, the giver. Joe-the-Nose was a serial snitch, nothing worse on this planet, even at seven, so on the morality barometer the young criminal scored in the lukewarm zone — not as good as Jesus, not as bad as Joe.

The future art thief and his young friends learnt valuable lessons, that the tough part, the smite of the crime, sat not in the fear, the guilt, the punishment, but in the coldness of the grey-green eyes of the girls they loved.

Janie's Irish eyes were colder now than they had ever been.

He needed Janie, needed to know what to do with the picture, but she couldn't be both cause and solution, so he was left not knowing. Not knowing must have saved him from a hundred things a day, perhaps it would catch him from this fall.

Aimee would have taken him for an actor (she hated actors) had she not had proof of his being an art thief. Watching his back as he walked, she couldn't help admiring how someone so prominent, with his good looks and loping gait, would chance to go unnoticed. Maybe thieves had to be actors to avoid being unearthed, worms playing at flowers.

Sammy was, in fact, a recovering actor; he'd just left LA and, he hoped, the whole profession behind him. It wasn't a profession, it was a hobby where a few won prizes — that had become clear. LA had been nothing more than an extended vacation. The only fortunate aspect of Janie's death was that it coincided with his inauspicious return, covering his failure somewhat.

Following hot on the high heels of his initial big-break film, which had reached number twelve in the top grossing films for its first week and had then faded, came a whole lot of talk. The kind of talk that feels like action, being so damn energised, and big with promise, growing fatter with each call. Sammy hadn't landed another rôle.

When first swept out there over a year ago, plucked from the road and lent wings by his agent, he had been offered six weeks on a new sitcom, which he'd turned down, on the fanatic advice of the suits who loved him to the point of proffering nipple, in order to keep himself free for the film offers that never arrived. Six months after that and he would have sold his own mother for a walk-on in that same sitcom. Six weeks after that, he got two days on a commercial for sugar-free gum, but even his unsold mother would have had a hard time picking him out from the crowd. Since then, absolutely nothing, and he had to admit that he hadn't shone in the film except with some borrowed varnish lent by the whole hype. His mediocrity doubtless leaked out onto the celluloid surface when he tested, with fewer and fewer screen-tests as time laughed on. Money had become a problem, and he didn't fancy spending years dragging his personality from casting to casting only to wind up working as a production assistant ten years down the line, for a director fifteen years his junior. The decision to forget the whole damn business was an easy one — the whole damn business had long since forgotten him.

He remembered a time about a year before when his agent took a whole afternoon off to go shopping with him; a month ago the same woman couldn't find time to talk to him between one sip of her hazelnut coffee and the next. Witch. Still … no point tapping a dead vein. Film-world intensity didn't much suit him — he couldn't guess at the men who knew the man, let alone hint at an affiliation, couldn't talk the talk, couldn't suck the suck. The whole town had been fucking with him, fodder boy. Great face.

Aimee saw that her game was veering toward a small market, and quickened at the prospect of witnessing some brand new hollow of criminal action. In honour of this she fell back a couple of steps and half hid in a doorway, before continuing to track him with lighter feet.

Feeling upstaged and ignored by the carnival, Sammy wandered past the meat cabinets, which were strange with shapes and textures he didn't recognise as cow, sheep, or pig. These lumps of animal-on-trust made him remember how Janie died, and left him feeling slightly dizzy, an ill taste on his tongue. He tried to picture how she must look now.

There was one stall he'd always dropped in on while living in this neighbourhood, a herbal medicine counter manned by a Korean or a Chinese man, he couldn't tell which, but knew he had to differentiate in these circumstances. (Sammy prided himself on the fact that he had never called a Canadian 'American' by mistake.) He'd often bought the cold and flu infusion, and had missed it in LA as the air-conditioning in hotels and the proximity of his co-hopefuls at studio auditions left him susceptible to such things. He thought it typical of the disappointment he had felt living there that he had come down with more colds and snuffles than during the previous five New York winters and the twenty-odd Michigan ones preceding that. Today he looked along the jars for something different, an elixir, a cure-all for everything for all time; cocaine had let him down big-time on this one and now he was drastic in his need.

'Cold and flu, cold and flu,' the Asian repeated delightedly, proving his trainspotter's joy in the herbs of his prodigal customers. Dermatitis, asthma, cystitis.... What? No dusty

Judy May Murphy

little jar marked, 'The Whole Damn Fuck-Farm $5 The Lot'? He mostly wanted something that could predict his future weakness and prevent its manifesting itself; he needed firm ground, just for a couple of years, or even something to make him forget his weakness for more than a couple of hours.

'Cold and flu,' Sammy said reluctantly.

He wandered out of the market again, feeding Aimee's intrigue, convincing her that he knew he was being tailed and was cleverly dancing her off. He went into a mid-priced Polish restaurant two blocks over and ordered some bits, so Aimee sat near the door and did the same, first putting on her huge sunglasses in case he recognised her from the Janie café.

A good two hours were trifled away, each with small food and hot drinks and the newspapers stamped with the name of the restaurant on each page. Aimee tired soonest: having occupied herself in this way for most of the past year, its novelty value was on a par with ordinary bread. Just as she caved in and approached him to ask about the picture, he waved over a waiter and paid for his leisure. So, once more, she threaded him to her with an invisible string, and hurriedly threw down some money lest the string break with distance and the swing of the restaurant door.

She realised that the time for the service was coming up fast, but since Sammy and the Janie picture seemed to be moving in the general direction of the funeral home, she let him lead on — no point breaking a perfectly lovely tradition. When it became clear that he'd be passing the front door of her destination, she decided to leave any confrontation until the last moment; at least if he turned nasty there would be people she knew around.

He wondered, as he walked through the last few yards to this next and most awkward appointment, if he had been known as Sammy back then, or had he still been Dave? Or would he be Howard like the first time they all met? Didn't want to come across all show-biz at a time like this. Looking suddenly mildly baffled, he stepped inside.

Aimee stood outside a minute — too good to be true, he was a character in her world.

'Sammy, you got here.' The choice had been made.

'I went to that café, but I must have just missed you,' he said to the friends.

Hugging them more politely than keenly, smiling a non-smile, balancing pleased and not pleased, as dictated by the situation, conscious that his shirt was too bright to be respectful and hoping they would think it a coastal idiosyncrasy. They hugged him back with an equally measured warmth. The sight of them all together like old toys on a bedroom shelf — Fat Molly, Josh, Lucy, so familiar yet imperceptibly altered by the days — made him feel as if the past year had been stolen. None clearly took the lead as chief mourner; although Lucy ushered people around with more zeal, the rest commanded secondary rôles, hanging back from the condolence book, referring new arrivals on to others' grief.

'Aimee,' greeted Lucy, 'did you stay in the café all this time? I tried to call you.'

Aimee tried to duck away from Sammy's attention, at least until she worked out what an art thief was doing there. Not having seen her before, Sammy paid her no more mind than if she still stood in the shadow of a secret door.

Since Sammy was so evidently staring about him with due care, wondering which one was Italian Tony, Josh's tactful eyes directed him to the man who had poked Janie home the last few miles. Italian Tony and Sammy met in the middle to shake each other's hand firmly, to sniff the competition even as the prize lay dead. Like men, like mourners, they had nothing to say, so they parted, and ran at slow-walking pace into the small chapel, where the priest was settling into his responsibility, proclaiming heartfelt appreciation on behalf of a family he had never met, calling the deceased Jeannie half the time, Jane the other half, and reading her details from notes. Just as well no one was listening.

There was certainly grief but it didn't flow, as eager tears were held back and fake ones pushed out. Many of the mourners looked at the closed casket, a few at the priest out of a respect for protocol, if for no other reason, with some fixing on their feet as one or two cast around for old friends, or for hints as to how to comport themselves.

That the continuous swell of sniff on sniff was not the result of a mass session of 'a little half line for the pain' but was instead a common side-effect of tears, took Aimee a while to realise. She took the second last row, the better to watch the proceedings from there without seeming to skulk at the back. Sammy saw her for the first time in front and to the left of him — he'd placed himself at the very back in the far corner, a vestige of stupid-kid classroom custom. She wasn't crying, so he felt he didn't have permission. She wore huge great sunglasses to hide a sadness that didn't show even as he saw through the edge of the glasses right to the rim of her dry eye. Was it suitable for him then? Was it a good idea? His anger he knew he had to hide, but could he spin it out as sadness? Anybody? Please?

Until recently, Sammy and death had been on distant nodding terms — his Granny, his dog, neither of whom he'd been sorry to see go. There were hundreds of others he'd have sent off to death with a specially packed lunch, but the way of things has never been kind.

Suddenly the service was over and Sammy and Aimee wished they'd paid attention in case there was a conversation later. Italian Tony was straight out the door as if the smell of Janie had caught up with him, or perhaps the stink of his conscience drove him off. The boyfriend is always blamed; Sammy kept forgetting that he wasn't that man anymore.

Aimee split right after, stalking from the front this time.

Many went up and touched the casket, taking their inexorable leave, returning truths too critical to have to haul around for the rest of their days, whispering secrets, confessing in the hope she wouldn't haunt them. Others stayed looking at their shoes, probably accomplished as much.

Some presumed that leaving last meant that you suffered most, so they hung on until there were just a few left, including Sammy hidden seated in his corner, and Boots, a guy he used to know, standing at Janie's side as per history. Then the stragglers realised there was no one of consequence left to witness their disquiet and moved on, leaving just the two men and Janie. Sammy watched Boots bend over the casket and kiss it at the place where her lips would be, tears falling onto the polished wood.

Boots was holding the only flower in the place, and rested this on the casket to mark the kiss. During his high times Sammy had funked his way through many parties where he sat, all liberal and free, in the same room as couples making love, but this was different, this was too intimate, in his mouth he could taste the salt as it slipped from his watching eyes. He removed himself quietly out into the street to join the tail of the people-stream flowing into Happy.

Happy was the kind of place that expanded and contracted in mysterious ways; always full if only with a handful of people, there was never room for one more but one more would always fit. Italian Tony was in the corner with some woman, trying not to smile too much, freaking that he couldn't do some business.

At the bar sat three old guys with paunches like pregnancies, asses curved to the shape of the barstools, guys with words that screamed as loud as their false hair, oldies entirely made up of hops and barley fumes, held together by sticky spills and their need to keep it mixing. The influx threatened their safe little beerdom.

'They've come from the funeral of that girl. One that topped herself.'

'Nah, it wasn't a funeral. They're having the body shipped, so I guess it was like a prayer service or something.'

'They should burn it, save some money, burn the body and post the ashes back.'

'Or sprinkle them on the dance floor in Cheeko's?'

'Or in the stalls in the men's room, ha, ha!'

'Welcome home, baby!'

Sammy's eyes burned through to their pint-sized coterie, signalled a stop.

'Oh, I'm sorry, son, did you know her?'

'Know her? He had her!'

They didn't all tune in together.

They forgave themselves with the offer of a double whiskey (no hard feelings), which Sammy took over to Fat Molly, Josh, Lucy and the blonde woman who had taken off her sunglasses. He hoped she was new, or else things could be awkward; with his memory and luck she might even be his cousin, the old joke about having a great head for names but being rotten with faces couldn't always cover the insult, especially if it wasn't the face he should be remembering.

'Aimee,' she offered along with her hand.

'Thank God,' he almost said, swapping it for 'Sammy' just in time, and shaking her hand politely.

Aimee felt itchy in such civility. Everything felt polite, all the people comporting themselves in ways akin to shiny sensible shoes. Having dealt with the formalities at the funeral parlour, they now had to remember quickly how to talk to one another — the normal 'what have you been up to?' wouldn't cut. She decided to find out what the deal was with this Sammy the Con, and then shed them for home.

The hush became worse than any mistake that might eradicate it, and Sammy, having put his drink down too soon, had to start.

'Almost didn't make it, I thought it wasn't till tomorrow.'

'No, it's tomorrow that they're shipping the body back,' Josh explained. 'Her body back,' he self-corrected.

Lucy's manner was as prim as her frame and she had made the round of calls politely as etiquette required. Having gone west around the world starting with Dublin, by California she had found herself rather tired, so she succinctly and benevolently told Sammy, 'We'll be saying goodbye to Janie on the fifth.' Sammy had taken this as her euphemism for the service, a point which wasn't cleared up as he had phoned the taciturn Garth-the-bar for the time and location. Luckily, Lucy, as ever, had called a few times, as if conversations needed polishing or something.

Lucy flicked back her long black hair and got ready her defence, but fell silent again as Boots walked in, grey and sunken, like a vacuum sucking further in on itself, and made straight for the bar, one more action lived through, another aching moment done. His clothes were black but wrinkled and slightly damp, his whole look dark and contracted, his face too grey for a skin tone, his eyes too hot for seeing through.

'Boots seems very upset,' said Josh. 'I mean, more than I would have expected.'

'Who's Boots?' asked Aimee, craning for a glance at rabid grief. She knew Lucy and Josh, and had just met Fat Molly that day, but was too new to Happy ever to have known Boots. The bar had generations, about four per year, and your association was measured against who you knew and when.

'He's a friend,' Lucy told her, admitting him to the band on account of the day that was in it despite the fact that most had long since begun to consider him a social wart.

'He only just heard about it yesterday,' said Josh.

Lucy rushed in again to defend her competency, 'It's so hard to get a hold of him, he's always everywhere and nowhere and running between the two.'

Sammy wondered if Lucy's jet black hair had been specially dyed for the occasion; he seemed to remember it having been every other colour except the more natural ones.

'It's four days since the rest of us heard,' Fat Molly said, reminding them she was there, 'I was still a mess the day after I heard.'

Her constant self-referencing was bugging Aimee big time now. 'Me too, after Lucy called.' Aimee planted her own credentials while denying Fat Molly's singularity, 'We all were.'

Knowing it might still be too soon to kick in with the shared reminiscence, Sammy ventured: 'You said something about, er … how did she...?'

'A rope,' was all Fat Molly could manage.

They looked to Josh to take over. 'From a tree in Central Park,' he added, not fully taking up the rôle.

At this point Boots joined them and the talk went careful once more, caution emerging as more silence sweating. Not that he'd have noticed — to Boots they were all a waking dream, to be entertained even in their unreality. To them Boots looked undecided as to whether he was in this world or off with Janie in the new place. He was odd, drained of an inner essence and the normality it obliged, barely substantial enough to stand but no one thought to offer him their seat. They watched him rock a little with the air, holding his beer like a prop, not once thinking to maybe lift it to his mouth. In turn he watched Aimee who was a tiny mouthful away from emptying his glass completely.

'Such a terrible accident,' Lucy sighed in a cover-all manner.

No accident, the brutal intention occurred to them all, but none was brave enough to voice it.

'How long … are you staying?' Boots asked Sammy; their old rivalry had yet to burn itself out on the pyre.

Judy May Murphy

'A couple of days, I'm not sure. Maybe I'll even stay for a while.'

Mighty big luggage for a maybe.

'But ... don't they need you ... in LA, for the ... acting?'

Sammy abandoned his launch into the 'Hollywood is dead' thing, deciding it would prove too high-maintenance. A bad actor blames his town, but Sammy knew that it was all down to him, so the less said about that circus trip, the better.

'It's not really working out.'

'I'm sorry to hear it,' said Boots.

He was sorry but he was also not sorry, a bit like Sammy himself.

Hitting her leg against his half-concealed bags for the fifth time, Fat Molly asked, 'Howard ... er, Sammy I mean, where are you staying tonight?'

'Washington Square Park? I hadn't thought.'

'Well, my place may not be up to much but at least it's indoors.'

'Thanks, Fat Molly.'

All Fat Molly wanted was a fortnightly happy-ever-after, a man to love her for all time until the next man came along. She was between men at that time, a dangerous hiatus — she was lethal as a child between feeds, a lion short on blood, a lush between bars. The Moll was getting twitchy, her huge brown eyes had the target companion in sight. She hadn't the courage to face the dark alone, or the sounds, or the animals that came out when she was on her own, the ones that asked her why she didn't have a man.

And poor Sammy thought it was a simple invitation to sleep over.

Aimee decided she'd go along too. She wasn't letting the picture out of her sight, and she knew what Molly's agenda was and that another woman would be about as odious a presence as rotting cabbage in a cake shop. She invited herself by saying to Sammy, loud enough for all: 'That's fascinating, but let's discuss it further at Fat Molly's place, it's getting very noisy here.' And before the elected hostess could find a way to twist things back the way she wanted, the three of them were sitting on the sofa-bed and armchair in her apartment.

Fat Molly was too nervous to risk asking Sammy questions about LA, worried that she might fail in comparison, nervous, too, that her own life had played out too dull to be news. Equally afraid to talk about Janie, or to give Aimee a chance to impress, she turned to the universal babysitter to bail her out.

'Do you mind if I switch on the TV? There was this hold-up in the bank across the road from work, one of the girls got talked to for the news.'

At first she thought she'd found it but it was something else; still, it was noise so she left it running. All three watched a local news story unfold of the robbery of an art work from the café, Sammy with his breath held, Aimee thrilled that she hadn't confronted him, the secret double bound, as if she were stealing from the thief.

'Hey, that's where we were earlier,' said Fat Molly. 'I wonder if it had already been stolen by then.'

The report concluded with the mandatory confusion as to why this 'other' type of person, so unlike the viewer and the broadcaster, committed these heinous criminal acts.

'No ransom has been requested, nor has the café received any indication that the theft was intended as some sort of misguided political statement. It is thought unlikely that the thief is an avid art collector as no offer was made to buy it first. Cindy Sherman is considered to be a cornerstone of the postmodern movement. So the question remains, "Why did he do it?"'

Sammy didn't know.

It was growing heavy in him. The deed blurred, the reasons unexamined, implications were not even attendant in him, except perhaps as a dull dread, blood in the sand, drunk fathers on the doorstep at dawn.

The thunder rolled a little closer, carried in on the television waves.

Could well be that he was overestimating the importance of the theft's being broadcast. It was a slow newsday; perhaps the next item would be about some lost cat. That would put the whole thing into civilised perspective.

'An eighty-one-year-old woman is in hospital tonight after a brutal....'

My life is over, he thought.

Fat Molly got up to make some dinner as soon as it became clear that Aimee was comfortable. As she baked and prepared things she chattered through the last year's biography of everyone she and Sammy knew. She was one of the only people in New York who baked cakes without using either packet mix or microwave — class that was, a hint of hometown homecoming queen. Knowing that she might be bringing someone home, but not knowing who, she had a carrot cake ready to go, all grated, mixed and beaten into submission, ready for the heat of Molly's oven.

They ate fancyleaf salad and spinach bread, chased down by the cake, and drank a bottle of red wine whose origin and age (unlike its volume) meant nothing to them.

'You're a great cook, Fat Molly,' said Sammy. That's a proposal of marriage in some rustic quarters of the land.

After the fourth wedge of cake he excused himself for a moment, and took his luggage into the bathroom to check if he'd really messed up. Or had he only been dreaming? When he finally gathered the nerve to take the picture out of his bag — an ordinary large sports bag, not the wooden ark of the qualified art thief — one of its edges was torn and broken. The damage done was telling, proving to him that there was no going back, no making it all right again. Sticky tape and a lot of hard wishing would never get things back to the way they had been, only hours before. He quickly returned it to the bag, and just as quickly returned himself to the smell of Fat Molly's care. Safe. Safe like Janie.

His anger crept up as the terror subsided, if the stealing of this picture were important enough to appear on the news, why had it not been guarded better? Why was there no sign of the value which he thought was only projected by him? He had never heard of Cindy Sherman; no one had.

'Girls, have either you heard of Cindy Sherman?'

'No,' Aimee lied. 'Oh, wasn't she that one just on the news, the robbery?'

'Of course I've heard of Cindy Sherman. Next to Andreas Serrano, she's my favourite artist,' said Fat Molly as if she hung out with them on weekends.

Judy May Murphy

'Artist? I thought it was a photograph. A photograph.'
He could hear the voice of his lawyer through his own,
addressing the members of the jury.

'Photography is art,' she retorted.

'Since when? Since when was a photograph a work of art?'

'Since they started selling them, I guess,' offered Aimee.

Sinking further back into the cushions, a fresh bottle of
wine opened, they gradually found the conversational
concord which had been evading them till now; they
sutured the gaps which awkwardness had left gaping,
relaxing out the clumsiness of the newly strange.

'I still can't believe it,' said Sammy.

'We all thought that after that private clinic place she'd
be fine, I mean, they shouldn't have let her out until she was
cured. Right?'

'Right.'

Fat Molly was feeling like nothing now that the meal
was over. She feared that Janie was the focus again, as there
had never been room for the two of them together. She would
die if Janie stayed so big in their heads. All's fair in war.
Janie was a living corpse, dangerous in the mystery contained in its treated flesh; she had to be killed over again.

'I've been thinking,' Fat Molly said. 'How do we even
know it was Janie in the casket? What if the fact that it
obviously couldn't be left open was used as an excuse?
Maybe she was never in there.'

'Why could they obviously not leave it open?'

'Well, she looked so … defective before the, the whole
thing, so what must she have looked like after? Bulging eyes
and bruising, we had to be saved from that.'

Sammy realised he'd been trying to imagine her only as she was last year.

'I didn't see her after the hospital, or during.'

'Neither did I,' Aimee lied to ensure a better tale.

'She didn't look anything like you remember her,' said Molly. Knowing that one glimpse of a skilful depiction of Janie's dead body would fix her in a less romantic light, Molly began to reminisce, looking past them into the middle distance like an old-film virgin dreamer.

'It was so sad. Her hair had sort of grown back but not really, it was much thinner and patchy, like the grass under trees. I think it was lighter too, greying. Her face was really full at the cheeks and she was whiter than ever, like bleached even, spongy-looking.'

'How do you mean "grown back"?' asked Sammy.

Fat Molly only then understood that neither of them knew anything of Janie's breakdown, save perhaps the skeleton facts, so she settled into the telling. Travelling her mind through the scene toward the point that she would fill in for them, she allowed herself another glimpse of the door behind which she heard noises, and wondered how much she could endure remembering or should tell to her select little audience.

So Fat Molly said nothing of the kitchen door, locked, with Janie inside. She said nothing of the hour she had waited, twitching, for her to emerge, an hour completed with the grinding of a key in a lock, when out had walked Janie with her hair, eyebrows and lashes cut and plucked to nothing, her skin a grey-green, except in the hairless places where it roared red-pink and white. Alone, with her mad eyes off somewhere else, not looking at Molly, she had

crossed in a hair-plastered night-shirt to the sofa, and sat
there watching the blank television.

They were offered the PG version instead. 'When I
arrived in from work she had cut all her hair off, and when I
tried to comfort her, she wouldn't talk to me.'

The rest was easy to recount; most of it had already been
told to sympathetic listeners, who heard how, taking the
phone into the bathroom, she had called her own doctor,
then called the doctor who was covering for him. The part
where she sat and watched Janie, afraid to talk, to move, to
trigger the next event even as she bathed in a deep thrill to
see her like that, was cut with false images of Fat Molly
with hot milk and towels and kind words. So the doctor
arrived and he took care of everything else and Molly took
the applause over and over with each public telling.

The rest of the film ran on in Molly's head, Satan's cut,
she never let it air; it had been binned to protect Molly's
dormant shame, and the smallness of it made it hurt to
watch. So Sammy and Aimee were left outside again, never
to hear how the doorbell's ringing had started Janie
screaming, sort of yelping and gulping at the air, or how it
took the doctor a good ten minutes to calm her. The doctor
couldn't make Janie tell him about what happened, couldn't
stem the low humming sound that was coming from her
pursed-up lips. He turned to Fat Molly for some answers,
but beyond Janie's name, rank, and favourite cereal, she
decided she had nothing to tell him, only suggesting with a
jerk of her head that he look in the kitchen for clues. He was
in there for only seconds before coming out and phoning
somewhere for a bed. As they sat waiting for the ambulance,

he gave Molly details which she was to pass on to the family in the morning.

'So I was able to explain her whole mental history to the doctor. I almost saved her life, you might say. In fact, her parents even called me up to thank me, and everyone was saying that if it hadn't been for me she would have killed herself.'

'Poor Janie,' Sammy said, not knowing the correct response was 'Poor Molly.'

So she chose to add the part about cleaning up the kitchen the next morning, how anything with hair or candy-cake vomit on it went straight into the bin, and everything was washed down with all the micro-cleaners and mega-cleaners and lemon-and-pine-anything to hand. All true, except Lucy had done it.

'Jesus,' said Aimee.

That was good enough.

Molly the caring, considerate and brave, all that, yeah.

There was no more story and no more wine so Aimee left, taking careful note of the address, arriving home to a full ear of messages. She was bored by them in advance and so went back out to Happy to get wasted. Why not?

Shrieking phone lines all around the Village had been hurling gossip, questions, accusations and denials as the friends tried to make some sense of what had happened. They all knew not to phone Fat Molly, none had the stomach for a clash of that magnitude; they wanted a fight of the neophyte kind, wanted to eat pretzels and suck on a can at the same time, wanted bruised but not bloody.

Sammy had known that Janie had a breakdown or had tried to kill herself or something a few years previously, way before New York, but had never imagined what it might look like; the label was all he'd taken in. Now Sammy tried to imagine her breaking, his head was almost weeping, 'I don't know what she looks like.'

He sat looking out the window of Fat Molly's place with a cold bottle of beer, searching for her in everybody who passed, seeing the possibility of her look in every light eclipsed. If he couldn't find her, how could he ask forgiveness?

This Fat Molly thing, staying with her, knowing she wanted him, it was getting too tight even though he'd just arrived, like pinchy new shoes. Agony. He wasn't essentially doormat material, but he was fundamentally homeless, and being imprisoned with a wifelette and a chicken casserole wasn't the worst thing that had ever happened to him. The rooms in this city were too small, the buildings too close, running was impossible without smashing into something hard, like walls or women.

Fat Molly was smart enough to know that you put a man sleeping on the sofa if you want him to end up in your bed, but feared that years of friendship between them might mean that he would take the code literally and stay there. Sammy didn't know what he wanted or how to get it, and was just waiting for fate to step in and inspire or volunteer him. Without saying anything, Fat Molly put a duvet and pillow on the sofa and disappeared into the bedroom with some standard non-sexual goodnight, the type of goodnight you would not be ashamed to bestow on your most elderly relatives. Sammy interpreted this as a repudiation, a

That Girl from Happy

redrawing of the friendship divide, but before he had time to counter-manipulate, she was gone.

Since landing the film-rôle he had never had to go to bed alone. Even when tired, he would do whatever his fatigue would permit and then gently, or not so gently, depending on whether she was the vacantly optimistic or the vainly obstinate type, suggest it was now time she left. He felt that if he went to sleep with a smile and the words, 'yeah, tomorrow', on his lips he would be safe from bad dreams. His talisman tonight was a line of coke which he sneaked up his nose in the bathroom, both faucets running so Molly couldn't tell. He passed her on his way out, but she was too busy wondering if he had noticed how good she looked in baby-doll pyjamas and braided hair to wonder why his hand went straight to his nose and then quickly to his hair as he grinned and shuffled past her back to his sofa home.

This was the first time in over a year that he was to fall asleep without his libidinous night-cap. He would really have to get into masturbating, the chick stream would be drying up now that he was mortal again. He had always thought of masturbation as relief for the socially in-competent, as a playground slide into loneliness, but he had recently discovered how lonely it can be with someone beside you, particularly if that someone was anyone, so maybe the whole self-sufficiency thing needed rethinking. Fat Molly chose that exact moment to walk into his room, naked and perfect, her long, chestnut-coloured braids hiding nothing. But Sammy pretended to be fast asleep and she returned to her room, prepared to fight on tomorrow, to win out over Janie by claiming her erstwhile man.

Fat Molly hadn't been sleeping well these past few nights, she'd drift off only to be haunted by remembered sugar fancies, pink and yellow nursery cakes, which, just before the breakdown story started, had been left in Janie's kitchen cupboard, and had somehow been dropped from the story in the telling. But Molly would always forgive herself in the morning by convincing herself of her good intentions, she had merely pushed the girl along the road to professional intervention, nudged her along with a fresh cream-cake or twelve.

Sammy, Fat Molly, Aimee, Lucy, Josh, and all the rest of them, folded into the city like flakes they were, sifted in through beetling streets, carved up by the train-lines and spat out through turnstiles. The grieven friends had been scraped back.

True to the cut of the night it should have been raining, a black rain, but it wasn't.

Diffused through the city-mix once again, they had nothing on the outside to mark their loss. Death, for all its enormity, for all its brutal eternity, hadn't made them different, had awarded no medals, peddled no answers. With a pygmy lick of red-eye and a choke unseen in the throat, they sat, stood, slumped and tramped their way, rubber-souled normals once again, sleeve to sleeve, groin to butt with people who were unaware of there ever having been a Janie Jay, didn't know what happened, and wouldn't much care if they did. All with half-eye searched about in other faces for a hint that the world was hurting also, but all understood that the platform is a leveller, that the momentous is mean change when you're packed into the S, that prize-day is merely Tuesday, your favoured breast is just a small floppy mound, your best-ever friend is some starchy suit, your mother is just any prayerful woman from some-where else, your dead friend is a statistic read from *The Post* one time only; they humbled under the form of it.

Life sat massive as they hauled off home to their bug boxes, tired, and knowing that death might not feel so different, most went on capricious little wonderings, suicide fancied as they searched in their mirrors for support. All of them, those who had latched onto Janie through bodies and buildings they had long since ditched: people from Happy who couldn't, through identical glasses, remember how they'd first met her or when they last did; actors from the play; fringe people who had swept her up; incidental bright young meat from parties and cafés, guys who were girls when she met them first or maybe the other way; those who loved her better when she was alive and those who only loved her dead; all types, all twisted with it. Drinking and pilling.

'Time heals all pain,' the preacher had said, and some mothers concurred in little cards and phonecalls left on mats and trapped in machines. No one believed anyone that night.

Best clothes flung where mites could sniff the day off them, before the air could settle, the friends were sweating out dreams of breathing in soil, woken into false night by a smiling Janie, never-dead, shaking them gently with her claw. All manner of animals chewed through their dreams, paid no heed to such calming barricades as lovers, fresh linen or scented burning oils.

Those who slept on fuller gin bellies dreamed below the elixir-line till morning, so the dreams slipped out under-dreamt, spilled on the pillow for tomorrow night as drunken bloods subdued the beasts.

Time sat fat on the people's bedside tables between contact-lens cases, small change and tokens, invisible as most abstractions are, sagacious as only the once removed can be, ticking on over without pity. Pity had been eaten up earlier in the day, flimsy allowances.

When the friends woke from battle, Time granted them a beat before letting them remember. In need of the night's sleep they'd only just had, all would be early for work, or for whatever the day had schemed.

Only one lay through an untroubled, fitless night. She stole their peaceful sleeping to feed her eternal rest. A want of flowers couldn't bother her now; that they'd rebroken her neck to get it sitting plumb, that couldn't hurt. Her life's single major concern sat now consigned to a tidy box in an untidy room.

When Sammy woke up it was with immense relief that his arm, his back, his feet, touched nothing living, he was alone. Then as things tripped back into place, realisations slotted together, he remembered where he was and why, and looked around for Fat Molly, hoping to find her gone, hoping that she had made him breakfast before she left.

But convenient absence was not within her realm; while not exactly obstinate she was always somehow there.

While she waited for Sammy to come and eat breakfast she picked a little more over her hatred of Janie. Fat Molly's mother always told her to hold her enemies close. Why? So she could let them hurt her without stretching, cut her without reaching? Connection doesn't save you from someone, immunity cannot be found in biting on the poison. This she knew.

Fat Molly's unrequited Janie-based anger had grown as love does in the absence, even as reason says it might have diminished into a sympathetic surrender in a cessation of all pre-mortem hostilities. Such a well-nurtured hate, suckled early on empty concerns, so when fully grown it took nothing but the air to keep it active.

From the day Janie clicked her heels and hung, it had been variously called accident, disaster, sad news, tragedy, mishap, unfortunate occurrence — the Fuck. Cheap party trick, that's what it was and Molly knew it like she knew all desperation's games. It was another device of Janie's, death, the ultimate bluff.

It had started for Fat Molly even before it had started, just as it would never finish even after the end. Less than two years, could that be right?

She had been much the same then as today, working for a reasonable pittance in a café bar where occasionally trendy people would hang out; pilfering coffee beans, smiling for tips, scraping to afford to dress like them, nip-and-tucking with the notes to make the bills. Janie brought in more rent, but the cost was huge.

She wished to Christ she'd never hung up on that girl who said she was working the sex lines, she might have been a safer bet, probably looked like a manatee, most of them do.

Fat Molly hadn't wanted to share at all, but her fear of eviction outweighed her fear of domination or personal trespass, only just. An enormous concern from the off, a six-foot-sixer of a worry, her first cut of misgiving had been well founded (albeit as a self-fulfilling foreboding) but misplaced.

What would Janie Kelly be like? Janie's actual size, and that projected by her demeanour, were merely the inaugural misgivings in a series of high anxieties which had bloomed like algae from the moment the new room-mate had been located. It was as if the deal with Molly mutated Janie, made her plastic perfect to the point of abnormality.

'Did you find a room-mate yet?'

'Yeah. She's a working actress.'

'Great, can't wait to meet her; what does she look like?'

'No idea. She's Irish though.'

'Excellent, I love Ireland.'

Just as no one is allowed not to like Ireland, their preference of Janie over Fat Molly seemed, to the latter, completely assured. The 'actress' part doubled the glamour, sat down twice as hard on Molly's nerves.

Actress, no, the image didn't augur well. You think, okay, so, firstly self-absorbed, secondly beautiful, willowy and talented, so as not to make a fault of the self-absorption, thirdly — oh, what's the word? — 'eloquent,' with or without the help of Shakespeare (she had to stop counting). Actresses usually laughed with the only loud laugh in existence that doesn't sound like a drain, and twinkled stuff everywhere, eyes, hair, teeth, oh yes, white teeth like new tiling ... Moll had sat for days in the dark making up a monster, so that when the real creature arrived on the doorstep, confusion and disappointment muddied up what should have been pure bolt relief.

The wispy girl standing there couldn't nearly compete with her predicted self. Not close to equalling the romance, lustre and kick of the European cities she'd abandoned, instead she seemed to have taken on the character of an airport terminal, all the jet-set run off her, melted, leaving a slightly worn person at the door, pretty but manageable. Her skin was so white, as if she'd long ago had a bad quarrel with the sun, her face was a perfect oval with only slightly protruding cheekbones, her features were the sort that didn't come out to meet you, rather inviting you into their careful size. Three large travel-bags hung from the tiniest of shoulders, straining beneath a neck so slim it seemed threatened by the weight of her long hair. And those clothes — still, maybe they were fashionable somewhere. Then, to rest the worries for a while, to keep them simmering only slightly.

Gradually Molly's defences were re-erected, new battles waged. Two days after Janie arrived in New York the apartment had become the location of this territorial struggle, each to assert her taste in the place; she with the most vases would win. The resulting mix of bold primaries and burnished antique failed completely, and the place looked like a five-year-old left to dress herself. The struggle wasn't lost on Janie either, who, being far less competitive, thought they should have stuck to more primitive methods of territorial claim, and pissed in the corners for a few weeks.

Still, Molly reassured herself in her mother's voice, it would only be for a few months, a year at most, and she would keep close watch for harm.

Big mistake, sharing someone's present-time, thinking they can be shaken off easy as a shower of rainwater when really they continue on with you, limpets on your rocky past, and there stick so comfy cosy with the achievement you thought was yours alone, starring in your dramas, stalwart through your legends and munching on your pie. Janie was victorious in that awful American institution 'popularity', and now its longevity (not normally a pre-requisite to the condition) had joined in promoting her to the status of legend. From their entangled days all the good stuff had been Janie's. Can you take it with you? They say not, but Molly, thinking about how Janie still felt like such a threat, had started to wonder already. Quietly from the other side, munch.

This pie of Molly's is a metaphysical one, it has to be said, especially if we are to speak of Janie calmly biting out small mouthfuls, good as it would have been had it been real, tasty-pumpkin-cherry-beef.

Janie was short, and thinner than cheap washing-up liquid. Even after she moved out, Molly often thought of her at mealtimes. It seemed that she survived on what she absorbed from table or counter to toilet, before all five-foot-two of her would hurl out melons, chocolates, whole lobsters, things she never even ate but felt guilty about anyway. Molly thought that if she did the same, she'd end up exactly like Janie, that Janie had started out in Ireland a good five-feet-ten-inches tall but had puked herself out so much, she'd shrunk, until eventually she could think of nothing else, which made her easier to live with. Molly used to imagine, when she needed Janie smaller still, that after a few more years Janie would be able to lose herself between coffee cups or in the pocket of a jacket in some lost-and-found. After, came the thought that maybe then she'd get together with all the other shrunken people and do over someone tall like Molly, but for then her safety was assured as long as she only spent money on milk and not food.

Skimmed it would have to be, Molly had an eating derangement of her own, no need to borrow her roommate's disease. Difference being, Molly just wouldn't put it in, and was amazed at Janie's ingenuity, such capacious moves, to have it and to purge the ramifications. But Molly was afraid of the food passing through a second time — it sort of doubled the reality of it.

So she kept it simple, two hours daily of self-inflicted high-impact hell, aerobic agonies in different gyms a short jog away from each other, not that it was anyone's business anyway, free weights in the closet, enough steps up to the apartment door to warrant an elevator, a physical job, effusive hand, arm and head gestures, difficult shoes. No fat, not even the natural grease off her fingers licked, no full portions, only quarter servings spread to cover small delft, no food after eight o'clock at night and no special snack planned for seven-thirty (salad with Sammy had been an exception, one not even permitted on Thanksgiving). Breakfast was the devil, as over-excessive as an everyday Christmas, avoidable, therefore avoided. She would eat chicken, no skin, boiled, broiled or just touched by the light, bread with massive great pockets of air in it, naked bread and salad with dressing on the side where it stayed, nothing that looked fat in case it was catching, so no apples, potatoes or mango. Just one will

Judy May Murphy

be fine, just a half please, no thanks, I ate a short while ago, they look lovely though, usually I'd have one. Can't eat, won't eat. No sugar ever, sugar was a sly friend to fat, mutating into lard as soon as it was down your throat and out of sight. Cake-eating was a trick, she would mush it between her fingers and replace it on the plate, leaving you with one eighth of the original volume, all the original cake, and the deceit rounded off with a reference to finishing it later.

As she collected possible breakfast ingredients together she wondered if Janie used to eat breakfast with Sammy, and, if so, did she use the special trick for observant guests? If they see you pour a bowl of cereal it never occurs to them that you mightn't follow through with the rest of the business, so in their head you already ate it, as you stir it into oblivion or flush it away.

She had wanted to know how much Janie weighed when she died, but knew not to ask. Without this information she couldn't fight her, didn't have the grounds on which she could compete. The phone rang, scratched into her wondering.

Out leaked the foe through the telephone line.

'How do you mean?' Fat Molly said over and over. 'But she's dead. What? How?' Increasingly irate, and with enough bark and frequency to deny the person at the end any possibility of giving a rational explanation without seeming leaden, vague or mistaken. 'Yeah,' the conversation finished.

With Sammy unaware in the shower, she started to clear the previous night's plates and glasses, the habit of a martyr causing her to do it loudly.

At dinner parties Janie would quietly collect the plates as a means of getting away from the table and nearer to the bathroom. They all knew though, slapping down fives before the meal, bets as to how many minutes she would sit at table before running to stick her head in the bowl. It was curious to most of them, as if she was content to feed her face but not her stomach, as if ghosts were living there with sick hunger, ready to feed off whatever scraps she threw down that direction. Between themselves they called her Thumbulimia or Little Hughy. Molly was more simple, they just called her Fat to her face, not realising that their 'sarcasm' anchored and confirmed her conviction each time.

Food was the main currency in the Janie–Molly household, an inversion of the normal market price — less was more, deficiency a wealth, physical weakness a sign of moral and mental strength — but it made its own internal logic: self-justifying, self-reflexive, self-destructive, self-control, selfish, self.

After Janie had started seeing Sammy, the two women would barely speak, not even to argue, dealing through messages left, communicating their emotional states through paltry concessions or empty challenges, plastic bags either left neatly in a corner, or contents scattered on the carpet, or on the armchair, blocking access. All behaviour was passively confrontational, laughing wildly on the phone, sulking, singing, tripping over undrawn battle-lines all the while.

Molly smiled at the sound of a man in her shower, and, leaving the dishes to soak, she lit her first cigarette of the day. She was new to smoking and had to keep reminding herself to light up. She'd give the place a good scrub when they got back, the incentive was singing off-key.

She remembered how Janie would usually stay in the kitchen for as long as possible to punish herself, and then go and work out with the vacuum cleaner, the scrubbing brush, the duster, next-door's lawnmower. If they'd actually had a lawn this would have been less bizarre. Because of her room-mate's diligence Molly only ever had to do emergency washing-up, like when Sammy or some other target wanted coffee, and she'd scrape dutifully away at a mug until it was presentable in the half-light of possible romance.

The lease had conveniently run out when Janie was in the hospital, so Janie discharged herself into an apartment of her own where she didn't have to hold back, she could sick up and wipe down as much as she wanted, unwatched by critical eyes. Fat Molly had already settled solo in the place where she now played hostess.

Sammy was scrubbing like a nun with crabs, he couldn't get the day to come clean. Raw, skin-slapped to the muscle-bound bone, he knew he had to run. He would wait until she'd gone to work and just take the picture and go, stash it in a locker. If he stayed longer he'd let some detail slip, it could only get worse with a woman. Decision made, but he couldn't trust it — he didn't have a rule for a time like this. He knew, though, that instinct would take over and he'd run with his torn sneakers flying and his candy-apple hands pumping away until he found the safety of a bale of hay, like Chicago, maybe.

Across town three people missed the same phonecall as the one that vexed Fat Molly, through being in their shower and alone in the apartment. Josh was one of these but Lucy called him a short while after. She liked to call Josh to reassure herself that he had dumped his ex and wasn't having loads of sex with her for old times' sake. Lucy thought that because Josh was bi- and could theoretically fancy anyone in the world that wasn't close family, then the odds of him fancying her were somehow increased. Not true — he didn't, wouldn't, at this stage couldn't, think of Lucy in that way, especially as she seemed to him to cast herself in the rôle of his surrogate mother. As he had no use for the original, the surrogate found herself sadly underused.

She offered to come by and collect him, but she'd be on foot anyway so there didn't seem to him to be much point. He told her he'd see her there, then began the task of finding a set of clothes that didn't contain more residue of dope than detergent. He sighed as he realised all the studs would have to come out again, no point calling attention. He shaved around the thin lines of goatee, gotta make the effort, man.

He felt kind of mellow about the whole Janie thing, sad maybe, as she must have hurt bad to have stuff like this happen to her, but it put a dent in a week which he liked to live smooth, and left him bereft of his clown rôle a while. With his nonchalance that many confused with wisdom, he skinned up, smoked, rinsed with mouthwash to rid himself of his own peculiar morning breath and left his solo commune for the precinct.

Morning in New York meant lunchtime in Dublin. A middle-aged woman sat in the bath, water cooled, half its volume cried by her. Her husband hovered by the door with a tray he feared would be untouched by teatime. The phone rang and he hurried to answer, hearing from the stairs the howl he had grown used to since a few days before.

'Have her parents been informed?' Lucy asked the cop.

He nodded and kept his mind on the bowling; McKenzie hadn't been playing well, but if this day kept up he'd turn in a lousy game himself tonight. Jesus, if she smoked, he could breathe her second-hand poison gas as she yapped, might calm him. His aunt had a little parrot like that, pity about it.

'It was a wrong number.'

'What?'

Sammy emerged, one towel around his waist, the other drying his hair; he hadn't heard. They had to go anyway and Fat Molly knew it.

'We've had a phonecall' she backtracked, 'from the police.'

The towel in his hands crunched into a ball and his eyes peered huge through his damp curls. It took her three shots to tell him the details of the call, so hard was she trying to get the balance between over- and under-stating the fact.

She linked arms with him as they walked up the street, it felt to him like when he had walked old Mrs Castanella's embarrassing dog for a dollar, expect he couldn't strap Fat Molly to the back of his bike.

They were around the corner from the precinct and Sammy was realising, about twenty minutes after it should have hit him, that this meant he couldn't make a run for it now, not without calling notice to himself. Molly slowly read his silence as boredom, wishing she was dead instead of Janie — Janie was doing it wormy from the inside, she was returning and reclaiming him. She was suddenly afraid that Janie was winning again.

She gave her wretched complexity a work-out on the first poor bastard (bar Sammy) who dared to speak to her.

They told the desk clerk why they were there.

'Would you just take a seat there, please, and someone will speak to you shortly,' he said with no attempt to disguise that he said the same thing twenty times an hour, every hour of every working day. Now and again you got one of these.

'Look, you asked me, us, to come here. I don't want to be here, so why should I have to wait? I do have other things to do, you know.'

Sammy took a small step away from her; two girls nearby who knew her slightly, turned and hid themselves in conversation. The muscles in her face pushed up into her forehead and her volume grew with every word, so that when the clerk replied in the same voice as he had started with, it sounded like he was whispering.

'I realise you're upset, but just take a seat please, Ma'am.'

Twenty or so people were now unsure as to whether or not to acknowledge each other under the circumstances, a funeral reunion was not a usual event; there was no known etiquette. They had been spared the funeral parlour and now sat on benches in a long, broad corridor with green shiny walls, the men mostly wearing the same clothes as the day before, the women having modelled themselves for the most part into apprentice-lawyer types. The shock, which had with the days relented into grief, had now hardened into shock again, leaving a long row of faces not sure what shapes to wear.

They had the book of condolences at the desk, a register of regrets, surrounded by clumps of people offering advice on work numbers for the absent many. Some denying in the new crisis that they had enough affinity to need to be there, the most intense mourners now the casually bitter. The romance of death deserted them as real day-to-day input was required.

Lucy had not forfeited her rôle as secretary general to the dead, and had explained to anyone within earshot about how lots of Janie's friends were on tour with *Riders to the Sea*. She stood at the top of the queue, bending the ear of the poor short-straw cop who had stopped replying, 'Yes Ma'am' a half hour before, and was not interested in her ideas for intercepting the actors' tour bus by calling every diner and bar along the tour route. Lucy was pathologically helpful.

Boots was off in a corner, alone, pacing in small circles, mumbling to himself. Wrapping himself up for his own safekeeping in a mantra — intoned admissions, very soft, a dirge of accusations whispered back toward his head. No one had the access code. All those who used to call Boots a friend didn't even try to say hello. Despite the same confused, tufted hair, and the clothes so baggy they seemed to hang there on a prayer, he seemed to them to be a different person from the Boots who used to find their eaten texts, bring whiskey and hook them up to the web with calm assertions as to the simplicity of his magic. Those who'd never known him kept an even greater distance on account of the smell.

There were at least two dozen friends now, and obviously more on the way. Some had begun to voice their astonishment, to reiterate the tragedy of it all, first the hanging, now this. They couldn't believe it, just couldn't believe it, and two minutes' silence later just couldn't believe it again.

America knows that it is better to be a dead legend than a living nothing. Janie, Janie, Janie Jay, hours and pages and hundreds of minds of Janie — what a small sacrifice death must be for all this fame. What fun she was, was great big fun. One great big fucking surprise after another. How lucky Fat Molly was to have known her; without Janie she might never have known the importance of contentment. As it was now, she might never know contentment, but at least she was hugely aware of its importance.

So Janie knew how to make an exit too, might have guessed. Her arrival had been akin to an alien visitation, she had landed with all the impact of a fallen house, she was strange and vulnerable and, therefore, according to the laws of reception, both desirable and approachable. Janie's perceived emotional frailty and presumed sense of cultural bewilderment brought out the mothering-minion side in many a together person. Weeks later she was still having the direction of the traffic on cross-streets explained. Knowing her appeal, and furiously protecting her sense of what she'd grown up as, Janie clung fast to her Dublin accent, anchored it on her palate, refused to let her tongue trip to a different dance, used Irish terms even when American ones came faster into her head. She wore jumpers in the cold, ate aubergines, courgettes, porridge, said chips instead of fries, crisps instead of chips, woke at half-nine, left the house at twenty to ten, walked along the pavement, bought a bottle of foundation in the chemist, always said, 'Jayzus', never 'Jeez'. She refused to visit an Irish bar, saying these were to an Irish person as sherbet to a junkie. They didn't understand. On Saint Patrick's Day, in reaction to their surprise that she hadn't worn green, she explained that Saint Patrick's Day was an American celebration of something that didn't exist.

Judy May Murphy

So, not even conforming to their understanding of Irishness, she kept herself an enigma, and they practically built paths for her to go down on her American journey.

Against all the innate rivalry of the profession, she was told by someone about the audition at the East Village Theatre Bar; an advance copy of the script was procured by a different someone, and by the time she got the part, a great many people were congratulating themselves on a charitable act successfully executed. After a packed-out run of a half-year of weekend performances, the production moved into a large off-Broadway theatre, and the celebrations were those of a community come into fortune, and more people gathered round to help. They all got their sly hours of latent parenting done, so when Janie achieved any degree of independence they admired her as you would a child on the first day of school.

Yelling at a cop when you've not been accused is not the happiest of tactics, especially not the best idea when you have the art world's version of America's Most Wanted sleeping on your sofa and sitting at your elbow, but yell Fat Molly did, and loudly and long. They listened to it from the corridor to the cells and even outside — hell, people standing in the future could probably hear. However, fear cannot be reasoned with. Sammy was glad that all the attention was on her, but not so pleased that there was any attention to contend with at all. After a moment of particularly intense amplification, Lucy entered to explain that it must be the grief, and they all three yelled at her louder to fuck off.

Until she and Sammy were dismissed some fifteen minutes later, Molly continued to smear her anxiety into the clean apathy of the detective; she had found her way onto a list and, by association, so had he. The last thing he asked them was if they knew how to find Italian Tony; they didn't. Could they keep an eye out, ask him to come down?

'Certainly,' said Sammy.

'Sure, we'll do your job for you,' mumbled Molly under the sound of the opening door.

'I'm sorry about your friend.'

'Thank you,' said Sammy, and then wondered if this was the wrong thing to say, if Molly might take it to be treachery. It was worth it if it helped push him off that list.

As Sammy and Molly walked in silence down the corridor, it was already clear that her blistering anger was pure over-burn. While it had been to her mind as powerful and noble as the Olympic flame, she was now realising that a wax match would have done the job. Her unease and Sammy's incomprehension were conveniently covered by a large cop who came new to the scene, grabbing a clipboard as he loudly asked the disappearing desk clerk, 'That the girl with the jellybeans?'

'How do you mean with the jellybeans?' asked a French girl, thinking the lingo was defeating her.

'They found her in the Park, right? Same girl?'

The whole row nodded.

He laughed at the memory, knowing it was off, not caring.

'Coat pockets were crammed full of jellybeans, no fetish I ever saw had fuckin' jellybeans.'

Everyone stopped to listen.

'So ... what?' said Josh sarcastically. 'You think someone stole her body for the candy?'

'Na, we finished those off by early shift two days ago.'

Josh eyed his girth, 'Must get quite a few jellybean suicides — doughnut ones too?'

The cop sucked in his belly and narrowed his eyes.

'I'll take your statement in here.'

Just then Aimee walked in, wearing Janie's coat. She quickly read their looks and sighed, 'She gave it to me ages ago,' not stopping to entertain anyone's suspicion, and, with a quick word to the reappeared clerk, she jumped the queue.

'God, I hate her,' Fat Molly spat.

Sammy was surprised; he thought they'd all got on well the night before, but he didn't realise that because he was staying with Fat Molly and had known her longer, her hates, especially those pertaining to other women, especially blonde women, were supposed to be his also. So he just sent a quick 'Hi' to Aimee with his hand.

He walked Fat Molly to work, thinking first about Janie's coat and then about the jellybeans, back and forth with each, right step, left step: coat, candy, coat, candy. It was a good thing Fat Molly didn't need replying to as she reworked the past half hour, formed a new truth, one which rendered her reaction appropriate.

She worked the noon-to-nine and sometimes the nine-to-seven a.m. shifts in a franchised café-bar, with glass walls and tiny steel tables, high-backed metallic chairs, halogen lights, black olives served with every meal, staff in long, white linen aprons. They provided the usual hundred types of coffee, all traditional — no maple-nut-crunch or strawberry anything, just blends from different parcelled gardens of the world, served in different degrees of froth and intensity, all according to the person you thought you were. It was the type of place where expectation ruled, fuelled by sightings of young film stars months before, where people stayed only long enough to assure themselves they were not about to miss anything before moving on to somewhere with greater empty promise. If music was played, you wouldn't remember it, if someone said something funny, it somehow wouldn't be as funny as if they'd said it somewhere else. But, in its favour, you could look good against the décor and the clientèle, with a tall glass of coffee in your manicured hand. And the lights in the bathrooms weren't blue. Twenty-five minutes was the average stop, no one made it a home from home; in fact, the only person truly comfortable here was Fat Molly.

After a quick round of introductions where they all seemed to be called Tom and Lisa, and a roast beef on rye, he left for the apartment, escaping Fat Molly's cowering control and the overpowering smell of olives.

He wandered back, lost in the thought of Janie's eyes — he knew them to be a greenish blue-grey, and fixing on this solid fact caused his mind to fill them totally that colour, like a postcard of an elongated woman he'd seen on someone's icebox, one single colour, no white or black, just eye spaces with plain greenish sky behind them.

He tried to recall Janie's face but it wouldn't appear, and taking out the Sherman didn't help as it should. Gathering the lawless picture to him, despite his willing her to soak through to where she could be seen, his mind saw eyes of a single colour, painted eyes.

He stayed slumped with it like a boneless man into the armchair.

It was chewing at him big time. The Janie he'd projected onto the picture in the café the day before was heckling him from somewhere else. He still believed she lurked within its surface somewhere, although staring through tears and tiredness was proving futile. It gave nothing away, shadows winning, holding him fast in the conspiracy, trapped but unenlightened. He could guess, true to the way of life's rigging, that, in addition to things he knew about Janie, there were many he didn't. And, faithful to the form of it, he had no idea how they might be discovered. Cursing his idiocy he suddenly felt led again, the accomplice on a need to know, kept safely stupid. It was brain damage, pure grief.

He'd go out and score something; Garth-the-bar was always handy with the names.

Janie

Somewhere along the east coast of Ireland, there's a road, a snake of redbrick houses, damp and softly buckled, introduced with blue-flower driveways and overgrown lawnweed behind, a back-slide in a wealthy part of town. Most people walking this road would not look once at ivy-brim number eighty-seven, let alone waste a moment on a second glance. Nor would they have reason to unless on a visit, and a visit seldom happens to this half-asleep home. So none would ever lay a curious eye, by accident or by other, on the small side window in the grey slate roof, a single glazed window onto a difficult small soul.

Behind that window sits in quiet waiting, a small-for-her-age girl. Hers is a face closed against reading, the inner life severed from the outward show. She might well feel unhappy, lost in her sadness, and then perhaps she doesn't feel at all.

Anyone of older years, who might (on this fictitious visit) glance inside her room, would sigh for the innocence brinking, for the simplicity apparent in a girl-coloured life, and would wish themselves back in an unworn body, and smile for the modest concerns of youth. They may chance to put an idle question as to a favourite film, or to casual-banter on a popular show, but such patter would fall on a dream-deafened ear and be gone.

Her bedroom is not typical, but far along the lines of such. The wallpaper discounted down to near nothing, spill-proof and coming away at the corners and green. Shelves, chair, desk, self-assembled with parts to spare, made of wood cut from plastic trees, wardrobe too shallow for clothes to hang level, woodpigeon sentried on the roof above, window-frame that rattles in the wind and the sun, door that will stick a whit shy of closing and snag the twist carpet when open half-way, bookends and suncatchers, pink plastic hand-mirror, trinket-tin shaped like an old carousel, ragged teddy bear survivors of charity sales, a Chinese alarm clock, a shell.

Her parents buy her extra lamps and mirrors because she is a teenager and must own more things, a duvet to match nothing else in the room, and a record player which she never plays in case they hear her feelings in the words of songs. She once asked them for a cat, but cats are trouble and give nothing in return, so they gave her instead an off-white sheepskin rug which she holds to her face whenever warmth is thin. The rug smells of comfort, not the kind to dissolve under sweet self-yielding, but a resolute softness, such that even when the chill is absent from the air she tucks it under her bedtime chin where it will lie on her chest until knocked to the floor by a turbulent dream, and she is left without any shield against the difficult night.

In the difficult night she thinks of him, at night and through the day.

Our visitor would not be let to grope inside her thinking, so private is the want, so impossible to tell. She thinks of him whenever she is alone, and tries to when she is not. She thinks of him when she's hating that her parents have the

That Girl from Happy

gift of speech and that they abuse it with use. Uninterrupted, she thinks of him best when she's trudging late to school, and when she's wandering the long way home to string him further out. No invented conversations, just keeping her head around the fact of him. She thinks of him, brushing her teeth till they bleed, then accidentally thinks of teeth for a moment and back again in time to rinse. As mundane life closes in to crowd her passion, appearing as a practical reproach, she drifts her way back to the always matter of the boy.

She is not completely alone in her remembering, however, she keeps among the late-forgotten toys a few small souvenirs which play silent companion to the vigil she keeps. A stone — a 'lucky' one yet to prove itself so — and a piece of driftwood, doubtless pushed from his new shore, and a long, thin shell from the year before the loss of him, the one he handed her as they headed off home through the sleepy dawn.

But the shell is inconsiderate, no help whatsoever, and it seems, to a young mind brimful of broken faith, to be saying that it knew all along. It laughs at her from its object comfort, punishes her for the hope she poured into its shallow hold winter night after winter night. Now it still lies beside her every moment, hearing no hope anymore, watching her cry from far behind the trinket carousel.

She feels too impossible to be expected to continue, like the tiny sea-snails that the waves toss at will, so full of resolve yet wholly unable to remedy the fell devastation, to find the rock on which to draw closed a callused protective shell. Waking every morning before the sun is really ready, waking to a day packed with sickly defeat, she wretchedly tries to work some control, to somehow claim back the command she once held over pirates and spies, over fugitive stones, to reassert that determination which once let her take a fall and carry on. Janie strains to unhook her locked-in purpose, the key gone these long weeks now.

One day she calls directory inquiries, asking for the number; she is told it no longer exists. Are they anywhere else in the country? she asks, and the answer is no. That dark afternoon on the good sofa, doggedly buried in another adventure book where the young girl suffers big bad torment through to her victorious end, her own course grows wonderfully clear in her head. She lets the book fall, page unmarked, villain unchastened to the floor as she races upstairs to her room. Then, nested in the downy bed, her shirt lifted halfway, baring her skin, she takes up the unkind razor-backed shell and tells it all about her simple plan, explaining what her father says about first breaking some eggs.

With her small breath slightly flinching, she presses the long edge against her soft, clean stomach. Braving the cut will win for her surely the future she was destined; she will pay for him spoonful by spoonful in blood.

If her mother, or any, had chanced at this moment to peer through the nearly closed door, they could have wrenched the shell from her shaking hand and guided her to a different road. Instead, a red welted line rises up under the push along the razor-shell edge as she presses and pulls the shell to tear the skin, and the pain is so perfect, so in step with her heart that she finally feels understood.

Over the following days she learns her lessons quickly, learns which soap-powders best wash dried-in blood from a

That Girl from Happy

pinked and spattered fleece, learns how long it takes a broken skin to scab, learns a deeper silence.

Since discovering this tidy little way for easing the disorder of the world, she sticks by it until she is clinging to its deliverance daily, and there is rest from the heartbreaking inaction as she sneaks away upstairs during something vital like the news. Where once she waited, now she can effect. The precious cut will lead her to the mercy of the Lord, will win for her the glory, all agony passed, all blood forgotten in the glistening reward. The nuns have a name for it, call it contrition, and it must be true if it has a name.

The waistband of her school skirt plays against the wound. Each rub is like a dig in a private place, such humiliation in the mess of her skin, no longer smooth but now rough, no longer one white but different reds, purples, streaked with yellow when it chances to pus. Her shame written on her body, covered by a thin white shirt and a vile blue A-line skirt, chosen to keep her identical, now serving to hide her difference.

Every day after school, dragging her book-full bag and heavy shoes behind her through the garden gate, she believes a connection awaits, lying just ahead on the long hall table, hapless in the letter rack or scrawled in biro on the message pad below. Sometimes, when her heart and belly are redder than magic red, she can see through all the walls to where he is sitting drinking tea in the kitchen. She can see him in her father's chair, choosing a chocolate biscuit, and so she takes a careful interest in what biscuits are bought on the Saturday morning shop, and her mother believes her the most perfect daughter ever to have carried a grocery bag. She can see him approving of the choice she has made. Trudge breaking into an eager step, her stomach a hatch of scab lines, hurt plenty enough for some small sign, she runs the last few yards of the geranium path. But the kitchen is empty. Only her mother standing there to ask about her nothing day. No letter, no phonecall, no clue as to the finding of him appears from the late afternoon. So she eats his biscuit for him.

On Thursday nights her parents and their tweeded few friends attend the bridge drive at the golf course down the road, leaving her with a can of Fanta and a video as surrogate until their return. On these nights she sits at the kitchen table and pours herself into a letter to the boy, no longer written in the special code but in her natural hand, growing more honest with each missive unsent. She explains how he must come for her now, he must save her from her dreadful life before she drowns in its very days. Now that her messages remain on land, uncollected by gulls or waves, she must hide them all away from her mother's caring. In the letters she calls him the boat-boy to keep him safe from others' knowing, and now to keep him further safe, and her, she buries him with the dust under the floor. She has cut a square in her bedroom carpet and sawn out a piece of the floorboard below using the hacksaw blade which her father's fine intentions would never miss in a century.

One ordinary Thursday night, when her parents return with their laughing from bridge, she side-steps the replay of each and every hand, and on upstairs to an early bed. She has been writing to him for the past hour and more, pleading with him one more time to rescue her, but it is all moving further away and she knows what she must do to stop the grief from running her to madness. First, lying as always, she cuts a new line from chest to waist, but this time it is not enough. She takes a bottle from the shelf, Listerine for washing her ritual clean, and, steeling her will, one fist clenching, she pours the smarting liquid over the freshly opened skin. It stings like a hundred million swords, and for a moment she is taken by a different pain, owned by it entirely. A change is as good as a rest, as her father says, as if he invented the phrase.

If only she could turn back time, not by years but by a tiny pinch to before they left for bridge that night, then she might not scavenge through their every semi-secret place, their every drawer, every file, address book, postcard and letter, for news of where his family might be. It is too late now to unknow. Her punishment lay in her parents' bedside table where she stumbled on a brochure for the Algarve sun, a book of people, shiny tanned with nowhere better else to be. It was as if they had just sucked dry her ocean and torn down her beach forever, but she knows that protesting their impending surprise would only draw them closer to her truth.

By the time they break the treat to her, as a birthday gift, she has rehearsed a naturally delighted response. She will not be going back. Well, maybe next year, she thinks, but next year is never.

One late spring morning when the cuts are deeper as her longing has become, and she has not taken breakfast because her mother chews cereal so loud, Janie passes out in the heat of the school chapel. Gradual as clouds it comes over her, first hot and breathless as the saints around the altar begin to sway, she feels strangely light, then the saints bow down and she faints out cold and heavy, her head not hurting as it hits against the wooden pew. She comes around in the sacristy behind the sacred tabernacle, waking to the sound of her classmates praying the prayer of the Father, candles lit behind the white-veiled nuns, with the gardener who has carried her there watching from the door for his release back to roses.

She holds her hand over the clothes that cover the secret, worried that the nuns in their starched righteousness might decipher the idioms of pain, but of course they are unable, being fluent only in the suffering of Christ, a limited rhetoric. Since ever she could hear, Janie has been made aware that the agony on the cross was her fault also, so it seems best not to remind them of her culpability, best not to hint at anguish in any shape or form. At least she is not in Africa, or Protestant, or any number of things they would inform her were far worse than what she bore. 'Monthlies, my dear, offer it up.'

From now on she brings toast to school in her pocket, and eats it in the toilets away from all eyes and all sound. Those who see her feet standing sideways on in the stall believe she must be smoking, admire her maturity, and think what a fabulous life she must have.

All during lessons she is pen-and-ink perfect, crosses every 't', dots every 'i', smiley-faces every 'o' to keep her invisible, immune to the renown of teacher's reproach. To her classmates it seems as if she wears the teachers' colours, complies with their design. So her best friend finds a new best friend, leaving her with only best enemies and girls who have to be nice to her because their mothers also play bridge. She hides in the back field before the first bell, heading straight for the gates when home-time sounds.

The less she speaks, the more she fears that the next words might be the ones to tell. That, being so large and everywhere, her longing might slip out, jockeyed to a mundane thought. And so, spouting small at first, she slowly starts to pattern over her truth with mouthfuls of colourful nothings, narrating the surface of life aloud. Until over time the idle prate becomes a constant babble, hosing the multitude with words, so that if one day her guard might falter, and some freak brainstorm let the real issue fall into view, then none could discern it in the endless shower.

Some of the friends drift back.

Secretive, sullen, giddy, removed — her parents check off each stage in their handbook of life as the years pass, and Janie Kelly finds herself sixteen, and new concerns arise to burden the old.

She finds a plausible boyfriend from the boys' school, or rather she declines to refuse the first thing in trousers brave enough to ask. Her longing is now grown so large it needs hiding behind a whole other person. Not caring enough to mind that she deceives him when they kiss, sometimes she surrenders to the ordinary of day-to-day, sometimes she even smiles. It seems strange that she has grown no taller since that summer, nor wider, nor stronger, and is smaller than most girls three years below. Often she wonders if the cutting keeps her small; she imagines that her petulant body has gone on a work-to-rule, and she'll forever be the size of that summer.

Her parents seem no different either, they still talk too loud on the telephone, as if they don't really understand the concept. '... so happy in school, I've never heard a bad word said. It's only wonderful, top of her year....' her mother reports to an aunt from the west. 'It's marvellous not to have to worry, she's just doing so well....'

Janie listens from upstairs in her tired little room, on her small bed, with her newly sharpened shell touching ready against skin still red from foreign sun. Touching against her inner thigh now that her stomach is hard as leather from some two dozen months of blood-level sadness; the toast crumbs sit hard in her pocket, digging into her as always with her skirt pulled up over her hip. A new half-full bottle of Listerine, a well-chewed pen, a clean sheet of paper, the small square of carpet taken from its patch, the shell pressing ready. Ready now. Doing so well.

In the middle of the night when Janie is the only person in the world not sleeping, she gets up, puts on her father's suede coat and goes down to the sea to make sure. The strand, this stretch of grit-sand and water so different from her past summer beach, is wide and long, shallow and calm as a mud splat, with lug-wormed, saturated sand, smelling of the waste of the whole city, two pipe chimneys huffing smoke out into the grey air. No place for a child-woman living on a dream.

Dear Boat-Boy,

I.S.M.Y.L.

I know that cutting yourself sounds like a really mental thing to do, and if I read a story about someone doing it then I'd want to rescue them from it and let them know that everything was all right. But with me it's different, there's a purpose, it's not a waste or a damaging thing. I know for certain that things will get back to how they were when we were younger and that it's only a matter of time, and all of the scraping open will stop then. It's just for now, and it really does work, it really makes me feel better.

When this panic thing comes up, you can't do anything, it's bigger than you. It's as if you go to a different place where the usual things don't matter one tiny bit, and the things from before the panic don't seem real. Panic isn't exactly the right word, but you really have to do something because you have to. It hurts so much and it takes over your head. And then after you cut yourself, or just scratch a scab open if you're in school or walking down the road, then it's doubly good because it keeps on hurting a bit and so you feel like you're still doing something, like it's being taken care of for as long as it hurts. I got too scared to do deeper cuts, so when it got more panicky, then I started to pour stuff on it like mouthwash, or vinegar, or shampoo, anything stingy. But the shampoo gave me a rash and Mum asked about the vinegar smell so I told her we're allowed to go to the chipper at lunch now we're in 5th year. I think she believed me because now she doesn't bother me about bringing sandwiches either. So I mostly use Listerine which is good because I have to rinse my mouth out more too because my breath is getting really bad. Probably because Mum still uses so much onions in things. I'm definitely going to tell her I don't like omelettes any more.

Janie

P.S. I don't know if I will send all of these once I have your address, I will probably type them out first.

Aimee

I still feel mouldering dirty. But it's not like I fondled up the dead partner, is it, so what's to feel odious about?

There there there we have it, grubbied up the blameless page again, pissed in my own creative juices. Down under load, plugged up with glut, my cognitive processes junked to the core, full heavy with what I should have been saying when I was a bedwet kid, but the house régime was such then that it didn't get said. So now it comes, and then some and how.

As it stands, it's all about to fall, the risk is running hard that the mind of the times will refuse my spoils for their lack of bridle action, but at least I'm getting it out. Foul fucking language, nothing like it, a dose of Epsom salts for the mind. One occupational predicament when ordering words, the balance between clenching and release.

The greatest have died early from the pressure of noxious declarations blocking up their passages unsaid, so the problem's nothing new. Rather than let leak a 'bollocks' or a 'fuck', the Brontë sisters took ladylike to their beds, no, their chambers, couldn't even mention beds.

Then, over the heath in the opposite direction entirely, we have the present camp, with their portable computers aimed at the world, fingers fiddling in their laps. These writers of more recent days, whose minds decompose under passion, the mellifluous progeny to be spurted straight from the fountainhead, escaping in black without any recomposition (dextrous or otherwise) in honour of the receiver. These are so hasty-keen on the flush, that any good stuff also recedes down the pan.

Sometimes when you read a piece, usually in a thin magazine, its autonomy validated with Xerox striping, you realise that the writer's lame ambition is to knock your college ass sideways with their bravery and freedom, using 'fuck' and 'shit' and 'wank' at least once in every line, and you know that they have soundly (if unwisely) positioned themselves for the life-task of shaking you from your middle-American suburban vocab comfort. Shake it then, you make me tired, the world is too old and so are we. What we do, us wordies, is a simple waste, an idle adultery against our real life discourse, a nothing. Words have power only when forbidden, like last century or when you're a kid. In their benign estate they have lost the push to thrust into academic insurrection, internal revolt, or giggly naughty with the cover drawn closed. Cunt. See, nothing.

When I was younger, a good deal younger (in my defence), I spent wonderland hours in Barnes and Noble on a trip to the city, thumbing furtively through all the dictionaries until I found one that extensively defined the word 'vagina'. This one I then bought and took home to reaffirm and advance my schoolyard education. But I'm older now and world-worn and can't afford to get a cheap hit from words like that, but I do overuse them, I know it, it's just sometimes they seem to be the only words for the job. Grubby little doing needs dirty little phrasing. So it's not so much that my writing needs sanitising, it's my day-to-day wants scrubbing up, and quickly before I die of it. I already have a lumpy rash.

Should have kicked for a touch of reality, some less ethereal profession that would define me in advance so I wouldn't have to work so hard at parties. Dentistry, accountancy, hairdressing, so I'd barely have to dribble out tripe concerning split ends and crowns, nevermore to drown in the shallows of my own cocktail conversation about whether I am what I write. Talking to people at social functions, funerals or parties is a very ill-thought-out convention. The mingle isn't me. Instead I lurk half-hung behind my conversation-proof expression, or duck behind some bespectacled shrimp canapé, out of the line of inquisitive fire.

'A writer, a writer! I'd love to have been a writer. What is it you write, Aimee, fact or fiction?' someone will inevitably projectile inquire of me. Truman and Hunter spilled pages of liquored prose on that one.

Fact or fiction? I found out the convoluted way, way back after Jimmy Saunders finger-fucked me in the fields and I wasn't sure if I was still a virgin, and my best friend asked me about it in the company of a girl I didn't like and another whom I wanted to impress: Truth is Impossible.

Impossible, not just because I'm perverted by what's expected of me, it goes further. My ass should be in a sling four days out of five, considering my ignorant demeanour, so I reckon I'm probably saved by an intrinsic warp, that I'm fitted with my own special full-time funky delusion just to get me through. In which case it's all fucked, all of it fiction, unfathomable, everything I say a lie, my whole

That Girl from Happy

fatuous life blankets of whites, and the best I can do is try to litter the trail with the odd brutal veracity.

Here's one from after Happy.

I'm practically disintegrating mid-keel, falling out from this guy's apartment, some Prep who'd kindly offered to slake the remainder of my Old-Crow craving on the understanding that I'd quench a few of his. Confident I'd have him whiskied to the nuts, drenched to saturation point before he'd make a half-way promising grab, I went along for the detour. By 2 a.m. he was out fish-cold and stayed that way, so I left. He wouldn't even wake to say goodbye, just half-opened a snotty eye and mumbled 'okay'. I left a note to say I was glad I hadn't fucked him, then still unpaid attention-wise (fine not to walk me to my door, but they should at least walk me to theirs), I swiped his much-mentioned deep-sea-diver's watch; now I can be punctual up to a depth of a thousand feet. If he calls me on it, I'll say we went onto the roof and it cracked under the absence of pressure. I'd probably do that too.

I go to drop the prize off at my place and sleep off some of my less wholesome endeavours. I feel really dehydrated and I don't know if there's enough in the Manhattan reservoir to fix it; the orange juice was a good idea but I'm too juiced myself to open the damn thing.

Aimee the portable fold-away human, with my legs collapsed and my face now in broad contact with the over-carpet. Better sit up and breathe; at least with Janie I could put my hand against her mouth and feel for the want of breath in her. I wonder if she left a suicide note? Strange that no one mentioned that. I know I'd for definite scrawl a punishment note if I fixed on topping myself, only it'd probably run to volumes, by which time I might have gone off the idea. Perhaps she left a rough draft in with her papers.

Launching any project at three in the morning is always a mistake as you sleepwalk yourself into farrago, and I always full know it at the time, should time-lock my phone against such eventualities. Here I am, dripping drunk, hollowed out from the guy and the whiskey, and hoping the search for a note might fill the gap usually plugged with bad phonecalls.

I have to flay the soaked clothes from my limbs before they drown me. Tomorrow, I'll parade her clothes outdoors, disclose myself manifest new for the new life; today would have been too soon, some of them aren't ready. I have my bedtime routine down to a minute-and-a half flat; removing make-up is hugely overrated, it's while we're out of control, sleeping, that we need to look our best. I peel the sticky coloured lenses off my dry eyes and rinse down some medication, with water.

I waver at the sink and consider downing extra glad-caps tonight, but while the side-effects increase, the emotion always stabilises at numb, so I don't. It's like the emotional world is now divided, not into the happy and sad, but the chemical and the non-chemical, no matter what the mood. I didn't notice anything in Janie's bathroom, perhaps she rammed them all in to carry her feet down the last road, popped enough to sprout a set of angel-dusted wings to lift her to the final post. Stinge — she might have left some all the same, for those of us remaining to leaden-foot it down a few more days beyond her premature check-out.

For me in my big fat craving, my perpetual lack, prescription medication is a creamier lick when it's some other freak's Medicare you're shovelling down with a rum and coke chaser fast on, but it's a good three years since I last passed in a wink-tipped drugstore for a forty-two-year-old man with migraine and haemorrhoid woes. Dealing Retin-A used to pay my restaurant cheques, the rest kept me quiet for a time.

I never really found another hobby after that, and it all feels empty. We can only really tell that an empty space exists because of what surrounds it, defines and shapes it as a nothing: the doughnut makes the doughnut hole, the ritual makes the habit, the clouds and the horizon frame the sky, the stomach holds the hunger, feelings need pages to live in, or hearts, I guess, trends need charts, resistance is dependant on the striker and the line. I didn't know I was nothing until Janie made an edge. I guess my mother left me before my own borders were fixed.

In the bathroom mirror I can see a body but I can't reach it. Straining to picture what I'm about, squinting, I can tell that I'm a fusty little composite, a deceit, the gross sum of what I reflect, and it's been confirmed — being nothing isn't enough, there must be greater ways to be. Having no sensibilities of my own, as far as I can tell, at least none of the virtuous ones, I'm going to have to take hers on, suck on Janie pills for a time, borrow her purpose seeing as how she's done with it. Cling until it sticks.

With too much constriction and contractions for these drunken limbs to bear, I cram myself into her long, green, lace dress. Garbed up for the task, I plunge into the box

Judy May Murphy

recently filched from her place, hoping to uncover her purpose and better understand how to be Janie Jay.

In my first loose rummage I can make out reams of photographs and bits of notes and old letters, unfocused but there. What possessed me to quarry out so much stuff? Apart from a picture of an old beach-house, the photographs are shiny ones of alien-eyed teenagers taken on vacation, at dances and parties, all falling over from too much cheap drink so early in the night. Cider-looks dripping mistrust, hopeless wine passes, the dance you think is sexy as you shimmy deceived under beer, I know them all well from my own adolescence, know the types of stories that go with pictures like these. Deep-tanned to crimson and smiling, they cling to each other as if they would otherwise fall off the photograph. I can't find Janie in any of them.

Letters from her mother, countersigned by her dad, tell me enough about her family to understand why she had to leave. Although her mother's only ever news was that she had none, the woman had an amazing facility for stretching this to a few tissue-thin pages. In my blur I start to think it's the same letter sent over and over but each time with different coloured dresses in the window of Pamela Scott's. I bet that's like JC Penny.

At least they were in English, though. I can't read the next pages, found folded together in a plastic pouch, neatly written in faded pencil and seeping biro. Must be from a child, but they don't make sense and, unless I've developed a rare form of drink-related dyslexia, they must be in Gaelic. Next out of the magic trunk is a piece of driftwood the size of my hand, not your normal dried red rose, but then, not your usual girl. I balance it on the window ledge; at last some non-fungal plant life in the place.

The dress is cutting off the flow of blood to my hands and they almost drop the next bundle of papers. 'The silence of the dawn is creeping....' Pages of song lyrics, still being worked on, still typical beyond belief. The type of words you know you really should throw away, but you've invested in them so much of your own inner truth that you hope against sense that it will ferment into a rich and original form, equal to your experience. But it only ever comes out looking like fourth-rate Simon and Garfunkel. Nothing will ever be learned about anyone from reading their song lyrics; they will only serve to strengthen notions of universal suffering — that is, the universal pain of having to read such junk. Bloated with hope, I write it myself, we all do, and one day we will all make enough money from one song to retire to a farm-house in the south of France. Fuck, it's going to be crowded.

With a difficulty only slightly linked to the Crow, as its size refuses to abandon its current residence, I wrench from the box a large brown envelope with the words LETTERS TO MYSELF printed in black magic marker on the outside, closed with a tight elastic band pinching its middle. Inside is a series of notes, hundreds of them, as if she's been collect-ing them over more than her one short lifetime, each one opening with the piteous 'Dear Me', and concluding with the equally wrenching 'Love, Me'. None of them are dated.

I tease one of them away from the masses with my disintegrating acrylic nails, and try to decipher the skinny black letters. Once I get used to the fact that a 't' and an 'f' are exactly the same, as are 'b's and 'lo's, we're cruising.

Dear Me,

I can't believe I can keep doing this to myself. I cannot hope to achieve what I set out to do, with one eye looking backwards. Yes, the boat-boy is the most important thing, but I have to move on in order to meet him at the finish, on prize day. I know this, I have had it out many times. There is no point resting on some cushion of old regret, and yet each time I try to take myself further along, I pull myself back again. I cannot meet the boat-boy with a life half dressed. I cannot go yet, it's not the time. If I open it all up now, if I tell someone or say it out loud, or even make a move, it will fall apart and the trouble would be for nothing. Hold firm.

Love, Me

Then, directly below, in blue ink this time:

Dear Me,

I'm being too hard on myself. If it wasn't for my strength, he'd be given up on entirely. If I don't stay strong, then, I'll end up in the wrong place, far from the possibility of him, and I'd blame me for not reminding myself. I almost told someone last week. Yes, sometimes I think I'm sailing further and further away, and that maybe if I don't open it up, soon it will be dead from lack of air. But for now, I will hold firm.

Love, Me

This is all a bit much, caffeine for the soul. I put Janie's letters to herself back in the envelope and hunt the edges of the box for anything that might look less of a psychologist's nightmare. Why did she write all that down, and why so upset about this boat-boy? Maybe when sober they make sense — that's not the way with most things but maybe this would be different. Are they a series of suicide notes? If I read them all, will it come into focus? If I sleep off this drink, will I?

There's a broken shell splintered over the bottom of the box, I must have crushed it when I landed back here with the clothes. The rest are unwritten New York postcards, leaving only that piece of paper I found under her pillow; I'd put it aside in my scramble for the photographs. It's an ordinary white sheet with a sail-boat printed in the top left-hand corner; underneath, in handwriting different from hers, it says, 'The future is written. He is so close you could almost touch him. In one week you will know.' I don't know how to take it. At a wild guess it must be from the boat-boy — with a logo like that, it's not such a grand leap of reason even with my whiskey head.

I stumble back onto a laundry bag, the note still in my hand. My head is full of dancing-fast teenagers, spinning with images of Janie swinging over them and visions of her tongue, and I'm standing in the sea with the waves pounding at the backs of my legs, my adrenalin pumping strong enough for me take them all on at once. I start pacing the room but this just makes the pictures come faster, everyone red and crying, my hands and scalp now sweating and my breathing getting shallow, the smell of yesterday's curry leftovers joining the assault.

In an effort to move the curry out to the hallway where my neighbours can enjoy its eastern pungency, I spill it all over myself and a posh part of the mountain. She smiles at my weakness.

I get straight into bed just before passing out.

Sitting in Happy, nursing a cure, I idle my head through the day that brought me here, before it all dulls into forgotten. Landing myself a date with a stranger wasn't even up there on the weirdness poll, such abnormal winds have been sweeping through. I could swear, adding it all up, that I clipped in an extra day on the sly. Just can't believe I've only woken once out of that putrid, malted sleep. And still a way to go before I'm back there, before I can avenge myself of the demon people who were biting through my lifelines last night.

Getting away isn't as easy as it once was, sleep no longer calm or helpful, waking up tired. Isn't it weird when you dream about people you know? It's as if you've borrowed them without permission while they were sleeping. This is why I usually confess to people when I have dreamt about them, although I usually lie about what I had them do.

I left the bed, the big wet body-print testimony to the night's battle, stinking sweetly already like the memory it drafted.

I pulled on the Janie dress again, which I had discarded sometime during the half-headed curry scrape-up. I caught myself reflected in the window. I looked unfortunately not unlike an eco-goth princess, all black-smudged eyes, tousled hair and long green dress. I could get free into some clubs with a look like this, provided I disentangled the Twinkie wrapper from my hair.

Priority number one: had to get to the laundromat. Correction — priority number one: gargle with antiseptic mouthwash and take a shower; shame they don't make mint-flavoured whiskey. Off with the dress again, breathe.

I showered and changed into something ordinary — jeans and things — tied my hair back and sat up on the table to give the letters another try. The first one I pulled out was short.

Dear Me,

The boat-boy can save me.

Love, Me

Who was this boat-boy? She seemed a little obsessed. The rest of the letters would tell me.

I felt alone, a thing which rarely happens to me. I always am alone, just I hardly ever feel it; with Janie around I felt as if I always had someone.

I couldn't go to any of the usual places for breakfast; I hadn't the will to invent myself sufficiently for the display, and this place now stank too badly to bring more food back. There was a candy-bar-and-coffee-vending machine in the laundromat which sort of solved everything, except for the alone thing. I brought the letters with me to read as I waited.

Hauling half the garment district behind me as I walked the short journey to the laundromat, I sacked my head for every image taken that day in her apartment, laid them all end-to-end before my inner eye, but found nothing that could be this boat-boy. Could be it was a pet-name for one of the obvious men. Italian Tony? Please not Italian Tony. Or Sammy? Or some other actor? But the intensity and volume of her obsession, and the suggestion that he was somehow unattainable, seemed to mitigate against that possibility. Perhaps he is a secret God, omnipotent, franchised even, one that can make sense out of me. I wish I was Janie, I could do with a God. There simply must be more clues in such a mountain of belief and affirmation, she must give a name somewhere. Please, Janie's God, don't turn this into some Nancy Drew thing, I haven't the luck for it.

The day had been up for a good while, and was easeful now following the people's rush to work. Winter slipped off the brownstone, the paining cold had finally softened and I couldn't even remember how bad it had felt. Even the wind had slowed down to a point where you could race it down the street and never have to push yourself past a brisk trot. The smells of garlic and fresh-baked bread, meat and oranges, puffed out onto the sidewalks, clashing with piss smells and worse, carried under your nose by the breeze.

Even so early, the bouncing pleasures volunteered by the local girls marked out the minutes, a lazy screech of good-time promises followed by a concealed yawn, a flash of blue-veined dimpled flesh. While, in the background, in the comfort of cars, this late morning with their hoods down and singing some station or other as the need grew and phonecalls were made to still-sleeping brothers, the hard men waited for their missys' fresh-pumped milk. The Johns scuttled on past to the rhythm of mild shame, the wind kept pace. It was almost too warm for the coat I was wearing, but not quite. Too soon for it perhaps.

I have always done laundry like a freshman boy, everything all in together, top temperature, maximum spin, strongest bleach and a lot of hope that the machine would know better than I did. Well, no, of course I knew better, but with so many clothes and so little patience, hey, something's gotta give. A mistake could be easily turned into an effect, if worn with purpose.

As I stuffed the clothes into the machine, this guy at the next machine over smiled in recognition of the take-out curry smell, looked as if he'd had a rough old night himself. I smiled back so that I could borrow his detergent which I poured lump by lump in with the clothes.

Once the clothes were cooking away nicely, I bought breakfast, which had now withered down to a cup of white coffee since I couldn't get change and didn't want to ask that guy. I searched my bag for an errant cupcake, but was disappointed on that score, so I sat down with my coffee, facing this monster machine, and fished in my pocket for the letters.

They weren't there.

I retraced the path from the door, where I knew I had them last, to the machine. I turned the laundry bag inside out but there was nothing there either. It was becoming clear that the only other place they could be was in with the clothes, swimming away, soaking out the black and blue ink, bulking out the fibres 'til they weakened and tore. Maybe if I caught them now they could be rescued.

No stop button, a start but no stop, so I pressed all the others in different combinations, banging down on them in the hope of breaking the machine. Reaching to pull the pipes and wires from the back, my hand found only a single thick pipe which refused to move. And all the while I could hear gurgling, spinning, and sloshing sounds coming from inside, the sounds of the boat-boy drowning in the suds.

With my back and my legs, I slammed the machine full against the wall, but it was familiar with this move as a form of encouragement, and kept on churning. I went to prise open the lid which would not give me anything but a broken bloody thumbnail, so I body-slammed harder. The hook-backed, smiling old lady who worked there seldom looked up from her card games, but was now standing over me like a query, smile straightened to a harsh line, storming away at me in her own language. I couldn't understand her words and she couldn't understand my rage. I slid to the ground and slouched beside the machine and turned the air dark blue as she scolded me in a mother-tongue.

The guy with the detergent had fled, I thought, to the safety of a diner or home, but he appeared again some minutes later with a small bottle of vodka, which he handed to me, saying, 'I do that all the time. I think it would be cheaper to fly my sister up once a week to do my washing for me. What I have in there,' he said, pointing at a particularly virulent machine which was frothing alarmingly, 'is collection number three this year.' I took a swig from the vodka bottle, then poured a dose into my coffee cup, not taking my eyes off his machine which was now bubbling over onto the floor.

That Girl from Happy

'Your laundry has rabies.'

I got slightly out of it on this guy's booze, as he did, watching his trail of suds reach the door as my own trail died a watery death in the next machine. I sat there for an hour, King Canute and her plastic cup of vodka. We didn't talk, we just drank, nice manners on a guy not to bug you.

Half-standing, half-swaying, I realised as I sorted through the damp clothes that I hadn't come across the envelope. I searched through them again and still no sign. A sodden mass of brown paper was offered by the vodka guy with a mumbled apology.

'Sorry, was it important?'

'It was, a bit.'

There was no way of separating out and reading the whiter-than-white flattened brick inside. Pity, I had thought until then that we could have had something there, me and that bleach-and-vodka guy.

'Would you like to have dinner with me?'

'Sure.' Defeat has never blunted my appetite.

'Can you cook?' he asked me, and, I swear, I thought I didn't hear him right.

'Sorry?'

'Maybe we could have dinner at your place?'

I never cook, not for me, and certainly not for men. It's not like cooking dinner is the same sort of affectionate gesture as buying flowers or chocolates: it is a promise to fail at everything else. Although you think you are free and doing your own thing, you are planning menus in your head, chopping things which would have been okay left unchopped, passing him your confidence on a plate. Girls

— Listen to me, NEVER COOK, only enter the kitchen to fetch large knives.

'No.'

'Okay, it's just I don't usually eat out, so I don't know where's good.'

Living in New York and never eating out, the guy should be sent to a lab for checking — he was already pickled plenty from the vodka.

'That's kind of rare. Who are you anyway, the bastard child of Chef Boyardee?'

'Just a guy content to uphold the stately institution of the ketchup and tuna sandwich.'

'How about we go to a place called Screeching Lindy's? It's just down a couple of blocks.'

'Sounds like a gay place.'

'You'll be sitting down to eat, don't worry.'

'Okay. I'll meet you here at eight.'

This kind of shit never happens to me, never. Must be the coat doing the business.

'My name's Dec,' he yelled from across the road.

'Janie,' I shouted back, and it felt a little more like truth.

Arriving back with the clean laundry I found some re-dial-happy cop had called three times. So someone stole the stinking body, big fucking deal. It's not like she needed it now, nor did they for all their fussing. If some bastard took it, he or she must have had a need and I salute that.

I brushed my teeth to impair the fumes, kept the coat on, and struck out for the precinct which was easy enough to find. I've never been in trouble, officially. Yeah, I know

That Girl from Happy

how this whole thing sounds, way too Kojak or whoever they have now. But this was me — well, not me but close by.

Janie's body was slated to get fried this morning so the ashes could get sent back to her folks to feed the roses or whatever, but when they went to get it, it was gone. So now we all had to go along to the precinct down the street from the funeral place and answer questions. They reckon this could mean she was murdered and the murderer was covering their tracks. They didn't exactly say that but I know the way it goes.

I don't do waiting rooms as a matter of principle, so I didn't intend to hang around. Although I'm excellent at waiting on station platforms, in cafés or outside stores, I'm inclined to clench up in a sort of personality paralysis if I'm left sitting in a waiting room (even if the magazines are under a year old). After twenty minutes I'd be no help to anyone, so I planned to spin the usual — an appointment with a gynaecologist. The embarrassment generally hurries men along. With women you have to say it's with the breast clinic and their own fears transmute to sympathy; either way, you're in. I'm not in the slightest bit impatient, but waiting for something that has already arrived is a thing I did enough of in my younger days; for eighteen years I delayed gratification and the world was no better for the wait. Now I'll move on a minute if I want.

Last there, everyone turned as I walked in, I felt about as popular as luncheon meat. Sammy looked at me as if I was wearing her pelt and not just her coat.

'She gave it to me weeks ago.'

Fat Molly's mouth was pursed so tight the upper and
lower lips might soon swap places. Could look good with
those big brown eyes, but as it is she looks like a mild dose
of flu dressed up; those eyes are too wet — you'd think she
was practising to be old and the haze and the yellow would
come later. Trust Molly Tightass, afraid I look too good in
it, afraid I was a better friend to the star. Might just steal her
man to watch her lose it. She's too tall for the damn coat
anyway so what's her problem? She so obviously hates me.
That's funny.

'So, did I do it?'
    'Did you?'
    'With these arms?'
    'Do you know this Italian Tony?'
    'Not well.'
    'What's he like?'
    'Sort of … there. Not the kind of person you'd have
anything bad to say about.' (At least, not with a conscience
as bloodied as mine.) 'He's nice enough. I guess I'd feel bad
about speaking ill of those who used to date the dead.'
    Deep sigh and please would I call if I heard anything.
He was straining for a cigarette-break, I know the signs.
    'You don't really give a shit, do you?' I smiled.
    'No.'
    'I guess it could have been worse; you could have gone
into nursing.'
    'I like being a cop because I get to put little girls in cages.'
    'Point taken. Can I go?'
    I wonder if cops are allowed to flirt like that?

As I left, I asked the desk clerk if it was true what my cop had told me about the jellybeans and was there anything else on her when she died. I'd counted on some degree of mystery, secrecy, solemn regulation, a tight hold on clues only the thief would know, so being given the information was a big old bore. A compass, he told me, which was sent back to her parents after the initial autopsy. Not so perverse but not bad as pieces of the puzzle go.

As I turned to leave, some freak-ass was lurking in my space, so close he stopped me turning fully around, all tufted brown hair and wilder than wild eyes — I could focus no detail that near. Pulling back a step along the counter, I saw it was Boots, looking worse in daylight than he had in Happy. His arm had followed my retreat and now tugged at the coat, pulling it right off me. He didn't say anything but his breathing was louder than when most people speak, he just kept tugging at the sleeve which wouldn't give, and I let him. I sort of felt protected by the coat because it had been hers, it was my force shield, it still smelled like her, but once it was gone, I would be vulnerable again, as good as naked but without the added attention.

'It's mine,' he said. 'I gave it away.'

'You gave it away,' I said. 'It's mine.'

Stand-off, a good forty seconds of looking at each other unblinking. Here was a man who was either very slow or very stubborn. I gave him stubborn. The coat was a man's coat, a green suede one with a tattoo-like pattern burned into one of the sleeves. It was one of those camouflages that works by not integrating you, a discordant disguise, making you untouchable because it makes you so different. When they look, they can't see you, they can only see the coat. Only most of the people in this corridor looked and saw Janie.

I think that is what would scare me most, to be the same as the multitude, that would make me feel unprotected. If I were ever going to carry out an assassination, I would dress in one of those dumb chicken outfits, like people wear for handing out advertising leaflets for fast-food chicken-shacks. Everyone would be looking, but it would be the suit they'd be thinking about, not me. Me they'd have me down for a half-wit, so, again, advantage. Also, it would be embarrassing for the cops giving a press conference, saying they were on the lookout for a nine-foot chicken, God, the very thought has me half-way to the dress-hire store already.

I don't mean to suggest that the coat made me look like a chicken, or an assassin either, but at least that would be something. Watched by those who missed her, I was feeling right then like a gap of a person, a space where Janie should be only they put me there instead. Maybe one day they'll like that it's me.

Most of them looked like they had levelled out, used up their annual quota of sad. As he sank into a bench, Boots looked like he had done the same and had also borrowed heavily on his future whack of despair. If he made it to the future I reckoned he'd have a fuck-load of laughing to get done to catch up with the rest of the by-no-means exuberant population. I tend to kind of seize up if things get rancid, hyperventilating and developing some rather nasty eczema around my elbows and knees, that's how I do it. I hadn't cried at the news, the service or anytime since — in fact, I can't remember when I last cried — but this man right here looked as if he was forming two sharp ridges down his cheeks from the river of hard tears running through them. As I kept looking at his face, behind the trouble I could almost see the years of apple pie plumping out the cells, and could tell his pain was recent, not more than a few months in, clawing inwards, burrowing against the decades of fat bliss.

He looked the picture of misery hunched over. I wanted to kick him in the ribs, get him moving out of that sorry pit he was sat in. But I've never been one for rescuing stray dogs so I decided to leave him where he was; no doubt some spongy bleeding heart or other would mop him up and dry him down.

Boots now took in a deep breath and held it for an age; some insects have shorter reproductive lives than the length of that held breath. He was holding back the goods, keeping back the wildness of his thoughts until they burned his mouth from the inside and he had to let them out, burning whisper like a jet flame.

'They killed her. I know it was them. They came for her again and took her away to kill her over and over, to punish her. And me.'

'Right, whatever. I'm not the arraignment lady today, so go tell your story to the uniform.'

Killed her over and over, I could see it all played out in my head. It's supposed to be so easy, this dying, people do it every day. I pulled the coat further around me as I walked away.

I accidentally turned the wrong way when I left the building, not like me to do that; it made me think about the compass. New York is the one place where direction is clear, it's charted in the layout and etched onto every New Yorker's mind. So, a compass?

I guess it was for personal navigation, like how some people use over-scheduling to dictate their day, or how my father and step-mom have always had money, using that to steer them through their lives. When you have money, you have to hang out in particular places, send your kids to great boarding schools, wear your predestined hat a certain way, eat and drink the impossible, bubbles and aspic. I tend to lurch, don't much mind where I wind up as long as it's not boring. Far too many people adopt the school-marriage-kids construct, living just a half-day from Bedlam and a good six months beyond their means. Some spin the bottle, some chase fame and other such spooks. You'd only need an actual compass to get you through the mazes if you had nothing else, if all the other constructs had deserted you. Perhaps you need extra assistance to find your way to death.

One thing was certain in this strangeness — they seemed to think Italian Tony was a key, one I hoped would remain lost to them as it probably opened a way to me. Doubtless he'd be steering wide of Happy, knowing how certain people would be stalking him, scouring those now-notorious drinking grounds for the arrival of their suspect of choice, so I headed straight for his apartment.

Sat there on the subway, I figured Italian Tony could take this thing two ways: run to Atlanta and hide out with a brother he probably had stashed there — somehow seems likely — or mingle until familiarity dusted over people's suspicions, obliterated the tracks. Middle-men like Italian Tony carry a philosophy which says that everyone takes responsibility for themselves, conscience persuades them that they are a stepping stone, protecting those who really deal from getting their feet wet. So guilt wouldn't be an issue, but incarceration would.

He answered the door and, as his look of recognition didn't double as a welcome, I broke the moment quickly.

'Did I leave my underwear here by any chance?'

I was joking, but he said yes and went off to fetch it, and came back with a black lace basque with underwiring and panel support. I had no idea I had such great taste. I'd stepped too far into the hallway for him to have power over my access.

'I need to talk to you and I think it would be safer here.'

He hustled me into the same kitchen I'd been deported from hungry only a few mornings before.

'If it's about Janie's body, I already know.'

'So then, you know that they think it was something to do with you?'

'They have my name on file, on account of a few mis-understandings, so even if they couldn't pin this other thing on me, they'd use it as a way of getting me for something else they think I might have done.'

'I didn't give them your address if that's what you're wondering.'

'They already have it, they're just trying to find out who knows me enough, and who might be pussy enough to dummy in a set-up.'

The doorbell rang; he looked at me as if I might know who it was.

'Another trick they have is to follow you when you leave.'

Judy May Murphy

'Shit.'

He went out to determine just how much of a greenhorn I was, but the visitor made it in with less trouble than I'd had, and as long as they weren't looking for ladies' underwear all was safe. A man was saying he'd got the address from Garth in Happy, that Garth said to say it was cool.

In walked Sammy.

What a beautiful boring-looking man, one of those tanned and cut gym-monkeys, with the sort of smouldering eyes that did nothing but smoulder, which wears a little thin even after the six seconds I had been watching him. His hair was impressive though, shoulder length, wavy and black; he sort of pushed it back with his fingertips, then dragged it forward again to how it had been, so you knew it was a nervous reflex rather than a hairdressing manoeuvre. He gave me a qualified smile as Italian Tony tried to choreograph the situation, looking across to the other room then back to the two of us. After nothing but a spiked coffee my stomach argued that the jerk still owed me.

'I'm starving, you wouldn't have any crackers or anything?'

'Sure. Help yourself — there's stuff in the icebox and in those cabinets up there.'

I knew already. He excused them both for a minute and left to trade in the bedroom.

Helping myself to cereal, I took the opportunity to poke around a little, but the whole place was dressed in innocence. Two sets of weighing scales but that's not even a misdemeanour.

Sammy and his hair came back in.

'How did you get on, in the ... earlier?' he asked.

'Fine. They just asked me a bunch of questions, about Italian Tony mostly.'

The condemned himself re-entered the room.

'Yeah, man. They seem to be looking to talk to you.'

'I wouldn't worry,' was what I meant to say, but I'd just ladled in some cereal so it came out completely retarded. I swallowed and tried again, 'I wouldn't worry, they always suspect the people closest to the victim.'

'Well, yeah, that's me out of it then,' Italian Tony said in a voice that dismissed all argument.

While in the other room, the two probably hadn't even mentioned Janie, I just knew they hadn't, although it was she who had brought them together in a roundabout if radical way. I was hoping the coat might bother them but they probably didn't even notice.

Italian Tony had obviously licked the wooden spoon, sniffed the cookies some; he was buzzing like an amp, managing to turn standing still into an aerobic activity, and saying 'yeah' in all the wrong places.

Sammy was playing with his hair again.

Looking perturbedly at Italian Tony, he said, 'Maybe they think you might be a connection, you know.' And I thought to myself how Sammy wasn't going to be much help in the untangling department, but he hit the button somehow and Italian Tony was off.

'Like if drugs were in it? You'd all love that, fucking love it if it was drugs, that way everyone's off the hook. And anyway, why then would I steal the body, yeah? To draw the stuff back out, distil it from her blood and resell it?' He was flying up the gears. 'I mean, yeah, get real, people. I know a junk fiend who'd suck it from his sister's hole if that were the only way, but even he'd be more likely to steal the brass from the casket and sell that for his shit.'

'Good point,' said Sammy.

'And so nicely put,' I added.

While smart enough to be able to articulate a defence, he wasn't smart enough to sit on it. 'That girl, ask that girl, the one thinks she's in charge of life, she saw the certificate after the autopsy, she told me, no trace.' He then put out his cigarette and made to go, except it was his place and he couldn't.

Having broken silence in such a major way, Italian Tony's poise faltered and he buried his head and shoulders in the icebox, rummaging for his lost composure amongst the old salsa dips and salad dressing.

Sammy nudged me on the arm. He had written across the palm of his hand, 'Meet me in Happy Friday night 8.30?' and then quickly returned it to a fist to keep Italian Tony from seeing as he emerged from his chill cloister with a single beer. Jesus, that man could peel and eat oranges in his pocket.

I'd just finished off his Nut 'n' Honey.

'Thanks for that, grocery-flow problem.'

'Did you want to take something for later?'

'No thanks, I'll be fine.'

Obviously sucking up to me, must be nervous about something, or perhaps this was his latest method of displacement; anyway, I'd already put half a slab of cooked ham in my bag. I wanted to say something, to mention her, but nothing would fit into the conversation. That type of sweeping her under the carpet was worse to my mind than any actual stashing of the body might be.

'I'll call by if I hear any more news. Good to meet you again, Sammy. I'm sure I'll see you around soon.'

His hand went to his curls as he read my consent.

On reaching the corner, I turned back to see him on the doorstep, shaking hands with Italian Tony. No dealer I ever knew shook hands with the buyer except as a pass. Perhaps they had finally mentioned Janie.

Which brings me here to Happy, late afternoon, content that my circus has been strung out, wondering about it. Italian Tony was choice target for their keen accusation, serves him right for being bullseye with the other stuff, but I know where he was the night she died, and I know he never hated her enough to take the risk. Having the guts to shift powder bags is toy courage, it breaks when stood beside a body ten times its own weight in death.

Lucy made me laugh with her pitchforked shit-heap information, probably called it clues, hoping one of the drear fucking facts she showered down on that underpaid cop might just catch the killer and save the day. Hurrah! Hurrah for Lucy the Cunt! Poor little Lucy, so much talk, so little mind, must ask her about the autopsy though, problem is, I just hate being arranged so any conversation is a trial. I wonder if she's taken Boots on, brought him home for mittened, chicken-noodle-caring soup. Maybe he'd be no use to her and just trouble her carpets, probably couldn't enter her listed and checked-off world; present-and-correct was a thing he could hardly manage at this stage. Boots, a man gone natural, one for the farm. What he said though, 'to punish her', just those words, they bothered me. How could he possibly know anything she had done, anything that might need punishing?

Ah, it's enough to drive a girl to the devil. Anyway this Dec guy thinks he has a date with Janie, so I'm off to oblige.

Ladymen and guymen rarely mix; poor bastard would probably choke on his spoon at the sight of a way-tall man in a cowgirl outfit, don't want to kill him off on a first date so instead I bring him to this Italian place busy enough to cover any gaps in the getting-to-know-you racket, and famed for its pumpkin ravioli.

He's on time, which denies me my usual moments of cold regret. When we get there the Maître d' talks to Dec about whether Madam would like her coat hung up, and I wish we'd gone to my initial choice where everyone is girlfriend, no distinctions. Here it's the same old scene, tiny kingdom ruled by the boys' brigade, with only a few, very loud women competing on their own terms (I mean being unnecessarily aggressive). Such places are arenas for the socially competitive, life reduced to a big-pig arm-wrestle meet. I have such low tolerance for success that their intensity always causes me to over-order on the wine and slump in counter-aspect to their lunge. There the men sit unrestrained by self-doubt, suited to their image, making their plans for success, as women play bit-parts, friends waved to, possibilities treated and waitresses ordered. And as they buy each other dinner with money that should be everybody's (no, I insist), the women sit there worrying about their weight. If we were smart, we would stay home and write a bestseller, plan a revolution, find a cure for cancer. But we are most of us not smart, so we go to jazz-ballet class instead, to tone up our inner thighs, and then eat salad. I'm depressed for us sometimes, more depressed when I order salad.

Dec's slight unease is a comfort to me. He's cute but not in a soap-opera way. I mentally sketch the letter I would write were I a dutiful daughter and could be sure she'd remember who I was:

> *Dear Mom No. 2, I have met a boy. He has brown hair, so straight it continually falls over his eyes, so he seems to be shyly peering out from a curtain with light flecks through it. He's taller than Dad but not as tall as Uncle Peter, which I guess makes him five eleven. His eyes are the darkest blue I've ever seen on a person, and his skin is slightly tan. Please send money.*

Won't ever happen though.

It's so nice to eat with a person like this; you aren't put off your food by a slight cast in their eye or a mole the size of Alaska — things like this do matter even if the popular opinion insists they don't. He keeps calling me Janie and each time it seeps a little deeper into me.

Life-story time, time to formulate your life. The obvious stuff. Has to be done. The best way is to keep any opinion out of it, otherwise you end up whining accidentally, going down sister-stole-your-doll roads. Sometimes I wonder, when I'm fully au fait with a guy's agonies with the ex,

Judy May Murphy

whether it's a date or therapy, or if people even differentiate.

'A writer, a good one, but under-earning.'

'Do you enjoy it?'

'Its kind of like eating — sometimes you enjoy it and sometimes you do it for maintenance.'

'But never for the money?'

'Hardly ever, not now.'

And not knowing enough about Janie's far-back history to chance taking her on completely, I go off into how I used to work for a weekly supplement on a paper, personal-interest lifestyle kind of stuff. How I was nothing special, on time and with the words in roughly the right order, very objective, they said, not too involved in the tragedy. Although I didn't admit it, a mass murderer or a homeless old lady were very much the same to me, someone else, no one, good for a few inches. It was a soft number, no digging for dirt, the stories were already there wrapped in people's lives, I just had to hack them open. Like lumberjacking, it felt, like felling and stacking sapling trees. It's not that I'm egocentric and blind to all but my own; in fact, my history doesn't interest me either, family and friends, with their rememories rolled out every damn time I show, have always been so much more dead wood to me, rows and rows of inanimates.

Then one day I seized up completely, and there I was believing oxidation wasn't possible without air. So I gave myself the axe, liberation from the tasks of social conservation, no more picking fruits and turning them into bite-sized media tarts, and didn't do much except exist from financial quarter to quarter when my trust fund interest would arrive. I let Dec believe I'm on welfare.

I'm done by the time the main course arrives, have all the Aimee stuff said, mildly annoyed that I don't have enough of a life to get me through dinner, but there you go. Confident of my performance up to this point, I divert from my own past and stray into an account of how I acted in a play off Broadway after leaving the paper, playing an old woman, in *Riders to the Sea* by J.M. Synge — had he heard of it?

'Yeah. My family's Irish.'

'Mine too.'

I imagine the coffin ships turning in their watery graves, and my four Russian grandparents coughing up ghostly borscht in dismay. And, as Dec orders a second bottle of wine, I hear the voice I'm claiming, clear as anything out of the rabble in the restaurant, 'There does be a power of young men floating around in the sea', and I wonder if the boat-boy was one of these, and lose the mood for telling my Janie life.

Dec's fun, not in the throwing-mashed-potatoes kind of way but he makes me laugh with his stories about the seven years he spent as a maintenance engineer for aeroplanes out in JFK, told with a deadpan face and a wry insight into the joke of day-to-day living; sounds like he made monotony into an artform. Thank God he doesn't play the perennial clown, that's something that can tire a date before its time. Instead, the pace calms right down as the story gets serious and he tells how he was caught blitzed to almost comatose on the job, and let a fuel hose leak onto a concourse. I swear I'll never fly again and he tells me he's seen things that would make you not want even to stand under a flight path. The union was his saviour, and although he had to be taken off the usual checking and safety, he still works for the same company in an office in Rockaway.

'I don't normally drink a lot, just all the time. I might have seven or eight drinks in a day but I start pretty much as soon as I wake up.'

He presents a theory that some people need lubricating more than others, on account of unresolved issues cranking them up until their interactions are like rough gear changes, that such people are so tight in their workings, keeping everything close in away from harm, and the drink bathes the knots of uncertainty, loosing them out.

'What are your unresolved things?' I ask.

'I don't know, shit about growing up without a mother, that's the obvious one, I guess. In fact, I think I just like drinking. So, great theory, huh?'

By dessert he points out that I too seem well seasoned in the drinking sphere.

'It's true, I'm no water baby. I can drink efficiently enough, usually if the people I'm with are going at it hard, but then I take a few days out to recover. But if you were drinking apple juice, I probably would, too. I'm an addict by proxy.'

'Bet you went to private school, one of those smelly rich Connecticut places, and had to drink fast before your dorm parents walked in. You can tell you're from money by the way you can sit in here like it was in your livingroom.'

If that were so, I'd be sitting on the floor.

'Yeah, New Hampshire, but I thought I'd rinsed all that out of me with the blow.'

'Prevalent upper-class delusion.'

'I'm not deluded, I'm too disappointed to be deluded. Besides, there's no such thing as class in America.'

'Only you guys can afford to think that.'

We shouldn't have mentioned money so close to getting the check; we quickly agree halves. We are most of us scarred from teenage years of family celebrations in Chinese or Greek restaurants recommended by families who didn't know any better either. Thank God my family was never the type to scour the bill asking, 'Who had the chicken?' If they had ever informed the waitress, 'I think you'll find we only had the one garlic bread', I would have run fast away to Africa and stayed. A semblance of dignity has always been worth more than the price of a side dish. However, possibly with his accusation of high social status ringing loudly in my self-respect, I now find myself at the end of this meal, saying to the waitress at the cash desk, 'No, I definitely only had one salad', and my family seems to me weak somehow. I am too harsh, I know this. But I also know I only had one salad.

Probably too polite to look at the state of the place, he stays watching me as we go into the room, and I suddenly wonder if maybe it doesn't just look bad, but has started to smell even worse, and hope the drink hits his olfactory bits as well as everywhere else. I sit down on a bag as an invitation for him to do the same. I hope he won't ask to use the bathroom; it's so close and I do so hate to hear a man pee when I'm on a date with him. His eyes are still on me and I start to rub at my forehead as if I have secret things written there. By now I'm sweating as much as the walls and I want more than anything to talk about her, and to tell him that he's lovely but I'm waiting for the boat-boy, but I guess I'm afraid of accidentally mentioning me in the process, the Aimee me, not the Janie one. Luckily he's now absorbed in the clothes and I can breathe deeper and slow.

Sitting on the softer laundry-bag, legs almost reaching the far wall, he eventually shifts his gaze from the Heap and starts to look around for any evidence of furniture. This makes me slightly edgy as I own less white goods and hardware than many homeless people. When I get nervously defensive, I talk. A lot.

'I'm getting a closet next week, a really big one. It's all going to be arranged into different sections with all the shoes in tight rows underneath. And some chairs, too, but I can't remember what type, I want ... what type I want. After that, I'm getting a bed, but I'll probably have moved into a bigger place by then, or a nicer one, anyway. I'm sorry I've no cookies or anything, I don't, I my friends don't like them so I rarely have any in, cookies I mean. I mean you only lose them in the bottom of your cup, cookies, still. But the closet should be good, anyway. I have a couple of Twinkies here somewhere though.'

I sound bi-polar, I sound the way someone does when they're about to go and give away the family car, manic as a high-power pressure cooker. It's him, he's doing this, he's looking at me, looking for something. So I reach for a pair of Janie shoes and change into them as we sit there.

'Look, we'll start over,' I say, half laughing, 'and this time I get to play a normal kind of host. Would you like some coffee?'

'Yes, please,' he says.

But as I stand to go and unearth the kettle, he grabs my hand and draws me close in a kiss that neither of us pulls away from for the next hour. When that man kisses a girl goodnight he is mighty thorough.

The smell from the room has now been replenished with fresh sweat, the rhythm of him paces my mind and I relax, my head in his right hand, my body arching over papers and rolling with him to the safety of the Heap, swelling, the pile moving under us, pressed down under the weight, clothes entangled everywhere, covering and uncovering forbidden flesh, inside me piercing the empty space. He calls 'Janie' softly, and I know she is smiling.

Finally, altogether still and happy.

'Regular or decaf?' I ask.

Judy May Murphy

Janie

She has stared at that horizon for many years in the beautiful Algarve, but every year it disappoints her, as her adventuring boy fails to appear over its distance in the little wooden boat.

Her parents are soaking up the wine bar with their breezers, now that they are best friends with the owners. They would like her to go to the local disco with the son of another absolutely lovely couple they met, so she is hiding out on the beach until said son is safely married, or slow dancing with some English girl at the very least. She is tired to the marrow of all this holiday fun. She does make an effort but there is only so much dancing her tan legs can endure, so much smiling her sun-blistered mouth can affect. So, she has escaped to talk with her boat-boy, and now imagines she sees him as a shape ambling slow as the heat down the road towards her.

Next comes the downturn as she sees it is only a local man strutting over to her, to tell her she is pretty and ask her to go for a drink, no doubt. It is time to turn back to the villa; she can dream until bedtime there.

'Do you have a light?' the man calls in stuccoed English from the road.

She does, and she fishes in her pockets for a matchbook from the bar. If he'd asked for a pen, a piece of string or a stamp, she could have said yes to that too. He joins her on the sand with none of the grinning and winking of the other local men, cups the flame with both hands, breathes in the spark until it takes, and then pushes her hard onto the sand.

She waits for a second for the joke to become clear, then in horror she wills herself to stand, or even crawl away, fights only with her mind to be somewhere else as he pulls up her short skirt and rips her bikini bottoms down to her feet, saying nothing, slips of ash drifting off in the breeze. She longs to drift off also but her arms and legs are unable to move, so in habit her hoping just calls for the boat-boy to come. He'll come running down that self-same road and save her, he has to become a body this time, he has to emerge from the prayer inside of which she has kept him locked away.

She feels nothing but a burning, stabbing pain between her legs and hears only the coughing, panting breath of the man as he thrusts in and out, one hand holding her hair, pinning her to the ground, the other holding the lit cigarette beside her eye lest she find the blood to move or shout. When his business is done, he pulls away as if he too feels she has caught fire. She doesn't even catch sight of the part of him he pushed inside her as his sarong falls back over his thighs and knees as he stands and takes another mighty pull on the cigarette. Janie lies there on the beach, feeling as if grains of sand were now running through her veins, and tells herself it isn't true as she watches him wander back up the road.

Knowing the lack of the boat-boy, knowing it completely for the chasm it is, she whimpers the horror of the endless toll. Why is he not beside her as in those summers before?

And as with her silent cries of years ago, nobody hears — not the boat-boy, not one single person in the world.

The loss of him now added to a loss of herself, she stumbles down to the sea to wash away the juices that run down her legs, not completely knowing what they are. No tears, only a single thought through her head, where could he be, why is he never here and her needing him enough to die of it? She tries to conjure him up as she has done for her comfort a thousand thousand times before, but she cannot feel the boat-boy in these gentle Mediterranean waves, cannot feel him underfoot since the sand is too soft, cannot smell him in the warm heavy air. Instead she is consumed by a shaking, as if she is a sickly animal outside herself, and is walled around inside by this musty, stabbing man who strode unbidden from the road and the night.

It is too much, the push too far. It is time for them to be together before the badness eats up everything good. Her boat-boy must be waiting for her under the sea, she thinks, that's where he has been all these long years.

And she will visit him there. She tidies her hair away from her face, and scrubs between her legs with handfuls of wet sand, before putting on her inexpert smile and setting out, her best foot forward, sinking.

An answer at last makes her light, so to weigh herself down she puts large scoops of sand in her pockets, and walks out to meet him.

Soon her shoes are heavy with sandwater and her lungs stop catching with each wave, and the thought of him folds in like the water blanket, a comfort as she wades out toward the very horizon which so disappointed her before.

That Girl from Happy

The water is tugging at her waist, its current starts to drag her out to the place she wants to be. The heavy sand of the seabed pulls in every direction, as she half-walks, half-floats toward her answer. The water over her shoulders, in her ears and mouth, hair spread on the surface; she hears a shout in the distance.

A curtain of seaweed opening and closing before her eyes, she is blinded by salt water, and as she slips beneath the sea she believes she sees salvation — his small boat come to fetch her.

She wakes up to the lack of him once again, in a shiny hospital ward with voices, her parents kindly chiding her for swimming at night, a rescue line running from her wrist. She has woken up without him so many hundred times before, but this time the loss is more terrible, and her after paying the price.

Yes, she agrees with them, so silly to go midnight swimming alone.

*

Over the years the redbrick road has sagged a little further into its slack foundations, towered over by the trees which have outgrown its careful size. This last half-day, a freak snow has fallen heavy on the city, making grey the cold roofing, grey the idle cars and the unpawed gardens, as a lazy rain comes calling to dirty the pure white fall. At the back of ivy-brim number eighty-seven, a frosted robin sits in ruffled hope for crumbs at the kitchen window. The house is

Judy May Murphy

as cold inside as out, ice forming in the vase of dead flowers on the sill.

No one sees the robin, as the only eyes watching him are blind to the view.

Head in her hands, a young woman stares dead cold ahead, covering her ears to stop the sound of waves, her pen falling back onto the blank sheets of paper on the ashwood table below.

She has been trying this last hour to write a letter, one like the many she had written for years before. But her pen will not lift her hand for the drafting, her head will not open for words to appear. She has been failing to write to him since the summer, and earlier today the child she had wished to the back of her mind began to kick inside her, as if asking to be let out into the world. How can she ever face the boat-boy, knowing she has carried another man's baby inside? Another comfort lost to the sea; never again will she talk to him in letters beneath the floor. She does not deserve him — she is a wickedness walking, a monstrous wrong.

Please be kind to her, she is only still so young, retarded by defeat, and cannot organise her value as unbroken people can. Her liquid eyes large in her shrunken face, her skin hangs tired from her empty frame, her face held on by her hands. Her ribs still carved but her hips now rounded, her cheekbones sharper than the razor-back shell. She knows she must eat, but that will confess the difference; she must hide her ever-growing stomach under bigger clothes, starve herself and the rotten child within.

As the hunger gnaws on her bones, a surge of despair has her reaching for the wooden bread-box, from which she

That Girl from Happy

takes one single slice of soft white bread. The hunger pushing, she folds the bread into her unsmiling mouth, straight
in past feeble teeth without toasting or spreading, barely
chewed on its way down to the child. Still standing there beside
the bread-box, the hunger strangely grown with feeding, she
takes two more slices, sandwiching a third, and these she
bolts in similar frenzy, neither tasting them nor feeling their
descent, and before she knows that she is eating at all, she
has devoured a small loaf. The robin waits for the crumbs to
be shaken from the bread-wrapper onto the ledge, while next
she eats a sugared scone, and two, the comfort calming to her.

She searches the fridge for any leftovers there, finding cold
pasta and a potato salad, eating quicker than they can be seen,
beginning to worry at the depth of her void. A smooth rich
cheese which she chews like a fruit, unable to stop, wondering, as she doesn't eat cheese and never did. Faster now, the
shiny biscuit tin: chocolate, jam-filled, custard creams all
crumbled into her need. The wetness sponged from her mouth,
the nuggets travel dry; she coughs as particles detour to her
lungs. Cereal, crunching bowlfuls after the milk runs out.

The hunger savagely crushed, still its compulsion keeps
on. In, and in, and in, to plug the way she is draining out
through every pore. The robin cocks his head and waits his
turn. Grunting softly as she fights to breathe through the
swallows, she spoons in a half-tub of softberry ice-cream,
the cold of it stinging her gums. Her stomach now hurts
and her temperature pushes to fever, sweat dripping and
shallow breath. Still this salmon-spawn need keeps her
feeding, she is master of nothing, caught in the flow, spoon
abandoned, she pulls in fistfuls of tomorrow's pre-cooked

beef stew, then upturns it onto the table and dips her face straight in.

Part of her sits beside the robin, outside, watching the view, marvelling at the wretched show.

Soon her parents will return; this distant thought drags her to the downstairs toilet, and, as she sticks first her finger, then her whole hand down as if to manually retrieve the overeaten food, it comes up so quickly that it exits through both mouth and nose, chunks and liquid, she can feel it even behind her eyes, and again it comes a second surge without her hand to beckon. She partly hopes to see the child emerge, to disappear forever with the vomited food. And a third wave, liquid and burning. And she is free of the food and the distress that fed it to her, the child still kicking inside. She has controlled the uncontrollable, salvaged at least one mistake.

She cries with relief, lines of mucus strung from nose to mouth to toilet-bowl to hand.

Then, feeling lighter than before she even entered the kitchen, she wipes herself clean, clears away the mess on the ashwood table and goes to sit as usual with normal magazines in the normal lounge, nothing new. Her parents return to a slightly happier daughter than theirs.

The following day, having stolen to the butcher's and remade the stew, she writes herself a letter to find out her own mind. So far is she from the person she thought she knew, she must place herself on a solid page before she can be sure of her doing.

Dear Me, she writes, amazed at the insight brought on by this beginning.

I have to get away from here, go to where the boat-boy is waiting, travel the lands we talked about, adventure in a distance.

Love, Me, she finishes, welcoming the plea.

From now on she will write only to herself; the circle closes smaller.

Dear Me,

I'm glad I didn't tell anyone because their fussing about it would be like it happening again. At least this way no one has taken my control.

I didn't think I'd do the food thing again but then I did, I'm sure its the only way to keep the extra weight from showing. But I know now that it is a danger and so it'll probably only happen when I have to eat a big dinner like for a family celebration or if someone makes me eat something that makes me feel sick. I'm not cutting, for obvious reasons.

Whatever happens, I have to keep going — otherwise it will all have been for nothing.

Love, Me

Judy May Murphy

Aimee

I have this lipstick-kiss tattoo on my right inner thigh. It looks exactly like a kiss mark, it's so damn sugar, and guys really go for the bisexual implications. I have another tattoo on my left calf; it's an old saying written in Japanese, but I can't remember what it is, something about a life lived in harmony. I should get it changed to say something about a life lived with your panties round your heels, and in English, so I can read it every day and remind myself.

Last night I slept with Dec again, at his place because he has a double bed and a non-malicious TV and VCR. He dug the tattoos, hadn't noticed them before, and we ate a monster bag of Dorito's and a tub of salsa afterward, and even watched some late movie before he fell asleep, so it wasn't too bad as sexual experiences go. Called me Janie. I'm so glad that I never got a heart, or that band-of-flowers anklet thing done — those are just so years ago, even an 'I Love Mom' would be a better option. Italian convicts are famed for getting 'Mother, Forgive Me' tattooed on their arms. If I had to list all the people I needed forgiveness from, I'd soon run out of body space.

I didn't get my bellybutton pierced either. I sort of played with the idea but the pain sounded very. A girl told me it was worse than her perineum tearing, a guy said it was worse than being hung upside down leather-hooded and drenched in hot paraffin wax, so I left his party as soon as I could.

As we under-thirties New Yorkers are a tribe, everyone is getting everything pierced, tattooed, cut, burned and scarred, with silicone horns and spikes embedded beneath our scalps, indulging in all manner of Orlonish procedures. I would be considered a little old-fashioned for not wearing jewellery on or through my genitalia, but I think that these things will age us when the next generation comes up smooth, unadorned and at least physically intact. I once heard two women in a café trying to work out if they were talking about the same guy called James. Rather than check if the other woman's James had the same colour hair or the same surname, she right out asked, 'Gold bar through his dick, right?' and the other one said, 'Yeah, about this big,' and indicated with her hands. I hope for his sake she was referring to the Albert not the James.

Dec was very non-trouble to sleep with and it's a welcome change to awake to an emotion that isn't some gradation of regret. He began his day with one of those vodka bottles he'd rescued me with, so, needing solid food as part of my diet I left him to it. Jesus guys, these days we don't insist you marry us after, but would breakfast be too much to ask for?

The sun is shining as I leave. I really wish it wouldn't do that. With the sun, out come the sun-slapped crazy people. These are everywhere today — young, white office-workers mostly, who think that a sunny day gives you licence to strip down to your underwear and offer your sandwiches to whoever is nearby and red and tender in the same places as you. Like we're all bonded by our inability to tan. Hope they wrinkle up like dicks.

On the trip between Dec's apartment and mine I roamed right into Boots, standing outside the precinct, still the hangdog, ever and ever the bone-clutch hound, and I wondered if they'd kept him sentinel, stuck there on some charge of devotion. I stopped and stood silent, marshalled alongside in crap allegiance, but as I don't buy into sacrifice as a general kick I quickly broke peace and asked him if he'd been home since I'd seen him two days before. He nodded, slack-necked and heavy headed, but it's hard to trust a person with a bloody whites to their eyes.

'Not even a week,' he said, those eyes wetting with tears.

Pedestrians were drawing great curves to walk around us, not sure which of us was the danger.

It was the sixth day in, his fourth, and Boots obviously considered himself immune to rest, he held his hands in a strange position like a scrubbed-up surgeon, as if they might otherwise give in to repose and the rest of his body follow suit. Sleep must have been wondering if maybe it was a job for the big man. What Boots really needed was a gravestone to pine alongside, his itinerant grief as lost in the world as the corpse was, a ghostly great pain too huge for any man to carry around. He pawed up to the wall of the precinct for support but found no asylum there, no fixed home-point to bleed into, the building looked ready to fall before it could support that weight. The Egyptians had it sorted: bury the slaves along with, fill in their sadness with sand.

Looking past my face, he quietly said, as if his voice first lifted the stay of life to let out the words, so quietly said that he knew the answers, that he suffered the knowing but they wouldn't even listen to its sound. As answers were the tallow to rub my need that morning I heard myself inviting him over to the shack, to talk it through, to off-load into my longing.

Reassuring myself that his current state vindicated any licence to criticise my own lax practices, I decided to stop for take-out on the way.

'Wait.'

I bought enough Chinese food to sustain the entire Shenzhen province. Death should really dull your propensity for food, sex, gossip — all those indulgences — as we slow in tandem with the corpse, but I was as hungry as a husband. Sex had been on tap the night before, of fine grade considering the measure, and now the eating factor had been catered for also. And gossip? Not that I'd be overly concerned about the morality of doling out information that wasn't mine to give, gossip entails frittering away small power for almost no return, not really my style.

Soon the food, the smelly mad dog Boots and I, were corralled inside the hairy little cell I call home. With some digger-like arm action I cleared a space in the centre of the room, only to uncover a hideous truth, a secret of old laid bare, a carpet more maroon than beige. I really would have to move on, and quickly before other realities caught up with me.

'Please, go ahead, sit.'

We got straight down to the serious stuff. Prawn balls, pork balls, spare ribs, fried rice, kung-po chicken, vegetable chop-suey chow mein, sweet-and-sour something, prawn crackers, and the last of the Twinkies which had lurked hidden, in case either of us should tire of the Oriental theme. We were too plain to pretend to be easy with chopsticks, so instead formed little shovels out of paper-foil lids, and put away a good chunk within the next five concentrated minutes, quiet but for lapping sounds like animal spoons. As I tangled on with the chow mein, shedding it as I ate (like leaves in fall to cover the maroon, strand by pasty strand), he started to talk, a grateful POW discharging his clandestine notions for an extra bowl of rice.

Paying no mind to my noodle offensive, he kicked off with how many were at the service, how they were connected to her, what rôle they played. He talked, ate, and breathed as a single action, the words ignited by the fuel and the air.

Eventually the stories grew larger and further from my own take: he believed Lucy was secretly Janie's sister so I knew I was in for a wild one. A sweat sat like wax on his forehead. Italian Tony was mentioned more frequently than most, the witness gathering evidence as he spoke, as one notion hitched itself along behind another — how Italian Tony hadn't known many people there, hadn't changed out of his work clothes, had left abruptly at the end. It sounded almost plausible until he put him in the CIA. As for Sammy being a doctor who deposited sly mechanisms in Janie's head at the hospital, that was a bit of a reach too. It was clear he was mad, convinced that everyone was trying to poison him with invisible, odourless gas. He managed to talk on the subject for almost an hour without directly mentioning Janie, until suddenly — 'I hope someone kept her green dress, the long green dress with lace, she was perfect in it.'

From where I sat, I could see the green dress; his view was obscured by the coat. Not wanting him to think me the master conspirator on account of the Janie clothes, I asked by way of diversion, 'How long did you know her?'

He had known her for a year and two months. Only when he said it did it strike him, as if he'd been seeing each day as a single grey pencil tick and only now saw the well-scarred incarcerating wall.

'Do you know where her body is now?' I asked, knowing as I pushed that it was too much. I had meant to say, 'Have some more kung-po', but it came out wrong.

Neither of us spoke for an age, all food and talk abandoned, we just both sort of stared into the wasteland of cartons, bags, and msg, which was now rivalling the Heap for a surgeon general's warning.

Cued from within by some rogue notion, he stood, thanked me with a gesture for the food, and made for the door; then, turning back, he began to speak with a sadness that showed he had given up scrapping with the world.

'We were supposed to be together a few days after, so you see I should be with her right now. With her, not this. No one knows her as well as I do and that's why they're hunting me too, because I wrote it all down right from the start, and that's what I wanted to tell them in the place, about the evil ones who came for her, kept her away from me. That's why I tried to give them the notebook but they wouldn't even look at it.'

'Could I maybe read the notebook? Perhaps I could help.'

'No, it's too dangerous and it's too late anyway,' he said to the door as he closed it behind him.

Judy May Murphy

I congratulated myself for lending credence to his paranoia as I followed in sneakers fifty yards behind, shadowing the shadow, tailing the dog.

In his creaky winding it took twenty minutes to journey a path that should have taken ten; with his hurting he needed to use up the day in the nugatory hope that the next one maybe wouldn't sting so. Once he got to the third floor of his building, he fumbled and fell with keys for such an age that I almost blew the gig, exasperation almost tipped me to it, one further slip I'd have stepped up from the floor below and busted the lock with one hand.

Once he'd opened the lock, I crept in his slow wake and saw the door left slightly open, the space inside rudely darkening with the maniacal sound of drapes pulled and screens wrenched shut. Uprooted planks of wood confused the entry, with unsettled dust billowing like so much filthy mist hanging like microflies around the wrested floorboards, while inside the open pit lay naked wires and pipes. I could hear Boots inside, the pile-up in his head impacting against innocuous surfaces, doubtless wrecking the same madness in there, and muttering in mad-dog whimpers, 'No. No. Under here, now I have it. Yes, under here, it's, must be.' He then flew briefly into sight. Jumping the gap between two rooms, he missed me standing at his door in plain sight. I must have been a pale sort of ghost to him considering, but I'd caught a glimpse of the surgical mask over his face and felt a part of me punctured by the show of him, two hands scratching his head as if to rid himself of it.

I walked backwards down the stairs, as he was more scary to me now with his madness proven, and ensconced myself in the café which sat directly across from his building, to hide and reassemble, camouflaged as a standard person with the usual coffee and facile intent within the norm. I loitered there through four coffees and a plate of something disguised as edible.

Boots was definitely milling for a hospital stay, not that such a sojourn had helped Janie all that much. I've never managed to quite unscuff the imprint from the kick of hearing (overhearing) that she'd been taken in for treatment; it was as if they'd stomped me with the same mosh that flattened her. I thought for a moment it was a heartbeat, but no.

The problem with the hospital was that Janie was too easily flaked, overly fragile to survive in the large hands of strangers, the brutal care of firm professionals too clinical to love her as Happy people did. It was way upstate and far off most people's road of experience, besides which she had barred any visit. So, while she wasted in the hospital I kept up storms of flowers, loading all kinds onto her, infiltrating the place with bits of me. Cards left unwritten, nothing to let her know who sent such veneration, to keep my integrity unalloyed, stainless in the flow. I would sometimes imagine she had died and I could send a dozen wreaths to carpet her grave.

One time, sending roses, I slipped up on a quart of lemon vodka and wrote, 'TO MY MOTHER' on the card, I just got so confused, jumbled the people anywise in my head until they were all the one same person, the person that transposed me. What a trip — enough white Russian to black out any light, dipso-facto, Janie became both the old woman Mauyra from the stage, and the old woman my mother would have grown into by now. I think I might have started out writing Mauyra and got lost after 'M'. Janie doubtless presumed it was from a stage daughter or a fan.

First time I saw her in the play I almost didn't. Got sidetracked down a French guy, you know how it is. I'd seen the guy waiting as arranged but then I bolted like he was infested — there's something about slip-on shoes I've never been able to reconcile — and kept running to the play in some feeble effort at rescuing my night. I arrived late and had to stand at the side in that way they have of punishing latecomers in a very grown-up fashion, and I remember assuming that Janie really was a shrunken old woman, a proper one with bunions and bad veins, so convincing, believable rather than plausible.

But more than that. She wore in her tiny head my mother's eyes.

They were so close to being hers, so near a likeness that I later called my sister for the first time that year, but she had never shown an interest in our real mother and asked me how I would know mother's eyes from any other. 'How would I not?' I asked her in return, and she said the kids were screaming and she had to go.

My only memory of my real mother is my single only memory of love, real love, not the kind you bargain for. It must have been soon before she died and because I was so young I can only recall shapes and how dark my room was compared to the light from which she stepped, dressed for day in the middle of the night. I can still feel her jewellery pressed against my face as she held me close against her. She was crying hard, coughing sobs and gulps, holding so tight that the crying didn't scare me, it just felt like more love; I cried a little too and then I must have fallen back asleep. Since then nothing in the love deal has come close, and I wanted it back whenever I saw Janie. I knew when Janie cried that she could love me, or at least teach me how to be that child again.

So I returned to the play on subsequent nights to watch the familiar eyes, and soon enough I found myself completely tangled by Janie's tripwire, manoeuvred from a distance by invisible strands. Many might wonder at my being wound in on such slender threads, but what can outvast a mother's gaze?

I hadn't yet penetrated Janie's people back then, so, at first chance, spinning my cheap trick of hanging coatless by the door then greeting new arrivals and helping them inside with their bottles, I crashed Janie's birthday. Fortunate for my mind-thirst, theirs was the leakiest cabal in town and I soaked up more than my requisite hooch, discovered more about Janie that night than since. I was told by various guests about the bulimia thing, how awful her room-mate was, her on–off relationship with Sammy and others. What really hit for century was the discovery that Janie was three years younger than me, born the week after my mother died.

'Coincidence' is merely a word employed to soften such formidable destiny, but I knew from then that Janie held the spirit of my mother, her same eyes crying over what I had become, loving me still. I phoned my sister again who told me to stop with the hippy shit. Haven't called her since. And just like in the play my mother had also lost two sons, not to the sea so much as to the gene pool, both gone by way of CF long before I arrived. 'Coincidence' is just their way of letting slip the links. Janie was the somehow link.

Half-watching for Boots, half-staring into my third cold coffee, which seemed deeper than the previous two as my caffeine craving faltered, that line about all those young men floating in the sea came back to me. The way that Janie used to say it, you'd swear that she put them there herself, so much anguish, so much regret, layers of it, years of it, as if the sea and the sadness had scuttled her mind.

I've never seen someone cry so well, so essentially and free with it, each performance a solid cascade of crying and prayers pouring from the ragged women left to continue in the world unbraced, without man or fish for sustenance. And with Janie you could always see real tears, gliding over the oily make-up to be absorbed by her shawl or by the dirt floor, or to hang there on the edge of her eye or caught on her skin through to curtain. I wanted that, to be able to cry that way.

I was half glad when I heard she hadn't been chosen to go on the theatre tour, but she soon started to look washed-up, shipwrecked with only margaritas for company, abandoned on the island while the others adventured abroad, left behind in Happy for the holidays. Perhaps without her nightly catharsis she became swamped by her pain, ruled under ancient sorrow rather than mistress of it.

The difference was perverse. From a person of pure nervous exuberance, she warped into torpid arrest, appending an ugly apathy which wore away the heart of her until she was barely discernible, an invisible, one of life's latent ladies, like she was some big embarrassing mistake of a person, struck off every register and not just the cast list. The keeper of my mother's soul was fading. Operating as always at a cold, clean distance, I watched her disappear.

I've always assumed that one day I, too, would be completely invisible. That I would sit aged forty in the corner of a shoe store with one shoe in my hand and watch the sales girls fail time and again to come and serve me. That I would then be so invisible, so unconnected with the world that it would let me try on a display shoe four sizes too small for me and not come to my rescue. Then I would officially be a middle-aged woman, the living dead. My current mother is made conspicuous by money but my aunt is invisible this way — I think she finds it a great relief, even if her shoes fit badly.

But Janie was too young; she distorted time with this premature transparency. I only wanted to urge her back to eminence, that's all I meant to do. Believe me, that's all I ever meant to do, to find her.

I will make Janie visible again. I will be all of us, I wear her like a coat and she will define me, like a mothering hold, and I will be someone at last.

Just as my back was giving out under the recline of modern plastic, Boots shambled out of his place and slowly back up the road, the same heavy cloud pinning his shoulders and a hot, damp look about him.

His door hung open like a sick mouth, unlocked this time as he'd jemmied the catch and the dead bolt, leaving them shattered in the hallway — must have gone to buy more virtuous replacements, unsullied defenders. I tried to think how the law sat on injuries received while breaking and entering, but arrived at his desk with both ankles intact and only the slightest asthma wheeze. I peeled open a curtain just enough that if I strained I could decipher figures, too afraid to permit full daylight in, in case daylight told or left traces.

Most of the notebooks were stuffed to bloating with computer material, designs for games and websites, pages of encoded ciphers, digital commands. I don't speak computer, and only have enough grasp of the mechanics to cough out term papers, but my misgivings were sopped up by an old-fashioned diary, penned instead of punched. I eased back against his pillow, shoes on his duvet as no self-respecting burglar ought, and began to leaf through. Snared by the first two lines I forgot that I sat on the keen edge of a danger, one that might call itself in while I was buried in the book.

He wrote with a young girl's hand, all clear and ballooning and even, different shades of blue and black dividing each sitting from the next. He had obviously begun to write his story during the months free of the prevailing rot. It read:

Um, goodness, how to do this? This is a story about the only love of my dumb life, an Irish girl called Janie Jay. I think it's maybe a story about me too, well it should be, yeah, but I've kind of disappeared or something, I've gotten buried inside of her and I don't know that if I wrote my story, it would be really much different from writing hers, you know?

OK, so you get here, you get to the Big old stinkin' Apple and you think to yourself, shit, I can't do this, yeah? I can't carry on with this, it's just too damn hard. Well, if you ask me, that's way worse that failing in your home town or in your school town or something, way worse. I mean, it's kinda like going to some high-class hotel to take a shit in the lobby. And everyone knows it, that when you arrive here all full of it, excitement and hope and stuff, and maybe with some money your folks gave you, you get here with one huge mother of a plan. You're gonna make a go of it, get all famous and rich, and your head gets off on thinking about it, and you start to think, yeah, I'll get laid by a whole bunch of really amazing people and all this great stuff is gonna happen. Absolutely everyone gets into the city thinking that way, everyone I ever met or heard about at least. So when Janie landed in New York, all pumping with it still, she'd be talking to you and it was like she was still some teenager or something, thinking it was cool to have a dream since she was older and was going to work really hard and all the rest, and probably some cash in her pocket too. I said to her, well, what if it didn't all go like she planned and she said no, that there'd have to be some huge volcano eruption in her apartment before she'd get stopped from making it big. That's what she said.

So as I remember it, she'd get dressed up so she'd look great but still like she wasn't trying or anything, and walk up and down streets, all around the parks, just days and days of walking, like she was collecting all these stories from every-where, a big headful of stuff to remember, meeting a Hispanic guy, or an African girl, getting burned sometimes and sometimes having it OK, some really funny stories, really funny, but at first she'd tell them about some other person and then she'd say it was her. It was like she was collecting them like a bag lady and her beercans, saving up all this shit for the book about her, or so she'd get to say it to *Vanity Fair* or whatever people read, *Vogue* maybe, or maybe for when she was an old lady and everybody else in the story was dead and she could totally tell it her way, so she'd come out of it really cool.

All kinds of stuff was new to her, food from Ethiopia or Thailand, S & M dives where you could just have a look or a touch, great big-deal after-show parties with really famous people hanging out. And all that time I bet she didn't think for one second that she was cruising away from, well, I don't know from what, from whatever would've made her happy. I'm not like saying she should have just stayed home and her life would have worked out fine, I'm just calling it like I see it, yeah?

And I am a bit of an expert on Janie, you'll see why later, a weekend DIY expert or something. If I'm gonna be straight up about it, and I do know I can get it twisted, then I'd have to tell you that she's pretty good-looking, has enough friends to make it look like she owns the most clothes on the planet, and is stubborn enough to come across like she deserves more clothes and more anything than anybody. But she's not really loud or anything, it's kind of hard to explain.

Her hair is shoulder-length and brown, but different kinds of brown at different times. She's absolutely tiny and has these big eyes which are, I'm not sure really, green and blue and grey, it depends on the mood she's in. She looks like she could fit inside your hand, but it's not exactly not true, she wouldn't let you near enough for that. She might look like a doll, but she's really cold. Not all the time, but if you try and get close she turns into a marble statue kind of thing, with her white skin and her not talking.

She definitely knows what she wants and how to get it. She's not some bitchy user or anything, but she did hitch herself up to the middle rungs of the ladder quicker than most. Problem is, it's in the middle where it gets hard to tell backwards from forwards, up from down, yeah? When the street stuff and the cold makes it feel like you're really living some adventure, and the whole glamour bit is sick after a while, and it all switches round as quick as you might turn a corner, well, I'm not blaming her really that she got it all wrong. We all sort of did.

I guess it was totally different for her family: her granny would've known black from white, up from down, anyone from that age had a handle on life. Her mother probably had it harder, mine did anyhow, it was all kind of grey and straight-line for them, so at least they didn't have to make a choice, just had to get through it, the whole grey existence thing. Now for Janie and the rest of us it's like we don't even know if it has a colour or a shape, don't know if it's retarded to ask, even. And when you do get an answer, it's changed before you can act on the thing. She once watched these morning-show experts who were arguing about if orange juice was good or bad for you, so she said fuck it, and drank orange juice every second day, just in case. That's kind of how she tried to keep a hold of it all, that way.

Hundreds of people know her — well OK, maybe a hundred, but it's like she's just swimming about in some piss-poor soup, like she's got no real friends, they'd all sell her out in a second. They're not really friends, they just borrow each other to hang out with, we all do sometimes. You'd swear we thought others could eat us.

When *Riders to the Sea*, that play, when it went off on tour, Janie was dumped from the cast and they gave her part to some famous actress that I'd never heard of; after that whole deal Janie looked stoned or something. She wasn't, but she looked like it pretty much all the time. I think she should have just gone home when that happened, I mean back to Ireland to get her head together. But she was so into the race by then, it was like going home would mean she failed.

If Janie ever sat herself down and had a real long think about it, she'd know that every high school in the world turns out one like her at least once a year and she'd know that she wasn't so special. I mean, yes she's special but not so special that she can carry on as if magic was supposed to look after her or something. Mostly though, in the early days, she was excited about things and she'd get off on her own hype and be really giddy like a kid. It did used to bug me when she'd say stuff like, 'I have to get famous' — she really would say that — and 'I have to have everyone know who I am and where I'm at.' It was like some skit from *Fame* or one of those other dancer films.

The first day I saw her was the day the snow stopped. It must have been February and had been snowing for the past three weeks non-stop, long enough for the novelty to have worn thin, I was well past it at least. The sidewalk outside my door was slippery as soaped glass, God I really hate the local kids sometimes. That day they really pissed me off and that was why I called in sick and went to Central Park like I was some tourist or something.

She was obviously pretty green or pretty weird because she walked out from the Ramble, like she didn't know what went on there, and then sat down on a bench and just stared at the squirrels forever, like she'd never seen a damn squirrel before. But I guess I'd seen girls before and I sat there for just as long looking at her. Even the fluffy animals are tough

That Girl from Happy

as a new bone here, she was the only really soft thing around for miles, smiling while they ate the bagel she gave them. Maybe it was the bagel she was so thrilled about, it was like she was three days old, everything was new. She walked on past my bench, stopping just past it, not looking at me but behind me at a large snow-dog a bunch of students had built on a hill.

'What are those dogs called, those Snoopy dogs, not bagels is it?'

'Beagles.'

'Oh yeah, I used to know that. Thanks.'

And she kept going. OK, so it won't go down in anyone else's history, but I swear she was the closest thing to Mary Tyler Moore I have ever seen, even with those chapped lips and old-man coat. The right hat can really do things for a person.

In this city you could start to think that you made people up, start to think you were losing it big time, because apart from your close friends and the man you buy your pizza from, other people are one-offs. There one day and then practically brand-new people when you meet them again — they've changed that much or else you have them so mixed up with the rest of the millions.

Fuck this for a karma vibe, but when I bumped into Janie a week later in another part of town, it was like a sign, it sounds dumb but that was how it felt. I thought that it must be fate and she was in charge of my future. Yeah, written down, it looks funny, but I still think it's true. Of course, mostly I just want to sleep with her, but with Janie it's always felt sort of spiritual. This is total crap, I know, but she does make you think that way, think of her in terms of a higher meaning or a bigger plan. Sometimes when she's wearing her long green dress and I'm out of it on Josh's hash, I swear I would follow her anywhere, Iowa even, no matter what it might cost to my bankbook or my body or my life. When I look at her, I see possibility tumbling out of her, and it makes me believe in the future. She's like a great big something ready to happen any day now. Or maybe it already happened and we missed it, maybe that play will be her last.

That second time we met was at a friend's party, and I was all excited at seeing her again but she was really different, completely down, but then if a week is a long time in politics it's a fucking age-and-a-half in the city. I remember reading some Thomas Hardy novel for school where all this stuff happened to some poor bastard over two generations and I remember thinking, wow, that's exactly what happened to me, only I got it done in a weekend. She could have suffered a life-altering tragedy between the first time and the second — it's possible, probable even, in this neighbourhood.

You guessed it, I'm a romantic, almost masochistically so, a romasochist maybe, and so I decided she needed rescuing. The only thing nearby I could possibly rescue her from was a sad bowl of cloudy fruit-and-wine punch which had one huge phallic banana and an old shrivelled lime floating around in it like old naked vacationers, as if it was all quite harmless. A cunning disguise.

'The only reason they aren't using Styrofoam cups is that they melted during a test-run before you got here.'

She looked. 'So just think of what it could do for me,' she said, dunking and draining the glass in one.

Excellent. She reminded me of a girl I knew in kindergarten who used to go on as if the world was one great big triple dare.

'Ah, a professional.'

Not by total chance, I had this large bottle of single malt and, seeing as how I was more charming and daring and fake back then, I took her by the hand. I kidded myself that I suited the part, my height and wide eyes making me look every bit the mad poet.

'I might be needing help with this one, Princess.'

'That's Princess Janie to you, son.'

'Janie? I would have thought maybe Kelly or Colleen.'

'Or Erin? Those are American names.'

'In that case I've probably got an American name too. I'm Sean.'

'So why do they call you Boots?'

'It's a computer thing.'

So she had been asking about me. Fine start, cool. She let me lead her out onto the roof where we sat on a damp mouldy mattress which had been left out after the summer, and, bit by bit, we drained the bottle over the next four hours, and the party just dissolved into noise and became something that was going on downstairs. She was all wrapped in my coat and looked so perfect that I told her she could keep it. Then I got kinda worried that she might take me up on the offer. To this day when I see her in that coat I remember my lesson in being some flash asshole.

OK, so we had just reached the moment when I should have kissed her when good old Fat Molly arrived up with a large Starbucks and a story about a stupid actor friend of hers. I'm telling ya, once that moment is dead, it's dead forever, but even though I know that, I still try to breathe life back into it for the rest of the night.

Most of our crowd are actors and some of them have even acted, but Fat Molly is different because even though she's the right kind of cute and skinny as a pin, she just cosied into being waitress and said 'OK I'll make the most of that.' Maybe she gave up the fight or maybe her fight changed and people like me can't see it.

Janie knocked back some of the coffee so that was the end of getting her wasted, and all my winking at Fat Molly to go talk to anybody downstairs was for shit — the girls seemed happy with this new threesome thing. And it wasn't like I could even offer to walk Janie home as the two of them lived together. Still, at least I wouldn't lose her next time, yeah? So fucking typical, one minute Romeo, next minute one of the three musketeers. I just kind of gave up and sat back on the mattress, freezing my pecs off in my new Armani shirt. My only Armani shirt, in case you get the wrong idea about me.

'OK, OK,' Fat Molly settled in. 'Do you remember Howard said he'd been chosen to do Shakespeare in the Park?'

'Yes,' I said. 'Despite the fact that they haven't even cast yet.' I have never believed any story about Howard. And why would I? They were normally success stories.

'Well, whatever, he can't do it now because ... guess!'

'He doesn't speak English?' Janie offered.

'No....'

'That's close though,' I said. 'You have to admit that's close. He's a corn-fed country hick with an accent to match,' I explained to Janie.

'With a name like Howard? Obviously not High-Church hick.'

'You're both hilarious.' Fat Molly couldn't wait for our interest any longer and decided to drop the bait thing and hand-feed us the goods. 'He's been cast in a big-budget Hollywood film. I swear, you'll have heard of the director but I can't remember the name right now — it's foreign.'

'The film or the director?'

'If it's the film, then your friend has a head start, him not speaking English and all.'

'No, it's an English language film, I mean the director.' Fat Molly was getting flustered now.

'The director doesn't speak English either?' I warmed to the task. 'Such a communication problem for such a large, important movie.'

'What have you two been drinking?'

'Duck Soup,' grinned Janie.

'Figures. I'm telling this story, I am. He's got six weeks on it and starts at the end of the month, and his agent doesn't want him to fill up his schedule with theatre as she's got big plans for him. There's sort of three other characters below the lead and then about five just below that and he's one of them, but it's a really good part.'

'Were you talking to him about it? Is he here?' I asked, now that it was clear I wasn't about to score.

'No, but Lucy and Josh were talking to him today, I met them at The Cellar earlier. Josh was spitting, it was so funny, he never gets freaked. He has even changed his name.'

'Josh was so mad he changed his name?'

'Howard changed his name because apparently there's some English actor with the same name who's doing quite well at the moment and he figures it might become a problem later on.'

'What did he change it to?'

'Jerry Jones.'

Janie almost choked on her coffee. 'Wait, you have a friend who must have hated his parents to distraction for calling him Howard, and then, given the chance to fix it, he decides on Jerry Jones?'

'She has a point, Fat Molly, that's not exactly a fuck-me fuck-me Hollywood name.'

'I reckon he hasn't landed a film rôle at all, he's just gone and joined the Witness Protection Scheme.'

'Isn't she great, Boots, don't you love her?'

'Absolutely.'

She smiled the smile from the park.

A week later it felt like she had been part of our crowd forever and people weren't calling her 'Fat Molly's new flatmate' or 'That girl Boots was talking to at the party' anymore, but at the time I had no idea how much time and money and sweat I'd be putting in to get it back to that. Howard, who'd changed his name to Jerry then changed his name to Dave and Janie seemed to be getting along just fine. Nobody's name is their name anymore — what is it they say? 'Diversity is the mother of reinvention,' or some shit like that, even Janie was now being called Janie Jay. When I saw that she was getting to know all these new people, I freaked and started these stupid daydreams about getting my tiny girl back home on the stinking mattress with me, but the papers had never gone through and I lost her to the soup.

It's now like there's a section missing, yeah? The part where I went from sitting waiting like some hungry tick, to sitting waiting like some born-to-it slave. If I knew how it happened I'd have drawn a map and got myself safely back to start. Right now I'm getting eaten by snakes in my brain and I wish to fuckin' Christ I'd stayed in my box with my computer and my magazines and notes, only going out to fuck distant cousins at weddings or whatever.

Every time I saw her I wanted her to want me. I wanted to mess with her hair when I came in. I wanted her to approve of me, I guess, to make an effort to look at me and smile a secret smile which other guys would notice and hate me for, and the more times I met her and this didn't happen I felt like my brain was cut, like I broke some bone in my head, yeah? Until I couldn't even speak to her, couldn't even walk up to her after a while, it was impossible. It was so stupid and it just got worse. Maybe if I had some surge-protection package — or some pride, even, would do the job. I jangled my stupid chains inside, where she couldn't see them.

Going to the play was total agony, too good to miss an hour watching her in spite of her old woman make-up, but the sting came during curtain-call and I was just another pair of idiot clapping-hands like some seal. Then in the bar after, I was just another idiot mouth telling her how great she was. I stopped going after my twelfth time, yeah I know, apart from anything the staff were starting to wonder if I was a bit soft, and out of manners I'd have to stay for the second half of the evening — a play she wasn't in so it bored the ass off me.

I've always been kind of 'stand-alone' — Beta, Amstrad, and the others knew this — but it was freaky to feel like you were that close to dying and no one gave a monkey's. I was now the guy in the cave on the hill or something. I knew I'd have to pull back from the action and get it together, so I didn't try to be her good friend, her boy-girlfriend; instead I set up camp at a distance and got ready for the wait.

Fuck. Boots was practically in the bed before I heard him, I just had time to hurl myself into the closet. What an obvious thing to do. If I was really concerned, I'd have high-tailed it out the window, or, with more sense of adventure, I'd have stood fixed for the fight, but I don't want to face off against anyone's wretched spirit, nor would I wish to ladder my hose. I hadn't managed to pick up the notebook which sat red and conspicuous as a butchered body on the white pillow. Concealed behind a row of over-starched office shirts, I tried to work out where he was. It sounded as if he had ventured no further than the front door where a short burst of grunts told of his displeasure over the new fortifications. I waited to hear him tramp back down the stairs before I fully exhaled the breath with which I'd flung myself from the bed.

As I started to read again, faster this time, shaking slightly and with half an ear angled to the door, I couldn't help wondering how much was true and how much he had thought about enough that it turned into something new, but perhaps that's the type of thing civilians don't have to concern themselves with. He certainly wasn't always as warped as his current demeanour might suggest. I read on.

That Girl from Happy

Reality's got fuck-all to do with it. Janie needed space to re-imagine me better than I am, stranger to lover is a pretty easy skip. I needed to work out what kind of guy she wanted, and then I could start to turn into him, yeah? But I didn't really know how to do that and still keep more than a breath's step away from her.

I haven't always been good about saying what's what, and thinking it out like this, all like a shrink or something, and mostly I just imagined what it would be like to kiss her, to touch her hand, to put a loose piece of her hair back behind her ear, and I'm not exactly proud of it but I would cry for hours, and then I'd slope off to the nearest 24-hour café and hope because I needed her to be there that she would be. But no, God did a runner ages back. I knew that already and this whole shit mess has been proving it. I bet the world is run by some bunch of people who just laugh at the rest of us. I tried to remember what it was like to touch her at that party but I'd forgotten by the day after as I didn't know I'd go and fall in love with her. I could only pretend that drinking from the same glass as her had been as cool as it would be if it happened now. I felt really good whenever I saw her wearing the coat I accidentally gave her, but then I felt like shit whenever she wasn't wearing it, like she was trying to hurt me, and by the summer it was like she hated me or something, like we'd never even been friends.

Some of the others said I was being obsessive, but they haven't a clue how it is, some people are just really into certain things. Like I eat the same type of breakfast cereal and nothing else for days or weeks until I force myself to eat a pizza and then it's nothing but pizza after that. I've seen every single episode of *Star Trek: The Next Generation*, but I guess that's not a thing to 'fess up to. Same with the graphics programs, sitting in my shorts through the night and the next day, keyboarding my ass off, that's when I'm not thinking about Janie. These days I do a lot of Janie programs too, but I haven't shown them out. OK, even if she thinks I'm not this big jokey ha-ha guy or a trendy freak boy like some of the shit she hangs out with, at least I can stick with something.

Man, it's fucked and I know it. When you're not totally your own person, when you're being run by some outside drive, it hurts like a bear, and at the same time it's your best buddy, so you don't want to wish it or smoke it away. It's like biting on an infected tooth, it controls you, yeah? So at first you think, OK just one bite, one program, one kiss, one bowl of goddamn cereal, and down the line you know it's kind of got you, and you know that everyone's laughing at you.

And all this time it was like I was some nasty germ and Janie was totally immune to me, and everyone else wanted me dead or gone so they could have her to themselves. I bet they'd love to find this notebook, they'd just love to talk about what a fuckwad I am and all their other shit they go on with about me.

Well, anyway, I pretty soon realised that I wasn't striking out on bumping into Janie — she was either avoiding me, or other people were trying to keep her away, she wasn't ever around any of the usual places. I know who it was too, that Howard-Jerry-Dave, or Sammy, that was his new name, and I think it's really weird that he has to keep changing it. It wasn't that they were going out together — there's no way she could really like him — it was all about that film crowd he was hanging out with. There's nothing wrong with that. I mean, if you're cold, you sit close to the fire, right? I'm glad really, because otherwise she might have an excuse to be unhappy, like how sometimes she'd look really hurt and just run off home or wherever. Or probably she didn't go home, she probably went to some amazing club or something that doesn't let real people like me inside, the kind of place with strobe lights that can give you little fits without you even knowing it.

So for the whole of fall and winter I was watching for her all the time but it was like she just vanished. Fat Molly didn't invite me up to the apartment anymore so I didn't even get to say 'Hi' as she was on her way out. Sammy left, he probably tried to bring her with him, but I checked with Josh and he said they broke up.

So I was really pushing it by now, really freaking it hard, running from one housewarming or birthday party to another, doing five dinners a night, I was stressed to bursting and got a note from my doctor so I could get a few weeks off work. But they were cleverer than me, and my timing was probably just an hour or so out, or a minute or something, so as I ran up 10th she was walking down 9th. I knew that as I was checking every face in Yaffa she was sitting smiling in DoJo's. So I got smarter still. I'd only sit at a table by a window, only stand at the highest place in a bar, only speak to people who knew her. But it was like the streets were getting longer, and the city wasn't just crowded anymore but was absolutely crawling with unknown bodies. I know I looked like shit — people took me aside and told me about rehab-centres or dealers, but they just wanted me out of the picture, or to be able to tell me what to do. I know their game.

Then I went and spent way too long thinking how to do the Valentine's Day thing, like how many hints to drop, how romantic or funny to make it, so I ended up missing it by a month, more even. Sending her an unsigned note seemed like the best idea I'd had, I thought: OK, that would do it, they'd see. I'm not wrong and now I could prove it, I could make her do things from a distance, like know she was in love with me. A long-distance sort of navigation deal, like getting into her brain while she was sleeping and leaving my footprints inside for the morning, yeah?

It's late April and I finally had the whole thing in place a few days back, so I took a sheet of paper, put a boat icon on it, like from the play, and wrote it with my left hand like my Dad used to do when he wrote Valentine's cards to my Mom. I wrote: 'The future is written. He is so close you could almost touch him. In one week you will know.' And said to myself: OK, finally, in a week's time I'll tell her it's me and everything will be perfect and all this shit will finish and no one will get in our way, like Sammy or any of her friends or her acting or anything. In one week she'd understand that I'm her fate forever and there's no good denying it. I folded and taped the page in case someone tried to read it first, then walked around to her apartment building and left it in her mailbox. I felt like I had just kissed her, you know?

So. It wasn't from the boat-boy, it was Boots, Jesus, now that's one for the learning-bank. I'd never have thought him capable, and I'd never have pegged the note for a bad love letter. Janie can't possibly have known, no one could unbend such convoluted dedication, no one could guess at such a singular meaning. It now seems far more sinister, perhaps this Byronic disposition makes Boots capable of greater destruction than ripping out the floor. I read on quickly, running for an answer.

It was a whole two days since I'd dropped it off when I wondered if someone had stolen it from her box, and maybe if I waited until the end of the week that would give them more time to do their damage. Then that night I was rescued by a message — it was so quick that I could have almost missed it, you know?

There were these two teenage girls sitting at the next table, and I was early after running from dinner with a group to have dessert with Josh's friend, Bill, down the road. God, they were so silly those girls, all with their giggling and names and more names, so I wasn't even listening until the message came, with one of them who kept on repeating to the other one, 'Call. You have no options left, just pick up the phone and call.' Bill arrived just then so it was good I heard it.

'Look, Bill, I'm really sorry, I can't stay, I'm really sorry. I have to do something.'

'I'm coming with you.'

For some reason then, I got to thinking about what my older sister told me after she had her baby, that the pain was so bad they could have wheeled her out into the middle of the high street to give birth and she wouldn't have cared. Well, I was sort of at that stage now — the privacy thing was so out the window by then so Bill came with me. I wasn't exactly giving birth, I mean, I didn't bleed all over the carpet or scream her name, but I didn't care anymore what he thought or what he could say or do to me or whatever. Like I started living without underwear like a jungle guy or something.

He didn't really understand the hurry to go up to my apartment and stare at the phone, so I said, 'Um, someone was supposed to phone and they didn't,' just so he wouldn't think it was weird.

And then, I think it was so some of the headache or the pain in my chest would go away, I said, 'I'm in love with Janie Kelly.'

'Who?'

And I thought for a second I had made her up and that was why I couldn't find her anymore.

'Janie Kelly.'

'I know the name, but I can't think…'

Maybe he really couldn't remember, but maybe he was fucking with me.

'Never mind, it's OK.'

'Oh, you mean Janie Jay. Haven't seen her about for months.'

Next day he rang me, said, 'You know you were talking about Janie Jay? Fat Molly and Lucy say she was in hospital for weeks, but she's been back for a while but in a different place. Lucy's doing her helpful thing and forwarding the mail and buying self-help books. I didn't tell anyone what you said, though.'

I fell off the arm of the chair when he said about the hospital, it really hurt.

This time I heard the downstairs door slam closed, and hurled the book back in its place and myself out of Boots' apartment and up to the next landing just as he shuffled round the corner.

It was clear that what for me was a co-opted itch was a tumour in Boots, and advancing long before Janie died. Adoration the size of that, a full-fuck obsessathon, has never been what you'd call a feature in my life. Well, maybe I can't throw those particular stones. Sounds as if he would have done anything to have her, absolutely anything, and I redoubled my ear for the sounds from the floor below and wished I'd just taken the notebook and spent my time rifling the drawers.

What was this becoming? Wearing Janie's too-small clothes, skipping round her friends — what was I achieving with all that dupe? Dress-up can't slide down through to the cells of me, the right shoes could never give me strength enough to die. Wearing her wanting, being called by her name in the middle of the night — how can such false libretto transform me into being the kind of person who has sizeable stretches of the civilised world wrenching and straining for a piece of her? When I find this boat-boy, then. I will know then, when her destiny becomes mine. Maybe the boat-boy could save me too. Janie was a person, no one ever writes about me.

Boots didn't leave at any stage over the next two hours, spending his time installing great fuck-off locks and bolts and probably alarms considering his (now appropriate) suspicion. God, I'd need an engineer to get back in there.

And then I remembered I had such a one to hand. On the fire escape I disturbed a couple having an argument; she was screaming at him about how he never or always or something.

Dec would be a safe bet for a bit of help, more of a guaranteed return than a wager, a double-down guy at the very least if you read him right. If you've got some private secret, a secret running off at the edges as life crowds in, then tell it to a drinker. If they chance to mouth it off, who's likely to believe them? Most would assume it's the good stuff flapping at random on their lips. The extra plus is that the drinker's own sauce clutch takes reflex precedence over anything you might brew, so they never appropriate your agenda, until after a while it blurs back into seclusion and is secret once again. And a drinker would most doubtless attempt even crazyman stuff while inflated to false bigness under swill.

When I landed back on his front step it had just hit 6.30 and there was no one inside. Being full-time idle I'd forgotten that Dec had spent the day at work, and could only trust he'd be returning home before whatever his evening had intended for him, so I sat for a while taking hope in the fact that he never ate out. I'm good at waiting, but only when I've full call on the issue. The trick is not to anticipate the endpoint, as that lengthens time, packs each second out with tiny disappointments in between, fattens them beyond endurance. As impatience has a tendency to run beyond boredom and into hostility, best too if you stop your head from holding the notion that a waiting period is time which

That Girl from Happy

the absent other steals from you; it must be thought of rather as time which you pilfer away from the rest of the universe. Sadly, like yesterday, such tactics don't work in waiting rooms or in the workplace as someone else owns and marks time while you're there.

Frankly, I don't know that I'd cope if I had to hold down a real job for any length of time, like a day or a week even. I'd always be calling in perturbed. When Mother One died she left my sister and me enough money that we could live uncomfortably on the interest, but my new mother (new as in the replacement, she's been hounding me full-time since I was twelve) has always clung to some righteous 'You-have-to-earn-it-yourself-or-you-won't-enjoy-it' crusade for the moral safekeeping of the almost rich. I noticed aloud at dinner one night that she did well enough without the operation of her little axiom, unless, I mused, she got paid for fucking my Dad as well as the odd day temping for him. Should have made a Christmas card out of that scene.

I should be more careful with my money, it's just that it's too divergent a task to keep one eye on the road and another on the trail of cash that flies off behind me, especially if my frequent bar-induced blindnesses are taken into considera-tion. So I tend to get over-comfortable at times, even when I feel a mere half-beat away from a horsehair shirt. I save myself from falling into Salvation Army territory by way of some stop-gap job or other (usually freelance crap articles that anyone more than a week in the country could write), as to start to dig into the bulk of the inheritance would bring down the wrath of the moneymen and they are all my father in different ties.

I'm starting to despise my Beat kind of life, hate that I can afford to be bohemian, ride down that rebel road in a taxi, make extended visits into the wasteland with my round-trip ticket hidden somewhere in the following month. Fun-money whispers to go down lazy roads so I've never had what you might call a purpose or plan. I spent too long in school, several schools, thinking one day I'd wake up with a way out. Instead, I'd wake up Tuesday afternoon, mad at missing a string of classes, or lunch, and rather than batter myself about the head with someone else's comprehensive lecture notes, I'd announce myself a fresh start and by the time the week rolled round once more, I'd be missing different classes in a whole new school. Always a school famed for its liberal arts so I wouldn't find myself rejected by future neurosurgeons or football stars. Overly evasive as to why I'd moved, I'd plant myself, enigma and all, mid-semester in creative writing and acting classes, amongst those who had already spent their mystery on affairs with each other. I'd have no handle on myself that I could pass to them so they would, rumour by rumour, construct me a history both destructive and huge. I had usually, in the anecdotal version of me, had an affair with a member of the faculty at my last college, who was a married man with five children, or a god-like genius, or a woman, depending on the inventor's fears. I had either tried to kill myself, or someone else, or someone's mother-wife-lover had tried to kill me (either garrotting me with his CKs, or bludgeoning me with a copy of Foucault if the narrator had ability). Whatever they wanted me to be, I became. I had no sense of myself, my accent wavered, my morals elasticised, my history contorted. The reflector of the world, I realised that I was writing all the time I was awake, rewriting with every small change in my mirror-led demeanour.

School out, I kept on standing there, aimless. My name is a screaming irony. So, before the writing thing took off, I became an 'actress' for want of anything to call myself; it's not like any action was expected of the term. I claimed to be a Method actress (partly to explain my lack of enthusiasm for life), whereas really I was more of a Method person, borrowing from fiction to give realism to my life, and not the other way round. When I landed in New York, following convention with a pretence at ambition, I found myself in the company of like souls — blonde, pretty, wealthy, bored and blitzed, as they constantly auditioned for the chance to audition for another blind-alley transfer out of town in the hope that the ride would loop them back to Broadway. They'd dance around on their bloodied toes, laughing with sung-out nodey throats, hanging by the tongue from some broke producer's butthole, tripping over their own need all the while, bruises the size of the Met on their sanity. So I went for that job on the newspaper instead, still not sure what I was at.

By then the creosote glitter of Dragbiz was serving as a timely distraction. I spent my nights with men who were more woman than I could ever be, in illegal clubs sipping negronis with the world and her well-taped wife. It was fun for a while on the groupie fag-hag fringes — an ardent fan whose abilities and biological assets posed little threat to whichever impotent old queen needed my attentions. The rest from sexual concerns was a welcome one, as they none of them fucked girls, congenital or otherwise.

As I sat there, missing those simple days, the sky let fall a rain shower, and, just minutes later, Dec arrived back. The sight of me, drenched in a schoolgirl-porn kind of Japanese way, rusting to the core and needing the shelter which he hadn't been there to provide, scared up in him a kindness which I cashed in for some dinner and a bath.

Rather than borrow a shirt and jeans, I lay naked as a promise under the sheets, so that, as the rain eased off and I announced (still sprawled in an unmitigated stasis) that I really had to be going, had to attend to some dull task, his antediluvian man-folly kicked in over reason and he offered to run the undisclosed errand himself. I thought it best to tell him my real name, in case he started to read the notebook before getting it back to me. He took it rather too well.

'So who have I been fucking?'

Fair enough question. 'My name's Aimee.'

He continued turning my damp clothes on the heater, nonplussed in a very non kind of way, sloughing off my grenade like a soft fruit had hit him and not very hard. 'I thought it was strange that you both had the same name.'

Both. So he knew about the other Janie, I mean, about Janie. I rapped on my bucket head for when I might have slipped, for a moment where I might have split us back in two and spoke of her as other. He smiled, a silence was unusual for me.

'I guess you couldn't see me through those Jackie O shades you had on.'

'You were at the funeral service?'

I found myself an unfuzzed glass and a trickle of vodka to dampen it with, and invited him onto his bed to confound me in greater comfort.

He explained that he had been at the service, although neither to mourn nor to nose into untimely death, but to accompany his friend Jim. Jim was a guy who stayed at the apartment whenever some lame event dragged him to the city. Dec would do anything for the man, every living day was a repay opportunity since Jim's was the strong sober arm of deliverance that had saved Dec from certain hidden-camera fame the day of the fuel leak on the concourse at JFK. The lies Jim told to efface his official report became convoluted and tightened enough that he felt he was choking, but rather than turn Dec in, he parted ways with the airport soon after, to go and work as a gardener in a private hospital upstate, run by a family friend. It turned out to be the same place where Janie did time. Dec was quick to assert that he had never met Janie, never even known about her until after she died, but his friend was staying over on the night of the service so they went to it together and then fucked off to a bar.

'Happy?'

'Sorry?'

'The name of the bar?'

But it was one lower down on the East Side. I asked whether Gardener Jim had known Janie well, wanted to put him on my witness list, but Dec wasn't sure. Apparently his title was that of gardener, and he did spend much of his time appended with a rake or a hoe, but his real function was to ensure that those people all-amiss didn't walk their troubles into the lake. Every day Janie would spend a long time looking into the water, so he whiled away enough yards of over-tended lawn in her company. Dec admitted that Gardener Jim was never one for talking, or listening much either, so the chance of his making someone's acquaintance, with less than a decade in which to accomplish the task, was very slim indeed.

'I wondered how bad your eyes looked behind the shades. Were you and Janie close?' he asked.

'Very. At the end.'

'Then, when I saw you in the laundromat the next day, I figured your troubles must be larger than a fucked-up wash cycle.'

And then we did that thing of reminiscing on our days-old history together, about fifty years ahead of when it might be appropriate, missing bits of it already and fluffing it out with explanations as to whether such a move or such a line was typical or new, until the notebook was forgotten under talk of who caught who. Which inevitably flowed toward the listing of, and disclosures regarding, past lovers (with me neglecting to mention Italian Tony). Which, as all roads lead to a place, led to the legendary telling of how you lost 'IT' — *Cherry Night in Yawndale High*, that badly rehearsed school play which passes for an epic production.

My virginity, like most, was shed gradually along the road, or lanes possibly, rather than lost to a single pedestrian moment, so in these tell-all situations I've never any great rite to refer to, no landmark tale to tell. The first time I got naked in a bed I wasn't sure if it counted as losing it — I'd wanted to ask but my mouth was full at the time. There was one

That Girl from Happy

technical instance I suppose, but even then I always messed with its mythic status, changing the details according to who I was discussing it with. I was bored with the telling of it by lunchtime the morning after, so Dec got a fairytale instead.

'I really need that notebook,' I finally said, challenging him to trust my lack of disclosure.

One hour and one notebook later.

'I'd forgotten how good that feels.' He smiled and opened a new bottle which he'd annexed during the crusade. Not many men could go out at this hour and return without a pizza in hand. It looked like a canned tuna dinner for me; he was too junked out on adrenaline to remember I needed to be fed. Hope he never gets a dog.

As he paced the three steps of room, out flooded a tumble of personal legend to make his virginity story seem tame, overly casual accounts of when he used to find hidden keys under flower-pots and stones and enter local people's houses to relieve them of their hire-purchase fun stuff while they were off at church, giving thanks.

'Used to deal some pot too.'

I just knew he had that entrepreneurial spirit in there somewhere.

Nothing too elaborate was required on this evening's venture — he just set off the fire alarm in the building, and Boots believed in the fire, being so sure they were out to destroy him. His neighbours were still persuading him to go back inside as Dec walked past with the notebook under his jacket.

'You're good,' I said with genuine admiration.

'And you're evil,' he said with equal deference. 'That poor guy.'

There was only one small addition to what text I had already pilfered, hardly worth Dec's trouble, so with him in the bottle but possibly half-watching, I started again on the third page and eventually switched to the new bit as he fell asleep. The handwriting was closed in like a cramp, as if Boots had written it with broken hands, the ink smudged in places, bruising up the text. I had to read it several times but the horror leaked through from the start.

... so much modems, so many questions, it had to stop, didn't want my head in modems.

Josh's new friend, don't know the name, just kept asking, wanted me drowsing, I stopped thinking of her when I answered, and look what happened. Janie, I said just to say her and he said what? he said sorry? but I had seen him talk to her at a party before. And Josh arrived when I said Janie and the friend said what and he said Josh did you know Janie and the friend said Sure yeah she's going out with Italian Tony now. No no no, more lies, all wrong, not that. No? said his friend and we said no.

She's dead, Josh said. No, I said laughing my last one Modems I said, about modems but it was too late.

You know she, you know, died. No. Yeah, Found hanging from a tree, what, did you not know? what? no and my head was all blood like their hands and black tongues talking. The door was right there and suddenly with the walls and everything changing position so it looked like I was falling they turned off all sound in the world with a switch they can do that. They put poison in my food because it lurched up out again of my mouth and somehow hit the road which was everywhere now and then they put the sound back only so loud to hurt my ears so much talking hearing the ocean that's when they took me I shouted to wake her up they fed me pills in my own room and I thought good I am dying but it was only sleep Waking up out of death means you have to stay and fight the evil Janie is dead Janie is dead Janie is dead

This went on for almost a page, the following pages were all scribbled out, to stop any more cruel story from coming, it seemed.

I had somehow managed to smear a great glob of mayo across the cover of the notebook which took me a good ten minutes to scrape and dab and plead out of existence. I assumed he'd be leaving it back in the morning, and settled down in the crook of my new sleeping partner for a much-needed early night.

'You're kidding! How many fires do you think the poor bastard can take? Okay, I'll leave it back, but I'll have to go now.'

Most couldn't eat a breakfast, knowing what I know, having done what I did. Most would never eat alone again.

'Full special, please.'

I am always empty. I concluded way back that there was some confusion or shortage when they were giving out hearts, and I got an extra stomach instead.

I did try to cry at the service. I hoped to drip out enough to give a redness to my face, or at least to make my eye-liner run in black snots like in the seventies, but then gave it up as a charlatan's job and wore those outsize dark glasses instead. In my world, self-constituted remorse is in famine-short supply so I'm fed my intensity from external sources, bled from others' prime emotions, my dead embers raked into cold fever by bits of letters and things said. Nothing seems to stem from inside me, everything is co-opted, everything false.

'Can you leave the eggs really runny?'

It has reached the point where I couldn't hope to operate with heart, I'm an undiluted stoic in the age of the hysteric, tin amongst feathers. It's always those who have that shouldn't. I would never abuse a heart as they do, those people who would be pleased to see me cry would say I was getting over it, having a 'good' cry. Any scrappy feeling I may chance to adopt stays jealously put, safe from the indignity of claiming a damp Kleenex as my own. What such soft counsel fails to understand is that catharsis is for people who actually want to get over something. Americans are the worst offenders; they splice open their blue hearts, black souls and red bankbooks on chat shows and theatre-style community self-help groups, open it all up and cry like baby babies, and then they're surprised to find there's nothing left, that it's all flown away. Thank you, I'll hold on to my hard-won bad bits, I just might need them some day.

Not engaging the hurt keeps it intact, a badness wrapped around the brainstem, where any damage would take years to emerge, by which time it would have bonded entirely. So, although mine is not a spontaneous condition, Janie Jay will be a long day growing inside, until such a time as she is fully realised within me.

The bacon is burnt, the potatoes cold in the middle. I push the grits to one side — I may be southern but I have never understood grits, it's too much like deformed oatmeal to succeed as anything else. A second coffee brings my head back to speed.

For fuck's sake, who am I kidding? I know what I'm at. I know that, with no public show, my particular can of worms can continue to masquerade as caviar. I'm a fake, ringing hollow.

'Another refill, please.'

I arrive home to sleep some more before meeting Sammy in Happy tonight. Definitely, yes, the place reeks like a giblet. I open the gash that serves for a window, but outdoors smells as bad so I close it again. I have no idea why he wants to meet.

Unknowing is a state in which I operate badly, but switching the power should be easy tonight, mere recreation once I'm in, a flick of the tongue. I'm not afraid of anything Sammy might have in his caboodle bag — a guy like that you could arm with the entire Pentagon arsenal and he'd hand it over to the enemy to ask them how it works. A vague plan, however, is always a good tactical defence against the arbitrary temper of the world. Location's on my side though, booze is my sovereign terrain. I'll start by being late, damage limitation by reducing the time during which it can be occasioned, after that I'll wing it. Wing it, great procedure, should have gone into the forces with a strategic brain like mine. Should go okay.

Only reason really I'm not snagged on hard drugs is I'm mostly too toasted to go seek them out. Bad move, babydoll, not your finest hour. Good thing my self-respect is independent of anything I hear or do or say. It was so not okay, I went and hammered myself to the point of occlusion, stoppered up my madness, renounced myself and my intention with the help of fluid friends. Had to after it blew. It all become badly infected, pus-packed, seeping runnied further out with every wrong word from my sore-crusty mouth.

Jesus Christ, I'm falling apart, not bursting at the seams but sort of chipping from the unbound edges, wearing thin at the other bits too from chafing and scratches. I can't even do this, I can't do this anymore. Sammy would run again seeing me like this. Janie would run. See Janie Jay run. Excuse me, forgive me.

Tonight I said some things, I started to care, and now it is all crashing down. I have been spinning inventions as if they were true fact. Now, my isolation gone, it hurts like needles, like all sound and all colour and all texture is breaking through my walls like a thousand heavy-armoured insects, tiny poisoned feet ripping through the careful membrane between me and the world I should never go out into again. I am sick. I have lost all control. I am taking her on and the pain of it is huge. I plant onions and wish roses to grow. I am sick.

Janie

*W*here else should she take a dark secret, where else but her childhood beach? No dead birds fly today, one good portent against the years.

To her wonder, the town still sits in blunt and quiet weary, squat in the grey light one endless cold summer more, and the village on the edge by the sea leans a little further, sinks a little deeper, towards the big grey water that it sucks on.

Seabirds cry loud their hunger, floating in the unsteady air as fog-sifted morning rains hit and slide off the salt rocks and plunge inland, to bore soft into the wooden houses of the hill and her bone-brittle leathery people, making them shine wet tarnish. The rocks are worn away only so much that a person long missing, returned perhaps from Tír na nÓg, might feel a slight difference and then put it down to a change in their head.

The wharf is now gone, claimed by a winter storm greedy for wood, sacrificed so the sea-monsters would not hunger for houses or boats. The dog that runs in the waves is speckled with white, the legacy of a grandparent, a locally famed white wolf-dog who was killed by a since-banished crazy girl as she tried to kill the maggots crawling on its back by hitting them hard and long with jagged stones.

The wind and the water, battle-weary, slap the coast in their tedious million million-year war, hit the rocks in a rhythm that the whole beach breathes to, fragments, compounds, creatures.

Harder with grit than even the sea-spit and strong beating air is the body of the woman who stands, her new thinness bending; louder than wave against stone is her breath as she watches. The sky threatens its mass, one grey sparse-woven cloth, uniform, more heavy than air is allowed to be, darker than daylight.

The hope that hangs forward off her slightly shoulders, ageing her beyond her eighteen years, is that heavy same hope she wore standing here when her past was lived for the first time through. The same, but different, but the same. She still carries in her face that ingrained mien of trust, a belief fused now into her countenance, firming her brow, widening eyes and even set lip. Different but the same and yet...

The sand is sodden, brown and cold. If sand had a memory, as faces do, each grain would slip aside, make way for their lone roamsome girl returned a woman, but she is a small particle in their years, she is not the first they've known. Her own heart is stale sand and yet it remembers, a heart like a sea-fruit sucked dry, no water for tears, no salt for scrubbing clean.

Less than a year ago she was standing on a foreign shore, colder and more brutal for all its sun. Now home to her own cold sea, no better place known to her for putting things to rest.

She continues to the caves, feet remembering the way, some sand parting. And goes inside.

That Girl from Happy

Right to the back where a wayward stranger eye or sun could never hope to reach. All is now to her as then was.

Brushing aside the spent sheaths, shells and packets, she falls on her knees and digs for a history, rips away delirious at the speed of swift tides, fingernails jagging, grazing her skin on rough sand, soothed as it brushes through mire, cut through the edges of layers. Spent, she scavenges on again, hour into next, smallest finger breaking, searching for the chance at happiness she hid there once, under the surface, away from knowing.

Trusting that her childhood was minded all these years by the visiting tides and the keepers of the dark, hoping the treasure might be disturbed by one single person only in the world, trusting against hope that he has left an imprint, some indication that he searched for her there. One sign only of her previous self, that will do, to make him real again, retrieve him from the years that consumed him.

Her arms now shake with the effort of exhuming a life, her body threatens to submit to the years.

Until slowly, out of dreaming it seems, out of a time more than a place, a tiny glint of silver pressed against a curve in the rock face. Emerging from the bed as her hands trowel wild with belief, until there in her hand, the pay-off for such long faith.

'Heinz' tells the label, spaghetti to prove she was here. With rust and dents to document that it all started long ago, provisions from a war not over, a war as bloody and exacting as the land against the sea.

She carries it up with her towards the house, not to ring on the door this time but to watch at a small distance, as time has made a stranger of her. She hangs back as Dowie used to, but the house is not there to play tomb to that age, replaced by a concrete viewing point by kindness of the county council. She holds harder to the tin, only the tin can tell.

She sits on the provided wooden bench, head down, looking past her feet to where pieces of loose straw are scattered, impacted through the mud. She is thinking, 'This is where the strawberry bed and cucumber frame used to stand', and cries at the space, for the space. Her mind walks her through the old yard, doors and rooms, plays for her the laughter they held.

Walking away now from the ruin to the road, she sits while the sun sets, watching from inside her second-hand, rusty car.

Once the light has faded enough so you would not know a friend at a glance, she takes a rucksack from the car and walks back to the beach. On her knees in the wet marram grass, a small torch shines weakly for her, the type she might have carried once tied to her belt, pulling adventure along in its yellow path. She is digging, but not for history this time.

Putting aside the plastic spoon doubled into spade, she pulls with blue-white fingers from the shallow hole a damp heavy swathe of cloth. Blankets which have lain there this last half decade and more, old of the farmhouse. Once soft and warm, half-promised for a youthful bride bed, now to compose a sodden shroud.

A shroud to hold the baby who is deeply resting in the bag, in the sand between clumps of grass.

She takes his stiffened body from the bag and wraps him carefully as mothers do their sleeping child, mindful with her offering of love.

This is the shell of her tiny son, a body so red for a time and now grey like stones. A body once loud with cries and now silent. She carries the newly robed child to the edge of the water, and places him beside her in the blue wooden boat which waits for them there as if it had been expecting her return. Anyone passing would think it a dying seabird she held so close, but the time for simple injury is gone now a long year.

Her parents would have understood, supposed a night of happy love turned to the bad. They would have held family forum, 'broken it' to the aunts, and told her too frequently that it was nothing of which to be ashamed. Begging her to stay with them, insistence dressed as kindly pleading, they'd have frocked out the spare room for a nursery. Painted it pink regardless of the gender of the child, pink like when their baby Janie was shaped there by nightlights, stuffed polar bears and lions and spinning suns-and-moons. Half hoping that she would remember, and then thank them as babies never can. They'd have taken down the cot which her father would have repainted in the front garden in imagined defiance of the neighbours' talk. Christening robes and baby blankets would have been washed by hand, bleached, softened and warmed.

Paintbrush, soap and crochet hooks did not announce this child. There was no name ready to welcome him, no name lying waiting in anyone's head. Conceived of the Devil, born in a locked room, hidden under layers of secrets

Judy May Murphy

before ever he was born and buried. He is indeed the child of a mother well practised in hiding everything away.

So far from cots and cradle beds is the canvas bag that held him since the day he first lived and died. A child worthy of soft quilts and white woollens, left now to rest in the mouldy, grey, scratch-wool blankets of a farmhouse. 'Jesus will save him now,' she is thinking. 'If he can turn water to wine, then surely in his infinite mercy, he will turn the sea to mother's milk.'

The bottom of the boat is his final room, the bottom of the ocean his final bed. Both blue, blue for a boy.

The blood of his birth had felt smooth, the weight of him warm, so unlike the chill salt water that touches her hands as she lowers her precious half-child off to Paradise, away from evil reach of the maker of him. 'I was once in a boat like this,' she remembers. 'When the time comes round again, I will go to them; until then, my boat-boy will keep my child.'

Dear Me,

There is a reason why things happen, and in the past, centuries ago, this type of thing was really quite common. It's only television and tabloids that really sensationalise everything, we are all spirits in animal skins, that's all. But I'm going to make sure that nothing was in vain.

I'm going to stay here in Dublin for long enough to save some money and train as an actress and maybe get a bit of experience, and them I'm going to go to LA or New York, probably not London as there are loads of Irish actresses there.

198

The reason most people don't make it is that they don't work hard enough or they don't have the life experience or the talent. I'm going to be really methodical and businesslike, and it shouldn't take more than a couple of years until I'm at least getting good parts in Broadway plays and maybe smaller parts in films. I wouldn't want to star in a film straightaway as that's the mistake a lot of actresses have made and they don't get a second chance if the film flops. Mum's really keen for me to go to New York instead of LA because the air-fares are cheaper. Dad just keeps going on about the great actresses in the Abbey, so I don't even discuss it with him any more.

I have to act. I have to use my pain to help others. I have to make sure I end up in a position where he knows how to contact me.

Love, Me

Judy May Murphy

The Friends

*S*ammy had long suspected that he might perhaps be a little dull, that he made connections micro-moments after everyone else, that what most took for his studied intensity or sultry magnetism might just be a rigid mask against his incognisance. He wasn't sure, though. Sammy always laughed at jokes during rather than after the punchline, and often only laughed for real after he got home and had a private little think. He'd been telling jokes himself for years on the basis of positive reaction, irrespective of the large breach in his own appreciation, always afraid that someone might solicit an explanation.

'You're being an asshole.'

There was no real resistance; you can't put up a fight without a weapon and Sammy was powerless against opinion, he believed Fat Molly completely because Fat Molly was the only person talking at the time. Sammy's tendency to concur with the last whim pitched toward the pot made many think him sycophantic; in fact, he wasn't smart enough for that — his crawling agreement was the unthinking action of an eager child. If you could belong to more than one church he would sign up under total conviction with them all, until the atheist told him not to. He knew this was a failing and hoped against patterns and histories that the next conviction would be the one to stick, that his head would spark into life and begin to make connection after connection, flooding him with the type of realisation which he suspected was intrinsic to the being of others. Then he could control the world, or at least his patch of it, and stop being swung like a rag doll, his straw stuffing scattered as they lobbed him where their persuasions willed, left him to fall stupid at their altars.

Perception for pedantry, a fair enough exchange under the circumstances; his was a purely cultivated intelligence, the sort that was powerless against the mutability of the women he ended up with. 'Molly. Fat Molly, come on, I didn't say you weren't welcome, I just said she's only expecting me.'

Although Molly didn't officially have a tail, she constantly feared it was being trodden on. Now she drew it in and quietly growled at the world in general. Janie hadn't been able to keep him from moving to LA, but the Moll was better — she would get him and keep him, that was the game. He took his jacket and left.

He was far too early for Happy but he had an errand to run first in an art supplies store uptown. He settled into the 6, a different silence, holding at slight distance the abundance of thoughts he needed to sort through, feeling them tangled in his hair. Needs must, he'd say hourly, and screw his effort hard to his plight, and (beer aside) take the situation by the scruff, only to watch it riddle away as it split into a myriad of unfathomable questions. When did the world get so slippery?

He had to get Janie back in the frame, have her back just one last time so he could ask forgiveness and be clean if not wise. He would fix his conscience up with some tape and glue, and that would be a start, now, wouldn't it? But even with his myopic take on personal psychology, Sammy knew that the real problem with the picture wasn't that it had a ragged corner, or even that it didn't look enough like Janie to be a discernible portrait of her, but that what had originally reminded him of her in the expression on the woman's face, in the whole feeling of the piece, was now faded. The night before he'd sat soaking in the image on and off for hours, but couldn't hit the vein that linked girl incarnate and girl depict. That perfect bond in his head between the two was now being replaced by memories of that feeling, and memories of failing to induce it as needed, until he couldn't even be sure that he'd sported the feeling in the first place. He now had a picture that merely abstractly mapped his recent confusions. Aimee seemed smart like Janie was — maybe she could shed some light through his ear a while.

He almost slid some singin'-'n'-dancin' kids a dollar before remembering that he would soon have just as much need of it; in fact, in another six weeks, even with Molly's patronage, he would be singing on the subway himself, or something similar like at trade shows.

Uptown can be taken for a strange new country, but once inside the art supply store he stood in a new world entirely. The smell, big smell like new houses, got you not just in the nose but in every damn orifice, from the tiniest pore to your drop-jaw mouth; it snaked up on the inside informing every cell that the body wouldn't be leaving without a freshly toxic bloodstream and a head like sickly heaven from the high. Then the next remove from the ordinary: colour taking up the assault from the front, all in different materials, tones, and finishes, aisle after aisle, Sammy blinking back the onslaught. Thousands of shades, so numerous they could only be realised adjacent to their nearly twin neighbours; so impossibly slight were the graduations between one tone and the next that he soon turned his dazed head from the complex of vari-stained papers and paints, recovered under bulldog clips and files. A secret rainbow factory, that's what Janie had called it, and he felt he was finding her again.

He stood choosing nothing, just looking and wondering vaguely what colour was. And all the time that smell, ever the smell of the toughest of rainbows. His back against the solvents he asked himself how gold was a colour. Was it just yellow with a lot more shine?

'We're closing now.'

What colour was Janie?

'Sir, please, we're closing now.'

Sammy grabbed some green and purple oil paints and added to these two palette-knives on his way to the cash desk, knowing only that they looked the part and that she would have known what they were for. He would have to work it out later. Had Janie just been a regular colour with a lot more shine?

Back on the subway, rocked back to present time, hiding his purchases away in various pockets, Sammy was impatient for the meeting with Aimee. However, no matter how many Janie links and ties he collected, how many particles of association he amassed, these could never be stuck together, with God's glue or any other kind, to make her whole and breathing. Perhaps only confession could save him now.

Sammy had no precedent for killing someone, so he'd find out in as roundabout a fashion as possible, what was to be done.

Having never fully realised that the point of a meeting time was to be there at that precise time, rather than to use the allocated hour as an indication that she should set out to get there, Aimee had been late for pretty much every appointment since her stepmother had stopped driving her places at age fifteen. Most who knew her knew this and would show up half an hour after they were meant to meet. But then Aimee would start to realise what they were doing and would herself wind life on that extra thirty minutes, result being that she would now be an hour late for any agreed appointment.

Sammy didn't know this and was growing angry at time for not moving slowly enough to let him catch up with himself. By the time he got to Happy at 8.45 he was sweaty, tense and pissed off and more than a little puzzled to see a very relaxed Aimee arriving at the same time. She offered no apology so neither did he.

Aimee was wearing, without evidence of the difficulty most would undergo wrapped in a living shroud, a slightly shorter, lighter version of Janie's green lace dress.

Happy was sparse for a Friday night, deemed unholy ground in spite of the liquid blessings it received on the night of the service. The friends had stayed away; association breeding accountability, guilt or mistrust were your two options, neither restful. Garth-the-bar greeted them with nothing more than an open ear, and each ordered and paid for their own vice.

Eager to carry through the enigmatic tone of the encounter (the note penned onto the hand had been pure *noir*, or was that farce?) Aimee chose the far corner booth usually favoured by enthusiastic lovers and those who owed money to the rest of the bar, a dark wooden box with frayed padded benches and the same yellow candle always unlit in its glass bottle. She pulled out a sachet of sugar which she poured without comment into her whiskey, then tasted, thoroughly, before looking at him long enough to recognise him ten years down the road, weighing him up ounce by ounce with the skill of someone used to both tea-dust and gold. Not sure if she was hoping he'd blurt the secret of the picture out or if she would, she wondered at his reason for wanting to meet her. There was no chemistry, that was certain, but perhaps he held more history than his deadish demeanour betrayed. She laughed bluntly at the set of his formal face and asked, 'Tell me then, why am I here? Not meaning to get so metaphysical so early in the evening.'

He'd presumed she would open with a stock sample, how long was he in town, where was he living, all that conversational warm-up trivia to help his mind get limber. This top-and-tailing the conversation, this slicing right into lean substance, was dangerous, his unmalleable sociability could snap under such a directly ingenuous style. He reinstated his own pace, realising that hers, if left to run, would slice his head right off his fabulous shoulders, that his brains would be shredded with her wit, and he had only ordered a beer.

'I didn't know you knew Italian Tony so well,' he said politely.

'I probably don't know him any better than you do.'

And then a big silence. That's the trouble with slow, it's so dangerously close to stop.

'I, eh, needed to talk to you about something, Aimee. I don't know if you usually tell the others — I mean Lucy and Josh and Italian Tony — I don't know if you tell them everything....'

'I usually tell people stuff they know already like what a windy day it is, but apart from that, they're on their own.'

'So they won't be hearing this conversation?'

'Not unless you talk a whole lot louder.'

A smart-ass chick, there was nothing worse, they were so high-maintenance attention-wise. She sat there, drinking far too quickly and wondering if he had paid for that navy shirt himself.

'Although I wouldn't put it past Boots to be lurking under this table,' she added in a mock mystery voice.

Sammy caught himself from looking and asked, 'What's the deal with him? Is he like having a nervous breakdown or something? I don't even remember them being such good friends.'

'Boots is still trying to cling onto her,' she explained. 'He needs to think that there's some big conspiracy, it's a way of keeping Janie in motion. You see, she was always some sort of a project for him, and Boots still needs that right now, to hold on to her. He just hasn't got the guts to let her go.'

Sammy was acutely aware of the tubes of paint weighing down his jacket, accusing him of the same lack of strength.

He couldn't have felt more guilty if he had the dead girl's very fingers sitting heavy in his pockets.

'I should have maybe brought him round to Italian Tony for a quick fix,' he grinned.

'Do you think Italian Tony did it?' again she speared straight to the meat.

'Did ... did what...?' he faltered. 'Take the, er, the body?'

'Or whatever,' Aimee said, relaxing forward, elbows on the table.

'Do you ... do you think she was killed?'

'Well, what do you think?'

Had Aimee guessed? He said nothing for a while, the pause seeming long even to him, and then, unable to find another road, asked what he had come to ask. 'Did Janie say anything about me before she died?'

He looked for a reaction, but she displayed nothing but calm and an irritating habit of slow-dunking the ice in her glass with a straw.

'Maybe you wouldn't know,' he continued, not granting her pause in return. 'Fat Molly said you didn't know Janie all that well.'

Feeling sidelined, Aimee smashed her tongue through his fairytale, from hurt place to mouth, bypassing reason; it felt like telling a naughty child there was no Santa Claus.

'We were lovers,' she said.

'You can't have been, she was straight,' he replied. 'I know that for a fact.'

Like most well-known facts, this one was conflagrating at a hundred miles an hour, dispersing the fixity of his history. She had finished her drink, downing the dregs of it

like some poor kid with a milkshake. She made for the bar
to buy two more drinks and some thinking time. By not
staying to confirm or deny, Aimee helped to speed up the
unravelling of his resolution, so he followed right behind her.

'A double Jack and a Grolsch, please,' she said.

'Make that two doubles, one with splash, no beer.
Thanks, Garth.'

They stayed standing at the bar. The smile and the
stance were gone, and his right hand now pushed back his
hair, over and over.

He didn't understand. Her eyes slipped down to the
floor, unable to meet his as she spelled it out, poured it out
dry onto the dust and beer-mats.

'We were together.'

He shook his head, a reflex. His eyes narrowed slightly
as he started to understand what she was telling him. His
hand went up to his hair which he coiled and pulled,
understanding slowly breeding disbelief, disbelief becoming
rejection, rejection becoming realisation, and the hand still
in the hair, twisting away.

As tendering any wild notion to Sammy was commen-
surate to preaching God's own truth, to his believing mind,
she had the only take on it worth having. Attracted to women.
He had seen her through a wooden head all the while.
Aimee had taken another piece of Janie away; soon there'd
be nothing left.

He wanted to shut Aimee down, switch her off like a
too-tough level on a game. He'd only come a-softly begging
for a reassuring word; he'd merely wanted discharge from
the heavy obligations to Janie's shop-worn soul. He'd

thought to give his conscience a quick rub with some dry persuasion, take a pill for his guilt. Rocks in the candy bag. Poor fool.

They stayed bar-bound, and laboured through another few awkward minutes, rushing round the previously aborted inanities and crass pleasantries, finishing on long goodbyes with counterfeit assurances that they would seek each other out again before long, so settling a seal of propitious completion on their night.

Once he was gone, the door still closing under its weight, she put her empty glass on the bar, drained his to empty also, and ordered another.

'One more for the load, Garth.'

Sammy ran on bursting lungs and broken nerve back to the apartment where Fat Molly had cooked an amazing buffet, just to make him feel bad. His stomach for an instant thought to join the insurrection, but it knew where its allegiance lay — not with the mind but with the gullet.

'I thought you might be hungry after your date or whatever it was,' she simpered, and served like a blue-rinse lady entertaining authority, casting Sammy in the rôle of pastor or chairman of the PTA. She garnished her hopelessness with an avocado and blue-cheese salad.

'I was really bored,' he said, rewriting in his own favour, mending his pride with the help of an oversized three-mushroom quiche, soon moving on to fresh hot cake.

'She's so aggressive. What kind of cake is this?'

'Poppy-seed with lemon frosting,' she replied un-aggressively.

'Are you sure these are poppy seeds?'

'Well, what else would they be?'

He examined one with the type of apprehension usually reserved for things that moved. 'I think we should try to grow one just to make sure.'

'But it's too late now, they're all damaged by the heat and the time they've spent away from the flower.'

The untrue seeds were catching between his teeth, as hard to shift as the expanding image of Janie lying naked with a woman. He abandoned the cake as soon as it was eaten and brought his overnight bag into the bathroom to search for new solace. No joy, not a line, but he did hit against a piece of paper, and with the fastidiousness of a regular user, scrutinised its folds for accidental reserves.

The scrap had been rotting there for months, clean but for ink, covered in Janie's last address, not more than a scrawl, written by a hand in a hurry. She had phoned it through to his answering machine, must have been just after she left the hospital. He hadn't used it, having had such vitally important things to do like, God knows, magazines to read, cappuccinos to drink, auditions to fail. It was hard now to make sense of what he had been doing out there, soaking up the sunshine, buying into body, climbing a ladder made of people who moved out there months before. The right sunglasses used to actually matter. What vicious kind of rods had fixed him there?

It was now midnight. Dry of cash, and credit cards ducking from disclosure in awkward corners of her bag, hiding out there from the advance of her rampant inebriation, Aimee left Happy for home. What she had said was eating her. Limbs in motion but the style of their moving wasn't right, like empty lead, all air where blood should be and too much trouble to pull along the road. They shook enough that she could watch the phenomenon at play, and this she did, bent almost double, clamped to a crossing sign one block over. Head greeting her knees, she stilled her self-hurt mind and rebel body, and craved for whatever could wipe tranquillity back in. Should have asked Italian Tony for some pills. Why did she say that they had been lovers? Was it because she wanted it to be true?

Sammy woke as every morning undefiled by dreams, fresh as the day, which he soon clouded with a cigarette and a vigorous run through the night before. The memory scrape of the bar encounter ignited his straw belly. He had given up smoking — in LA it's tantamount to jerking off in a crowded room — but as Molly lit up regularly he was exposed to passive smoking and figured if the detriment was mandatory he might as well take a pull on the pleasure now and then. A cigarette as restitution for lung cancer was hardly the most defensible rationale, but under the law of 'make the best of a bad situation', it triumphed to the extent that he was now buying his own. He answered the phone as Fat Molly was out.

At least it wasn't Aimee.

'Sammy? It's Lucy, about Janie. No more news I'm afraid, except that we've decided to have a celebration of her, a beach party up the coast, this Sunday, tomorrow. I realise this is absurdly short notice but I was really hoping you and Fat Molly....'

Had Lucy known about Janie and Aimee? What further deformities, he wondered, did they plan to work on his perception? Together would they storytell her down to nothing? He made no attempt to talk back, mortified at his lately realised butt-naked being, his self-image dismantled down to idiot spares. He was the new clown of the hour, the hapless fool who thought himself the lord of the dance.

Lucy talked on regardless, vitalised by her undertaking, brewing up some magic solution to it all, conjuring up plans which would eventually navigate all the friends to the sparkling city of everlasting satisfaction. She had no idea what this city might look like, but as it probably wouldn't be catered, she was gratified that most had agreed to bring food.

While Janie was alive, Lucy had always been needed, the friend-on-call, 24-hour emergency devotee, no whim too small, no foundering disquiet too far-fetched, no distance too large in the rain. A thousand randomly vagrant troubles could call her into action at any time, and it hurt to think that she wasn't called to duty for the big one.

Without solutions to conduct or a difficulty to nurse, she felt useless, the fairy godmother with the shitty arthritic wand. She had to admit that her service was bankrupt — she hadn't managed to find the body, or Italian Tony, or clues, or to mend any crack really, or recast any mould. She had always prided herself on the fact that she could work tiny magics, fix a heart with a tissue, fix a life with a well-chosen blueberry muffin. Boots was being needy, that was obvious, a right little nose-bleed since the news, but unfortunately taking Boots under her wing wasn't a possibility as Josh might get the wrong idea. Besides, he wasn't a good bet for the emotional reimbursement on recovery, but then neither was Janie in the end.

Her flown coop was certainly less desolate when occupied by an exhaustive cause, so there she was, over-planning, over-fixing, checking, talking her lonely way through to Sunday. 'And then we can just all talk about her, what she meant to us, what we wanted to say but didn't. Or even just get shit-faced in her honour.'

Sammy still listened, though she had started to blur in her copiousness. He was looking out for the spurious word, wondering whether to ask straight out why he had never been told about Janie and women, but afraid of blowing the impression if they assumed he already knew. Before the confusion could wreck his head, he got caught up in the details of Sunday.

'...this documentary on Discovery about funerals in New Orleans and they...'

'Sorry, Lucy, was that "bring chicken" or "don't bring chicken"?'

'Well, I was talking to Aimee — you know Aimee, don't you, she was there after the service? She's kind of sulky?'

He took down the directions, thinking the journey itself would take a fraction of the time and wondering how she knew the names of all those wrong exits and grocery stores. Then the phone numbers of pretty much everyone that ever existed, suggestions for how much gas money should be pitched in, based on a certain number sharing, and then Lucy had to hurry off the phone twenty-five minutes after she had first called, so much to Xerox, fax, sand to sieve no doubt. He still hadn't worked out the chicken thing.

And why a bonfire of all things? Burning seemed such a violence to Sammy, fire seemed to mark an end to everything. He always felt uncomfortably aware of its menace, knowing it could waste him in moments if it chose, and so the lighting of the village barbecue fire would every year concern him beyond its physical range. Fire sealed the frayed end of summer, signified the closing down of freedom and light. After it had eaten itself up (such an easy, yet savage thing to do) there was nothing to look forward to, anticipation all spent like the holiday dollar, nothing but school the next Monday and the deferred whopping now that other parents were no longer always around. It had burned Tommy Tyler's brother that one year; the screams stuck in his ears for weeks. Fire was friend to no one. No consolation ever rose from the ashes either, except maybe an over-burnt potato or asphyxiated fieldmouse.

But this time Sammy welcomed the decided end as the tired welcome sleep no matter how dribbled the pillow, a coarsely hewn completion better than endless extension and stir. Fire could smoke out his beetling delusions and burn a little sober reality in. Some coke wouldn't go amiss either. Perhaps he would let slip a secret or two of his own.

He tried to imagine the women Janie had been with, hating them. Then he started to worry that he might be homophobic, a terrible affliction in a large American city. No, it wasn't a sex thing, or gay thing, nor even a concern that he had been betrayed; his own guilt at leaving prohibited that. The dread that was ripping him up right then was that those he thought close could all be leading completely different lives from the ones he supposed. Were his folks happily (if turgidly) married? Perhaps his old man had affairs with the ladies at the golf club. His mother was more likely to be celibate, not much room in that tepee, and he hadn't read the leaflets she sent, but sex was probably a toxin or carcinogenic or an act of karmic sedition or whatever else she tried to counteract with powder sticks.

No, he couldn't afford to believe that the world worked like that. True there were some things that turned on you, like a chance shard of glass in your steak dinner, but that's all it was, a rare and unfortunate thing. It didn't mean you should spend the rest of your days puréeing your food on the off chance.

Guilt still in the driving seat, he was driven to Janie's last apartment. He or it pressed a random bell. The intercom clicked.

'Yes?'

'I'm looking for Janie.'

Unsure of the next line, he stood until the voice and the person appeared at the door. Twentyish, Jewish, with black hair and a grey sweatsuit, and more teeth in her head than Sammy had ever seen in one person.

'Janie doesn't live here anymore. She must have moved out last week. I'm from across the hallway. Are you a friend of hers?'

'Yes, I've been out of town and I thought I'd look her up again.'

'Well, she didn't leave a forwarding address and the landlord didn't say where she's gone to. But something arrived in the mail just this morning — it was addressed to a friend of Janie.'

'Which friend?'

'It just says that on the outside — "To a Friend of Janie" — I guess whoever sent it wants it passed on to her. Will you be seeing her?'

'Sure. I'll make certain she gets it.'

'Thanks, I'll just be a moment.'

She returned with a white package about the size of a postcard. 'Here you go. I was starting to worry she might be uncontactable or something.'

'So was I.'

He thanked her and said that he would probably have found Janie by the end of the week.

The envelope tore open easily; there was no letter inside, but a wad of newspaper the size of his palm. Out fell Janie in the form of a claddagh on a neck-chain. He held it so the light made a silhouette of the crowned heart with two tiny gold hands cupped around it. He knew it well — an old Irish friendship symbol. It had been a gift from some old family friends of hers back home. He knew she'd worn it since she was a small child, and remembered the morning the chain had snapped at the kitchen sink and dropped down the drain — from the sound of her, you'd have sworn she'd lost an arm. He'd had to take apart the U-bend to prevent her from atomising the whole block with the high-C vibrations from her screaming. She'd have made him pull apart the building if that's what it had taken.

He held the necklace in his pocketed hand and made for Happy. As he sat in the same booth as the night before, having shunned feeble beer, it being easier to go straight for the hard option, he noticed how the place looked shabbier in the dusty grey sunshine from the window over the door than ever it had in the kindness of electric light. More distortions, so which was the reality?

He had placed his new treasure on the table in front of him. It hadn't occurred to him that whoever sent the claddagh might still have the body that had worn it; his mind had been dragged back to nights when she had worn only that. He pored over it for inspiration, as it lay there in silence, witness to truth.

He placed the under-applied scrap of paper on the table beside the claddagh, a pitiful souvenir of a whole life, but at least he could be sure that these had been part of whatever it was they had together. And if it had been New Orleans instead of New York, this here collection and a pinch of voodoo dust would have been more than enough to bring her back.

'In the cauldron boil and bake; Eye of newt, and toe of frog, Wool of bat and, er, hair of dog … Hair of dog? Garth! Another vodka and tonic when you're ready.'

Nothing doing on the resurrection front. Could be he'd have to paint her his way from scratch: no smudges, smears, or extra detail from smarter brushes, no looking through another's jaundiced yellow eye. His Janie was his to paint, and may the gods of the happy ending strike all others dumb.

In walked Aimee, wrapped in trouble.

Judy May Murphy

Janie

*O*n the East of the island of Manhattan, around the square where the homeless once found home, there is a shabby little building with blacked-out windows and a front which makes it seem all boarded-up, two-by-foured in a final long goodnight. The second storey crumbles down to meet the ground floor, to ask for assistance in its worsening state. No one has been up there this last ten years. The front door is heavied by an iron grill, and painted — or left to wish itself — a greenish black with touches of dark brown. The door needs good strong shouldering to open it even the essential inch to glimpse a little inside.

Once inside, the single room is longer than wide and lower than tall, bolstered by girders and painted in a single coat of black, with the old walls peeping out from behind to see what new devices appear.

The old leather-panelled bar, where legends were spawned in the 1960s, is now a coat-check stand and a place to store the large chunks of plaster that sometimes fall from the ceiling and look too structurally vital to simply throw away. A medley of old sofa frames, amputee kitchen chairs, backless little office numbers, dilapidated bar stools and discarded ends of wood have been fashioned (with the aid of too much time and a glue-gun) into a bank of seats, holding eighty in comfort, two hundred on a Saturday night.

The stage is a brown-painted platform, the two slightly different shades meeting in the middle; it is gently sloping and the height of most knees from the ground. It sits idiot-still behind a blue velvet curtain before and after each act, except when the fire-safety officer appears and the curtain is sent to live rolled up in the park, minded by a kindly purple manboy on the beg.

The audience's way is patch-lit by lamps from the actors' homes, taped at intervals high along the playhouse walls. The stage lights were abandoned by a community group when the members all died of old age. They were fondly remembered in the first two playbills and fondly forgotten after that.

Anyone walking by the building at night with a good ear for a ghost, might chance to hear an old Irishwoman call in her broken voice from the past:

'He's gone now, God spare us, and we'll not see him again.'

And wonder who that person gone might be.

Anyone entering the building, that night or another, believing it maybe to be still a bar, or one of those illegal drag-queen clubs with a name like Pastry or Whore, would be surprised to walk in on a reserve of silence perforated by a destitute sound, the symphony of all that cuts, the voice of all mothers speaking, loud as the west wind in the wisdom of her years:

'If it was a hundred horses, or a thousand horses you had itself, what is the price of a thousand horses against a son where there is one son only?'

If they were to choose not to turn and run, but to stay instead for the telling, they would perhaps be glad, and would perhaps hear something of their own sorrow sung in her full lament:

'They're all gone now and there isn't anything more the sea can do to me ... I'll have no call now to be up crying and praying when the wind breaks from the south, and you can hear the surf is in the east, and the surf is in the west, making a great stir with the two noises, and they hitting one on the other.'

Night after night the old woman takes the stage, lurking at the edge of a deep, dark pit, and cries. She kneels on the straw-scattered boards, weeping the pain of generations, praying for an end to the suffering she bears. So lost is she that the audience becomes her.

'They're all together this time, and the end is come. What more can we want than that? No man at all can be living for ever, and we must be satisfied.' And with that she prays and she weeps.

Curtain call confuses her, drags her back to the present. The lights shine too brightly for her eyes yet tearful, the applause sounds too loud for her grief, she feels protected only by the latex rubber make-up as her younger skin sits back behind the wrinkled shield.

There are no dressing rooms behind or to the side of the stage, not even a cupboard so called, so she stands outside in the alley between the makeshift playhouse and the rear of the back-bumpered building, and rips away the countenance worn for her weeping. As the audience waits for the next part of the evening, a play which shows a happier Ireland (one which she doesn't know and doesn't perform), she waits until she is completely alone and the crying continues for the men in the sea as she stands with her old face in her hand.

She could go now, as she sometimes does, to a party, or a bar called Happy, or to fake a dinner with the man she sees, but tonight she runs home, her claddagh bouncing against her chest, and writes to herself for an answer.

Quietly she cries on for the loss of the boat-boy, the baby, and the person she should be, tears falling smaller now, smeared against the soft of her new face.

Perhaps later she will venture out again, to drink to keep the pain at bay, and touch up against the ugly surface, keeping one foot in the humdrum world lest she fall from life completely. At least the acting keeps her occupied if not terribly busy. She wishes other rôles would come: the faster she becomes known to the world, the sooner the boat-boy will arrive and stand in a queue of admirers, from where she will pluck him into forever. 'I have to get famous,' she says. 'I have to have everyone know who I am and where I'm at.' But the generous bank drafts which arrive, methodical as Monday from her parents and her aunts, remind her that she hasn't got there yet.

Dear Me,

It's just as well that Sammy is going away — he's not the one, but then that's probably why I went out with him in the first place. It's time to really get moving, I have to make the most of this play and use it to get auditions for others, otherwise the whole thing will grind to a halt. I must get my picture in the papers or a magazine. I can't believe I haven't got an agent yet, the director said that loads have been to the play but I think he's just saying that. I'm really starting to panic about it.

Fat Molly is being such a bitch, I mustn't let her win. Earlier I ate a pizza but managed to fix it on time. Must get another rôle, a really good one, someone my age.

Love, Me

Aimee

It was well gone noon and I just dragged myself, kicking, to waking from this dream where a fine clump of toadstool mushrooms, grey-brown translucent and long, were sprouting on the inside of my wrist just where the veins threatened to surface, as if they drank from the well of me. When I first felt them blooming there, escaping from my arm, I gazed as if to lick them, wondering if they were gills, and plucked one out. It came loose from the root, a tiny maggot nestling in the hole, tiny inside my wrist, but a new mushroom shot to full size from nothing, so I picked this one too. More grew and my wrist became a garden of pale rubbery meats and I could feel the writhing of the grubs below. The panic set in and I plucked and scraped and scratched with a blood fury, but still they came, more bonding with my body with every passing second, until each maggot became a squirming, pin-eyed little person, sucky mouth open, fists flailing. Then, falling through a wormhole, I awoke, drenched from the fervour, and rubbed my wrists raw, the imagined mushrooms and miniature sucklings stronger than the reality cast by the midday sun.

I had that weird acid taste in my mouth and went to look at myself in the mirror, as we all do in times of crisis. I looked like shit, for a blonde. This was one big Happy hangover.

Some stray segment of me, no doubt distancing itself as far as could be from the embarrassment of the rest of my indolent parts, had managed somewhere on the unsteady night road home to procure a large carton of orange juice which, dehydrated as I was from alcohol and a night of irrigating so much fungal growth, I stuck to now like a familiar on tit. Vitamins avoid me, I know I'll have a head cold by tonight.

I could hear the postman pouring his usual disappointments through the front door. Mail, I really must yawn, it's hard to get excited by mail — how anything can arrive in an envelope looking totally unabashed at being neither drugs nor money is beyond me. Besides, I figure, if it's good they would have phoned. Still, I went to claim my dispatches, to find out who needed what and how many millions I'd won.

Two or three years ago now, I'd met a woman about my age over several bottles of the bad. She kept in touch although I warned her I wasn't the greatest with the pen-pal thing. Surprisingly optimistic about my survival odds, and stubborn in the face of long-suspended replies, she wrote quite often. She had been staying in a Mennonite town as part of a post-graduate something, like they have to send students and experts into each part of the world to make sure it really is being inhabited full-time and with adequate amounts of ethnicity. Like the Amish, the Mennonites stave off modern, even as modern comes writhing up to claim them. They could have a point: if God meant us to have cars, he'd have given us hands to build them, or something.

I've been forgetting of late that the world is somewhat longer than Broadway and broader than Long Island by a good few miles, and now in dropped her missive to remind me that there was a planet going on, acres and oceans to escape to. I could knock this happening on the head and bail for any place where my spleen could comply with the oxygen levels, and my plastic keep pace with my inclination. Anyone might say that nothing physical tethered me here, but anyone might be mistaken. This Janie-gum had slimed my shoe and I was suckered here for a time, so I took my only available parole and escaped for a short while inside the letter.

Apart from her cancelling her e-mail server, a how-was-I? and the shock omission of her usual entreaties to reply, the letter was about the daughter of the house where she stayed, thirteen, obedient and respectful as only the oppressed can be, with her neatly tied-back hair and modest clothes like some paranoid father's ideal. Apparently the young girl's nights were spent as mine at that age, with pen and paper to author herself a liveable world beyond the family coop. Night after corn-shuck night, my friend would watch the predestined young girl create 'wish books' (for want of a proper term), flimsy clumsy pages bound in a sock darn, the same as all Mennonite girls made once the peas were re-counted, the hemming sewn and the barn-door firmly closed.

However, deliberately, and in full family view, she would hand-draw pictures of herself holding articles barred to her by her religion, illustrating the very urges and ambitions which were outlawed by her people, derided as obscenities, symbols of the lost. Page upon page of the girl wearing rings, watches, playing music, riding in a car, wearing fancy clothes with her hair hanging loose, sitting on Mexican boys' knees. On she'd dream, page after page, night after night. Until one year the ink would run dry in her pen, and they'd expect her to stop, and start with the babies and the like, but until then these small, dirty wishes were allowed.

It was a contained rebellion, the vaccine, the small jab of freedom in the arm to stop them from succumbing to the bigger expression. So said my anthropologist friend, who always seems to send a message buried not too deeply down but stated abstrusely enough not to condescend.

I'm more apologist than anthro anything, but, out to get some muffins to go with the juice, it struck me that I had my own wish books, already coloured in, glossed with seasonal choices, jewellery, shoes, clothes, cigarettes, drink, make-up, perfumes, and the faces and bodies of buffed and sweated men, replete with desires I've been coached into chasing since very, very young. Since long before I knew that they put tiny tastes on your tongue to teach you how to hunger.

As I never put aside my childish ways, only chronologically upgraded them, I was now, as I often am, carrying a copy of *Vogue* under my pale, scented arm. There is little I would add to these gloss-dipped wish journals, and it seems a shame that my wishes are the same as those of all their other readers, the other millions of individuals. It's tragic that I have to buy my hopes along with my Tic-Tacs, muffins and milk.

Such are the worst ever wishes, the attainable ones. No deep enchantment in their germ, only a ten-minute shopping buzz, acquisition orgasms, idiocy marked up to addictive highs, cheapened in the sales.

The boat-boy is a far better hope to hold to, the running him to ground a hidden goal, the origin of him masked, offside out of broadcast, and with no one hovering invisible over me brandishing an edit, an airbrush, or suspending my dream for more prosperous times. Don't get me wrong, I do realise that my current dreams are also not mine, but borrowed from Janie's journal, harvested from the dead girl's heart. Poor Janie, her 'dear me' letters were her wish book, and miserable me, I went and abluted her possibilities right down the wash-pipes with the sickness and the dirty vodka stains.

I haven't felt this excited since I still believed in Jesus. Holy, holy is the boat-boy. The boat-boy is the pusher, the fall, and will one day be the one who saves. 'In ancient times,' my post-friend extracted aloud one night, '"that which is imbued with holiness" had the same meaning as "that which is forbidden".'

Figures.

But if you don't get what you wish for, what happens then?

Then you sit foam-curlered and slippered all your life, sighing over the kind of hair you know you'll never achieve despite what they sell you in an English voice. Could be the boat-boy needs to stay hidden, maybe like the perfect cut he never was nor will be, I could wear my feet out walking the seas to find him. A capable danger abides in all ambition, and here was the danger in mine — if I didn't find him and move on up to the next plane of realisation, like Janie I'd be tied forever to a vision, like a Mennonite girl dreaming of riding Cadillac Mexican dick while her actual self is dough-sopped, kneading.

Hearts are given only to those who dare to hope. Hoping is beyond me, but I can tack myself on to Janie's and get fixed in the process. It's like ice-skating — the only way to learn is to borrow a pair of skates and let someone take you by the hand.

No other way out, I have to catch the dream-boat, the boat-boy is the most important thing. I have to move on up to meet him on the final line, my moment of reckoning coming on faster than a rope. The city currents are pulling me, I'm drifting further and further from him, confusing him in the sauce, and if I don't part the mass of it soon he will be dead from lack of rendition.

To blast it loose and now, is the only way, and if everything meets full obliteration in the storm of finding him, well then at least I'll have triumphed in some trick other than masturbating with coloured pens. It's a story to wind forward, the kind not naturally unfolding but gathering in on itself, puckered with countless doublings-over, the hiding of patterns parallel with the noticing them there.

My first step on this new resolve is a backward shuffle, to set things straight with Sammy. No chance of getting to the truth about the picture with such a big spent lie sitting in the road, bloating and stinking like a dead family pet in the sun.

I obsessed on my lie a while, and reached home still wrapped in disbelief that in one fell sentence I had forfeited whatever objective distance I might have claimed to the axis of my hinterland life. I could only conclude that I was now thoroughly snared along with all the other woes and wants of the bars and their bit freaks. Packed out to every inch of me with hate — hate for the me that built false annals into

Sammy's simplicity, and hate for the me that finished off the muffins too soon — I tried to call.

Calling Sammy, or rather, not calling Sammy, was taking me all day. My much-fingered phone would spasm and die if I punched the whole number before hanging up, touch-tone dialling should be upgraded to extrasensory dialling that makes the calls for you whenever your crap-resolve buckles under finger.

I loused that business good and large, I know it, I know it. But I don't know why I'm even the smallest bit surprised at fucking up bigger than republican line, because even the Lord in his retirement knows it's certified routine for me to fall monumentally on my upward ass, shoved down there by my own clumsy intrigue. I trip up over nothing — give me a level playing field and I will somehow manage to stand myself in a depression; give me a simple everyday problem and before too long I'll be calling in the psychiatric para-medics. Maybe I need professional help, should put Lucy on the payroll, she could clean up behind me with a damp amending cloth and large squirt of justification, the non-scouring kind.

I sat smeary there at the foot of the Heap and wondered if it was possible to clear it all away — or was it too far gone? I noticed some of my yesterday's clothes had some-how managed to find their way on there. Sometimes there's too many layers to hope to skin each hide away. As my foundation layer of scrumpy vice is dense enough for minor sins to forage on securely, any badness coheres to my crust entirely, so that coming clean is not an easy operation for me, washing off a sin feels like a sanding to the bone.

I had to take back from Sammy a sordid lie, and patch the hole it would leave with a piece of my pride. 'Making love to Janie' — I hadn't known I needed the connection enough to cripple history with such absolute contempt. What a big fat figment that was, considering how I bumped words with Janie once and once only, a single kink of conversation in such a long weld. I never even meant to talk to her: the parasite fares better when the host is unaware.

The accident occurred one night last year, one half flight down from a party. I was doing my usual usuals, ingesting the profligate tortures of the rabble from a distance, the easier to swallow from there, thinking myself a blind corner when, as if bingo-balled from nowhere, Janie popped her head around the door to rec the stairs for new arrivals.

'Were you at the play?' she asked, fighting to form the words through an animated difficulty, one natural to the quantity of hospitality she had already co-operated with. She said it again in case she had only thought it the first time, groping one hand against the sweaty door jamb as it held her hollow weight, staring through escaped strands of hair down the eight steps to where I sat. Until that instant it hadn't occurred to me that I could exist to her. Invisible as I'd remained during her conspicuous residence in my head, I thought she'd look at me and see only herself.

'Wouldn't it make you hate the sea?' I asked in reply, facetious in the shock of her address. 'You'd wonder why they all didn't just move inland to safety.'

She inhaled a breath, the weight of which seemed to draw her back inside, but it turned far back in the sway and brought her forward to tell me: 'There's no life in safety.

That Girl from Happy

People like that are of the sea. It may finally kill them but it's also what gives them life.'

She paused to work out if she had just spoken sense, grammatically at least.

With that, the spangled hoards arrived with feet that looked to crush me, and up pushed a loud flock of party people, dangling bottles which would loose them from the starting position and then dance them to the dawn of sexual disappointment and the final gasps of high. Janie was either swept adrift in their run or had migrated on ahead to the relative quiet of the matured madness inside.

Later on down the year, even when I came to know Italian Tony too well, that was to remain the only time Janie Jay and I spoke, and the first of two occasions we were together alone.

I never made love to her the next time either, I only kissed her. No, not only. I kissed her.

Lost in the memory, I accidentally dialled Sammy in full. Fat Molly was freaked to shitting her innards, she seemed to know it was me before I said. The epitome of wannabe girlfriend, taking such a generous message for him, my number, what it was in connection with, when would be a good time for him to call back, could she sit on his knee while he did so? I'm almost positive she sold me some insurance and windows in there somewhere. I hung up, half sorry and two-thirds not.

Then I remembered that she said she was expecting him in at any moment, a celebrated wifey term for, 'Go ask my tupperware ass, the little fucker's missing', so I knew exactly how to find him. Euphemism is often the most direct description, only the hidden really knows how to reveal.

The day-drinkers were few in Happy, so I saw him from the moment I stepped in.

Not looking as fresh as the last time we'd collided here, at least he was wearing a shirt that didn't want burning. I could almost understand why Janie went out with him, he sort of fills a space nicely, probably provided the basic services while she waited for her boat-boy to arrive. Any other man would guess at her elsewhere allegiance and try to fight for those corners of Janie that had been red-stickered for another years before.

I collected a drink first at the bar, to give him time to regroup his senses on seeing his fact-free historian arrive back at the dig, but not quite enough time to escape to the ease of the traffic outside. He came over as if uninterrupted from the last time and sat down beside me, no doubt believing that by actually choosing to fall off the cliff, it wouldn't hurt so bad.

'Your friend's expecting you home,' I said, starting low enough to suck the sawdust from the floor, an underhand trick to web a bar-fly for a while. No man alive would want to seem to jump to some girly's command. He was slurring drunk already, not badly, but badly for the hour.

'Hear about the fire?' he asked, knowing to set his own agenda.

'In Boots' apartment? I think it was just a drill.'

'No, I mean the one Lucy is organising, the picnic bonfire. She gave me your number, said your boyfriend might be driving us down if he has a car.'

That Girl from Happy

'She's gone and organised me a boyfriend too? The girl's insatiable.'

'She said she saw you guys in that Italian place between Jumelle's and Screeching Lindy's.'

'Oh, that boyfriend. We actually ate dessert so you can tell Lucy we're married already.'

'Sorry?'

'Never mind, I just wanted to talk to you about something I said last night.'

Our position at the bar placed us dead centre of an 'old-guy-Garth-old-lady' triangle, so I lowered my voice and moved in closer.

'I just wanted to tell you that I'm sorry if I upset you. I sometimes just say things under pressure, when I get hyper. And then I can't believe that it was my mouth that said them, and not someone else's, some enemy. When I was fourteen I told my home-room teacher I was pregnant, just to avoid getting into trouble for not doing my homework. I'm really capable of saying just about anything.'

'Oh, I didn't know. And did you keep the child?'

Jesus! this man was so trusting, he drove up the price of face-value, being so naïve. I lied, Sammy, that's what I'm telling you here, I am a liar. But I wasn't going to say it outright. If he couldn't think sideways at his stage in life, then wising him up to the twisted minds and vile tempers of the world might rent a pit open in him, one he'd fall inside from gazing down in horror at it all. Didn't want to wake the sleeping.

'No, it was a false alarm. What I'm trying to say is I don't want you to think badly of Janie.'

Maybe if I just left things at that, no point stirring up a whole ocean just to put one little pearl back in place. He drank like a puppet with one hand glued to the glass. The other hand seemed clenched hostile against me, but then I saw that the fist was holding a thin gold chain, the small medal or design hanging from the end. It can't have been his or else he'd be wearing it, tucked inside his shirt while on the crawl. Our drinking neighbours were now hanging by their half-deaf ears onto every word, but he didn't seem to notice as he continued on.

'It feels like I've woken up in the dark and put on the wrong socks.'

I was worried we were giving the audience a life.

'So I guess we better fall in with that Lucy thing,' I said. 'She left a message, something about a chicken and warm coat; I really shouldn't play those back until the morning. What day and everything?'

'Tomorrow evening, she says she'll get a map to me tonight. He does have a car, doesn't he?'

'I think he keeps it near work for driving out to his Dad's place, but if he doesn't, Lucy probably has a few lying spare. OK, names and times?'

'Come over to the apartment around seven, it'll just be me and Fat Molly, you and your boyfriend, and don't forget the chicken, Lucy mentioned that a lot. Can't wait to meet him. What's his name again?'

'Dec. The chicken just goes by its generic.'

I didn't really want to go, this was getting me down, but absolution is contingent on doing the penance, so I took his address. If I looked at it in a professional way, this bonfire party could be the perfect place for snooping through people's information — get them high and then dig about in their heads with a psychological plastic spade, see what stage they were at with the body and the boat-boy.

When he'd left to Mollify I finished another drink and put a hole in the next, this binge set to blast me from here to infirmity. This beach thing would bring it all to a head, maybe the cops would be there, Lucy probably had them all on her party list by now.

The journey down would have been some unrefundable hell only Dec was there to buddy on the mary-jane feel, on the whole fat deformity of the thing. Shame the car didn't run on talked-out saliva, as Fat Molly left not a scratch un-spoken in case someone stole in with an entertaining word. Weary ears aside, I'd have cherished every tiny chew of the inane had someone tipped me the wink as to the raw dimensions of the backward trip.

Any telling of the party would be hopeless now, I'd just colour it with stains it didn't wear at the time, but in true story style I'll start from the start.

It was as if Janie was calling to us, suffer little broken ones to come unto me, keep your deep-clouded eye on the road ahead, the kingdom will be yours for the drinking. Maps at the ready, the feral terrain of night lay ahead for us rambling pilgrims, especially Dec with his bigger make and his excellent know for a dram.

I watched from the hallway as Dec sat in his car outside, appraised by me of the insanity ahead, curious plenty and fixed for the journey down. Not one dab since lunch, he boasted. Full certain of the rum slake some time along, he was whistling some tune about a ribbon round a hat, and the ever-special thirst sang louder than anything. I laughed to myself, Dec was not a strong contender for the early return.

What a circus, I couldn't have wished for better, what tabloid fodder, scuttle-butt feed. There was a layman's holy Testament in this here canon's run — Janie's days-dead body snatched from final pause, celebration fires, burgers of remembrance, ragbone odds and ends and surplus tags of party folk, and drink flooding generous enough to baptise the most nefarious of beings. Janie-ville was for sure a land you might get lost in without trying, and stay lost in without much caring, a delicious wasteland, but then wasted is a word for those that cannot see.

Too fit to falter at the side of the road, Dec lightly punched the horn so it sounded not displeased, but hurried me and the others along.

My smile dragged me out ahead of the pavlova which followed in Fat Molly's arms. On the huge side, the pavlova hid its architect from waist to prissy face, a face which echoed loud the difficulty of her new shoes, nervous for her stately meringue in its double-cream glory, the pie of ages. It was without exaggeration the size of a small school-age child.

Sammy tumbled out after us some seconds later, having postponed the floss and brush-up for a broader time, and climbed into the musty old Ford with a handshake of first hello for Dec. Poor Sammy, his ideal rear-position choice and one-third of his remaining comfort was nudged aside by the pavlova, but he knew to defer to its superior presence.

Our initial short-term in capital gridlock proved a muck-mash, as every inane traffic-dodge came pouring out of Fat Molly in her fear for the freshness of her cakely friend, politely agreed and ignored by Dec, while I sat firmly on my remarks about the cake, which made for a very uncomfortable ride.

'And so I told him straight — didn't I, Sammy? — that if he wanted to find Italian Tony, he'd just have to do it himself, I mean, we weren't there to do his job for him....' Dec gave me a look like he was thinking how the pavlova was better company than its maker.

We stopped at a gas station for various forms of relief: bathroom, silence, beer and cigarettes enough to smoke us through till morning, and a lottery ticket to sweat and dig me out of my financial mismanagement.

'I know I have a memory like vodka through a net, but hasn't she told us that part about getting the doctor for Janie twice already?' wondered Dec aloud.

'Yes,' I confirmed, 'and possibly more than twice.'

Sammy got back in and his now palsied-looking smile established that not only was he familiar with the story, but the poor bastard was by now a veteran of the telling. Long old hour.

Down at the beach we could see stick figures on the sand; the wind was low and the tide high. It looked like Josh placing the first few pieces of skip-salvage wood. Drag a little, stack a little, smoke a little roll.

Lucy would have been the other early bird, anticipation worming through. Earlier, on the phone, she was predicting no one would bring anything but bottled, got weepy telling me about Josh's 28th, how she'd laboured like an indentured ant over fourteen kinds of dip only to be faith-fucked monumental style when nobody furnished her success with the badly promised *crudités* or chips. This time, she confided, none could junk her doing, the catering crown was rolling on home to Lucy and they'd see, those dipless monkeys, that Miss Molly was not the only chef to shine in the kitchen, lager limes were not the only fruit. And the first thing I noticed on getting out of Dec's car, was miles and miles of sand, sea, and trays of chocolate Rice Krispie squares.

It was eight-fifteen by now and seventy plus people stood on the beach squinting at the sea, checking their paper bags in at Food-point Lucy, introducing themselves to those who looked new, and seeking out vague friends and past mistakes.

Sammy had already drifted off toward madness, visiting only, trying to coax Boots toward lucidity with a beer, the innocuous ministering to the neurotic. Sammy delved in, talked, drank, and did normal for the two, as Boots, hair brushed but doubtless still stinking something rank, looked out to the ocean. Josh told me that Boots had travelled down with him under minimal resistance. Josh had such an affinity for the outcast, his best friend in grade school was probably the most farty boy on the bus.

Jumped up to boss-mode proper now the urban urbane had alighted into her agenda safe and sandy, Lucy's worry seemed assuaged. She'd planned on the phone to teetotal the night in case some emergency hit from the far side, but I watched as, soothed by the so-far-easy tilt on the array, she reached for a can. The place was rotten with unknown people. I didn't like them even before I heard them talk.

That Girl from Happy

'No way, if you pour gas over wood it stinks out the whole night.'

'I knew this guy who killed himself by drinking the gasoline from his fiancée's car after she dumped him.'

'No you didn't, you saw it on that show last week.'

'Oh, yeah. I thought I knew him.'

Genius.

At a far-enough throw to indulge a healthy volume, couples sandwich-bagged their road-trip altercations and hooked up with the mob either grudgingly reconciled, or sufficiently incensed to have louder, more perilous fun than their disposable spouse. The first anaesthetic layers had all but dried into the guests, and as the early bolters sought relief in the near privacy of the dunes, the beer boys tore off bottle-caps with every available tooth, key and heel, rip-flicked open cans and roughly ranged around the driftwood mound that Josh built. I just chilled with a starter can and watched as they fidgeted up and down, as they threw coats, car rugs, sleeping bags and a drunken nineteen-year-old in a broken circle for when their party legs finally gave way. This unfiltered DK Babydyke flunkied on at me about how cool Lucy was to have organised it all, 'absolutely marvellous'.

It suddenly hit me that it wasn't going to be like a party in the old Janie days, not like I thought it would be. I somehow thought I might get some of the adoration now that she wasn't there to collect it, not that I needed it, these were not the choice cuts of the human race. But it felt as if Janie had been rubbed out with a lame hand, leaving visible smudges. I could hear the lack of her, hear the voices that were not Janie's, hear no one calling her name, hear Lucy not asking Janie if she needed a beer, hear Boots not trying out something to say to her, hear other friends not asking for a light, hear strangers not asking for an intro, nothing, no Janie sound at all, just a screeching deficit. The amputated reflex left phantom pains, I suddenly hated the gap of it and switched to the half-litre of whiskey from my pocket.

Lucy was looking miserable but I knew that she didn't miss Janie, she missed herself, the Lucy bits that cared to keep razors blunt, pills unswallowed and buildings unjumped. As no one even had the decency to throw up yet, she was unable to prove herself essential, and I had to laugh — the famous Lucy reserves of stalwart condescension were seeping out to shit the mattress and show themselves for stinky and excess. One day it will dawn on our little Autarchick that the people can do their own doings without a Lucy standing helpful by to act as inspiration or an extra thumb.

As if to shake their autonomy in her miserable little face the people all horsed and tore gum and scratched and stirred with purpose, talked out guff while the tide washed closer in, while the city-bound wrote their names in the sand to be felt out by waves. No one needed to take charge of the sea.

'But I'm vegetarian.'

'Well, there might be other vegetarians here.'

'And what? I can eat them?'

'Oh, well, there's usually too much salad at these things. What was the name of your friend again?'

'The dead one, or the one that phoned?'

You couldn't make up shit like this. Lucy snagged me for a quick moan — as she'd predicted, no one had brought dip, though all vied for the office of chipster supreme, enough

Pringles and the like to stay snacking till the next New York potato famine, but a practical manbunch who looked just about smart enough to stand, had been devil-big clever on the hamburger front. I felt my stomach step closer to the food in solidarity, though not in a spirit of actual work, but I did explain to the industrious Dan that you could leave the skin on a sausage but had to remove the Saran Wrap from the ribs. No sooner was that sorted than I found myself gulping back a yawp of a laugh. Fat Molly was roaring at Sammy for the keys to Dec's car, as hostile grains of sand lodged in the fresh cream plasterwork of her acme construction, the whole landscape out to humiliate. And there was poor Sammy, still chatting madly to Boots in clumsy pursuit of a life-saving companion transplant.

More and still more came to people Lucy's composed tract of sand, scuffing the arrangement with their human shoes, no great Israelite hoards but enough to swell the ranks to over ninety, or to over twice forty-five, as a bifurcated crowd had bloomed, those who were of Janie and those who were not. I kept just outside, didn't feel as if I fitted in either. The camps were absolute as the Janie friends had magnetised, recounting corresponding stories about what dice went down at the shop, probably bitching about me, incidental kin, taking solace from like. Those who didn't know her slammed out jokes about Janie showing up in person, even scouting for some woman skank enough to look dead.

'OK,' I yelled, unable to take anymore, 'let's build this bloody fire.'

Which instantly realigned the crowd into muscle and meek.

The sky was darker now, and thick enough to hide the early stars. I noticed Boots, now alone, was staring so hard he could see past the night straight through to morning.

A few of the women, their mood growing smiling, and content to leave others take small glory for the food, started nitching sand-holes to keep their bottles cold, stopping only to denounce the over-efforts of their boys as they proved, by stacking high the pyre, that they were a superior make of men. Some superior brain set light to it before it was complete.

'Fuck me maybe for a fool, but is it us they want to impress?'

Wise up to it, girl, men only want to impress other men. They know that the ladies are on to them already, so they can only hope to fool their kind. A large placard which had once been a danger sign, a hardwood self-fulfilling prophesy felled by a high wind, was proving too heavy for the top of the fire and fell through the branches to the centre, letting fly sparks and shards of burning stick as it went down. The eager-beaver boys jump-fell back as if sharply hit, in vertical recoil like so many crazy beans, and after much shouting to cover their slight emasculation, they agreed that the fire was complete, and what a fine one. Arms folded across puffed chests, biggest bestest fire, boys in their back yard.

I was pleased to see Dec still sitting smoking his cigarette a small way off. As I went over to him, I was joined by Lucy, Josh and a couple of others; in fact, by the time we sat with Dec, we added up to a full Happy transplant, except of course for Italian Tony. I'd been keeping an eye out, almost convinced of a no-show, but part of me holding to my faith in the freshly tapped histrionic vein that seemed to run through all things Janie. I guess he was on all our minds as Josh started rehashing a two-week-old rumour that a large scoop of coke had found legs, just vanished into thin city air from Italian Tony's packing-plant home. Josh insisted (under proof of the force of the same insistence), that Janie must have used it to spur her to the final deed, 'must have' equalling 'did' in his self-reflexive reasoning. His conclusion, an equally circular presumption, was that Italian Tony had murdered her by leaving undercut stuff where she had access to it. Even when Lucy quoted the autopsy, negating any possibility that Janie cashed herself in after drugging it up to the gills, Josh stood firm.

'But that doesn't change the fact that there was stuff missing,' he gathered up the shreds of his argument and carried on weaving. Though not certain of the truth, he was sure that he was sure. 'I remember Italian Tony storming into Happy like a crazed mosquito....' Others agreed, disagreed, pitched their dime and Italian Tony grew with the fire's heat into Satan himself, fanned by their need for a devil to engage, all secure as this contra-virtue pushed them by his very existence closer into the woolly arms of angels.

I looked around for Boots — these energised contentions could set him to barking — but he remained away in the distance and further still from the shoreline he stood by.

The fire was now blazing like a fierce wind, gorging on the given stock of wood and soon to make its way through the reserves. The food was cooking on, much in the manner of the blame, doing its thing, spitting out juices in the mad heat inches from the flames, dripping its promise to fall on sand.

Another half-dozen of the Happy crew descended on us with coleslaw and apologies, their arrival doing nothing to calm the controversy as everyone had his or her own logic to emote. Sound went for broke as the justified louded it up in twos and threes, soldering an indefinite connection, their passion lumpen and ungratified. From Janie's family to chance strangers, all in turn fair blamed. Then some mimsy ass whined for peace, pooped out a moral take, 'It's supposed to be a celebration.'

Timely on the mood check, I'll give her that, Lucy put the brakes on the open ride to nowhere offering a burger and a million chocolate squares, slapping medium-rare ribs against the collective nose. My nose was twitching extra, and I wondered if Sammy had some talc. No chance of prizing him away from Fat Molly who was whining some media-corroborated concern about underdone meat to cover her opting out, and she sat with one arm free lest her tenure try to bolt, the other nobly holding a chocolate square for at least the next hour. For those like me who had to eat for biological reasons the stuff was great, even shut them all up for a bit.

I was pleased that Dec had avoided pointing any notion to the spat; he just sat there, sucking in information, disregarding hysterical leaps. But with a frequency common to nervous mothers, he kept looking out to the sea, probably out of concern for Boots, a concern that the fire alarm had addled the poor mutt to destruction. Boots still stood by the tideline, eyes to skyward, squaring the moon.

In time, deeper, colder night flew in, and there, by the grace of God or Lucy, sat me, Dec and the rest of the Janie-raked random collection, midway between the heat of the fire and the chill of the world, straddling notional life and death.

As we licked away at our grease-lathered lips and hand-wiped our salt chins, Josh rolled Christmas out early, stick shaped and welcome, like death's daddy handing out loaded cigars. And we began to smoke our demons into repose, and chowed on Lucy's vile attempt at baking, sugar mending hash hungers.

One of the newly arrived, a Spanish girl whose name I didn't catch during the twelve times she said it, mused at the scene. 'She must have been special. A special girl for all this.'

Was she? Apart from the fact that I needed her, needed to be her in the hope of being something, was she really all that special? The others granted it as given, answered, 'Very special', 'An amazing person', and led the newcomers over the emotional groundwork, but no one dissected the issue of 'special', afraid to deflate it with an impolitic dig of the scalpel.

As they all knew but none would say, Janie had not been the life and soul; she was funny in a Dorothy Parker kind of way, but no consummate sideshow. If stress was a funda-ment of special, she was there, fret-wound to snapping, bitten skin around her fingers, strung higher and tighter than telephone wire, such that the anxiety was infectious and you'd find your shoulders up around your ears purely on account of her proximity. Of course, for me, being my mother's reincarnation, she transcended all that, and she was like me in some ways, fit to dance holes in the dance-floor, to self-pollute to passing out, and then to meet and recover body and self-respect over too much coffee. Any quirks sat the easy side of odd. But special?

The crowd would pillow and blanket her whenever she fell, and even when she merely looked as if she might, which made plenty enough for Lucy and others like her. Janie was safe and snug as burdens go, made them feel all useful. Crude bind was that her death meant they'd failed, especially those impotent in caring, who'd been side-stepping contact since she left the hospital. The failure feeling was compounded when her body was stolen, hardening the bond between the forsaken dead and the careless living.

They didn't notice her as I did when she was alive, now Janie was infinitely more valuable because she was forever out of reach, human candy fallen down the drain. With the notions of murder, drugs and black markets now added to the pan, her value surged anew. Amazing. Incredible person.

Dead is a big difference, difference is special, Janie was a secular celebrity.

As if proving my thoughts as I had them, Josh turned loose his photographs of Janie now that he was way too shot to care if people cried.

'Where's your camera, Josh?' a question Fat Molly's disappointed vanity never failed to ask. As always, Josh shammed a smile kindly, and explained to Molly that he wasn't working that night, although the incentive to counter-order cappuccino from the skinny-ass fool was growing absolute under each such meeting.

Sammy passed the photos along unseen.

'Did she have any kids?' asked Bethany, a teenage mother of three.

'No, no kids. I guess that's one blessing,' said Lucy.

'How do you know?' Sammy jumped at Lucy, more in Fat Molly's style than his own.

'Well, she didn't.'

'That's a good thing,' nodded Bethany, no doubt thinking of the dearth of people to mind her own toddler brats who were probably at that moment painting the walls with Sunny Delight under the dubious charge of the telephone-trussed fourteen-year-old next-door.

'She doesn't look like the type to kill herself,' said the Spanish girl.

'Suicides don't have to look dead weeks in advance, you know,' Fat Molly sighed patronisingly.

'I think you're right,' Sammy said. 'She wouldn't have killed herself.'

'What then? She slipped?' Fat Molly snapped, waving Sammy's sudden theory off like flies. I was really starting to enjoy myself as he slowly picked his decapitated head off the sand and returned it to his neck, with no attempt to operate it this time.

'She was so wonderful, in her way,' sighed Fat Molly to soften her most recent barb.

Then, just as it built, the conversation reverted to things too mundane to be remembered, so I brought a plate of ribs down to Boots, more as an escape charge than a mercy mission. Not taking my offering, he passed me a sort of plastic patch, small and plain. I had no idea.

'Er, weird little patches for fifty?'

He had gone twitching into himself.

'Boots? What is this?'

He was glancing nervously back at the crowd.

'Do I eat it, fuck it, wear it, what? Hello?'

'It's for detecting poison gas, the type you can't smell or see. I can't remember the name of it.'

'Well, can you try and remember? I like to be on first-name terms with the enemy.'

'They know I'm onto them, and they're trying to get me before I have enough proof.'

'Who, Italian Tony and his friends?'

I sat a few feet upwind of him as he stood to exacting attention. We made for an improbable nightwatch as we scrutinised the waves, looking out over the sea for any seditious approach from the far side, and letting the noise of the campfire recede, until the less assiduous sentry (namely me) needed a refill. Besides, I was worried that my own natural isolation might be somehow related to his.

It was too dark away from the fire to see his face properly, and I was glad of this. His food had gone untouched and lay spoiled in the sand.

'Come on back to the fire, you might as well get poisoned on a full stomach — Lucy's making marshmallow sticks.'

His feet moved slowly, sinking a little in the sand as he followed me back, but his mind was still lost out over or under the waves somewhere.

A marshmallow cure for paranoid schizophrenia? Must fax the *American Journal of Psychiatric Medicine* with that one, get some award.

Leaving Boots at the edge of the fire with a beer, I went to grab the last of the spliff as it flew, and to chew the strangeness of the night with some fugee reveller a while.

The fire was stronger but had lost its youthful erratic inclination to flare and spit, so the more dextrous (a scant count at this stage) lobbed foil-wrapped fruit into its edges, the others co-ordinated adequate only to watching. I was getting squiffy, but Dec belonged to the able; lush as he was, his liver was quicker on account of the practice, hardened to the poison though devoted to the kick. Lucy, on the other hand, had swapped her self-possession for two small beers. She was twisting his ear so I just had to listen in.

'You see, I presumed,' she said, spitting out each bite of word, 'that an emergency would cancel out accents, but Mr Kelly could have been auditioning for a life in Japan....'

'Well, my Dad's Irish and we lived there when we were kids,' Dec said. 'So, I can catch the accent if it's flying slow. Did you talk to her parents often?'

'Only twice, once per crisis.'

'But why was she left here after the first time? Didn't they want to fetch her home to see a doctor there?'

He was good, getting the info from Lucy without getting helped.

'I reckon they'd worn through the Irish doctors and thought to give the Americans a turn. Anyway, it's pretty obvious now that she wanted to go all along — it was just a matter of time.'

'So why didn't you sing out when they were railing on that Italian Tony guy tonight? Jesus, they could lynch the poor bastard if he shows.'

I chimed in before Lucy's reasonableness had a chance to irritate me. 'With their way, the blame sits elsewhere,' I said. 'It's someone else's defect lurking at the end of the pointing finger. Italian Tony did it so we can all go home blessed, forgiven and free.'

The photographs bypassed us due to the lolling arrangements, but they had just reached the ash-smeared hand of the buzzcut blond, only to be recalled by Josh in haste before they could get as far as Boots. The blond guy had donated his efforts as chief stoker for the night, the excuse to flex a divested bicep or two, muscle up to single women and other availables who'd since paired off with the verbally articulate, and the semi-so. 'She was a tiny little thing,' he quietly said, surrendering her to the box.

To cover the cover-up, Lucy asked if anyone wanted more food, so, with an urgent need to compete, Fat Molly commanded Sammy to fetch the pavlova from the car. Dec said he'd go with him; the lock could be tricky at times. I said I'd go too, to make sure they didn't drop it.

Lucy then headed off alone by the shore, no doubt motivated by the couples who had headed for bouncy cars, or private pockets in the dunes to exfoliate their interesting bits, hoping Josh might follow. She'd told me earlier that if he didn't force himself on her, then she might just submit to him in any case, gracefully accepting, so making him believe he had offered. It worked with the coffee tab, why not with sex?

The fire was dimming, slow licks and soft molten bake of orange and touches of grey.

Retrieving a paper cup taped flat beneath the driver's seat, Dec opened up the amended water tank and scooped out the vodka he had stashed inside. He welcomed Sammy and me to his executive bar: 'Bottles are so conspicuous, don't you find?' The three of us then sat on the hood, backs against the windscreen, and drank.

'Sometimes it's better to drink alone, no one judging your alacrity or sizing your amount.'

And I felt so good to be included in his aloneness. However, our bartalk was abruptly cut back by this huge and blaring noise, the shouting from the beach so loud that we threw back the drink to return to the fun, forgetting the cake.

I later discovered that everyone had been watching Lucy at the water's edge, wondering if anything was wrong, as it was so unlike her to act unannounced without obvious practical reason.

So most were facing away when Boots went for a head-crash and felt into the fire. Josh was to tell me that he read it in his younger brother Adrian's eyes as they narrowed in a snap to close out the show, the fall too swift for him to voice the sight, save a sharp noise from his chest. In a second, all heads were back. Boots had both his hands in the fire and had left them there. He didn't scream with pain, or pull away, instinct had been overridden by conditioning, layers of fatter pain sheathed his nerves.

As we ran toward the fire, it felt like a large slice of forever before someone pulled him backwards away from it, although it was probably only a second or two. In those following moments as he lay there, shaking wildly, a hundred breaths were held and then let go, released in a rage of orders growing louder as we raced closer:

'Put his hands in the sea!' 'Salt water won't help!' 'God, what happened?' 'He's OK.' 'Call an ambulance. Who has a

phone?' 'Turn him on his back!' 'Jesus, what was he doing?'
— it all came through as a roar from the sea, the words too
stepped and layered to make sense.

We could see what madness had played out as we ran,
and on reaching the point of insanity, at the same time as
Lucy arrived unfit to command from the shore, Dec ripped
the extra shirt from around his waist, submerged it in a
cooler where the ice had relaxed into water, and wrapped it
around Boots' screaming hands. Everyone stepped back to
make room for his authority. He then hauled Boots up in a
fireman's lift and was halfway to the car before I came to
myself, grabbed the cooler, and ran in their track.

With that, the whole mob started running for the car,
almost the hundred together, save the blond guy who was
stamping out the fire, punishing it for what had just happened. The fire bled fruit and died. Some of the absconded
couples had heard and were emerging, tucking themselves
in as they ran, others oblivious.

Dec piled Boots into the passenger seat while I un-
ceremoniously threw the pavlova into Fat Molly's arms and
climbed into the back. Dec was already pulling out as Lucy
jumped in beside me. But then it was as if we all blinked
together only to wake into something different, a serious
world where fire hurt and people were heavy. I lashed a look
back and saw the crowd; they might have been sending us
off on a cruise, except no one was waving. I wished we
could take their enormity along, to mainstay the flight as we
drove like needles toward some style of redress or defeat.
We pushed on the first two minutes through the anacoustic
zone, total silence but for gasping, our lungs catching up

with the air we'd already breathed on the run. My ability to ride such an ebb was out cold, way far back on the beach somewhere, four or so hours behind me.

Lucy broke the silence with nothing helpful as Dec bruised his shoe against the gas, full-floored the pedal from the moment we hit solid road. Boots was panting shallow enough for a good view to the bottom of his pain, slumped against the passenger door, eyes wide open like a dead man's, his head flopped, face against the window, which buddy-breathed in tempo, fogging and clearing in time with his mouth. The damp shirt compress had fallen from the burn, given up the task entirely, so I vaulted over in beside the scalded thing, the closeness killing me. Lucy was all ideas about top buttons and pulses and butter so I had to ask in my pissy voice before she'd hand over the cooler, which she did after briefly talking it through with herself.

Dec said (less freight in his voice than mine) to keep his hands immersed, but the water had already grown warm from the burn, we could brew coffee from it before too long, and the vile object refused to comply with anything that might lead to his relief. You could see his hands changing, swellings and twitches, looking so red-ugly shiny that I didn't want them touching against any part of me, afraid they had caught enough fire to scorch and smoke-stain with the briefest contact, that the burn might catch and run mould-like over my skin.

Nursing isn't best accomplished from the house next door, but the thought of those blister fingers made me ill, and passing out would not have been helpful right then. So I stretched for the glove compartment, to fish out some gloves

Judy May Murphy

or a plastic bag, knowing it was an unnatural assumption, as if anything could live there except bathroom tissue and apple cores. Dec's arm reached across me as he saw what I attempted, and I presumed he was helping with the clasp. But before he could cross my reach, the book had already fallen out, resting on Boots' leg a moment before falling to the floor.

It went to that curbed quiet again.

The book lay larger than the Domesday roll on the floor of the car, not moving but working nonetheless. At the sight of his own Janie notebook having followed him there, proof of the conspiracy, Boots found the energy of the damned and opened the door to leave along the speeding highway. Unbeefed as he was on account of not eating, I found myself the stronger, and pulled him back in — a cruelty I knew, another barbarism loosed from my stow. Staring at it there under my stranglehold, seeing his handwriting large on the front, he started to whine, an anthem of the fucked with neither tune nor words nor end.

The true impetus hidden from where she sat knowing, Lucy declared his natural endorphins in decline. I had begun to feel a gob of pity in my throat and wondered if maybe mine were too, finally.

As surreptitiously as possible — mood, climate, décor, audience and the like considered — I kick-slid the notebook to Dec, with Boots watching it as if it were possessed. Once it was safely under the driver's seat (notebook and owner out of sight and out of mind, respectively), I relaxed back to a heart attack state. Boots looked at me for the traitor I possibly was as I held him by the elbows ducking his gaze, afraid that his look would burn me worse than his hands.

Soon came the odour of charred flesh, the smell of obsession, burning away nicely as it's supposed to. Lucy opened a window, two inches in case he could slip through, but the stench stayed where it belonged, in the company of evil.

The hospital was well signposted but Lucy navigated towards it as if she alone could read. Accident and Emergency shone for the finding. In she ran to pull at the first unfortunate and raise a reception committee, from orderlies to interns, fund managers, gastroenterologists — she'd stop nothing short of digging up Hippocrates himself. This we knew as we guided Boots to his next affliction.

As we and the medics converged at the doors, it was plain that none of the coats nearly matched us for disquiet. They were so toughened they could probably eat an omelette off the stomach of a plague victim, so we surrendered a large eggy slice of anxiety as they started with their tics and pins and touches, and their Latin and their numbers, to let us know they were expert enough. The cooler (which for some reason I now wished was a more respectful colour than red) had become a splint, holding the adventure in a ritual to stop the form of it from snapping altogether, serving us more than the burning man in its temperate state. So this we also handed over to their indifference along with its sorry appendage.

'He's done himself a mischief,' said Dec.

'Good job,' whistled the doctor looking at the water-covered hands.

'Does he mean us or Boots?' asked Dec as they disappeared off to attend to the fry.

'He means you with the water,' I said. 'Doctors aren't allowed to be sarcastic.'

'Well, you did most of it. I mainly just drove. Well done,' he said, 'and I mean that in a most doctorly way.'

He must have guessed that it didn't come natural. Women like Lucy, most women in fact, really want to ease the pain, in like Flynn with the one-hand hugs, sticky bandages and lukewarm sugared tea, making wheelchairs out of plastic cups and biscuit tins, or whatever. It's like they need a little lick at the infection, need to partake of the pain for the cleansing or the distraction or the attention it secures. But in my humble overdue book, a person's pain is just that, their pain, so I'm last in with the first aid, not so hot on the saving and remedy rôle. I often think I'm only called woman by the mercy of someone who judges on the basis of what could have been. Even Dec knew better.

'How did you know to do all that anyway?'

'We had emergency medical training for the airport job.'

I'd nicked a spliff which we stayed outside to smoke as Lucy entertained herself inside as nurse's little helper.

'Hairy moment back there with the notebook,' said Dec.

'I thought you were leaving that back the other morning?'

'I tried to. I was waiting outside his door for him to come out, then snuck a peek and got to reading it, and by the time he left I was so far in that I needed to finish. I prefer a book when I know the ending — it's much less draining that way. I planned to give him a ride home tonight and slip it back then.'

'So is his version of Janie the same as your friend's?'

'It's not really about Janie, though, is it?'

Just then a doctor called us in for a soft-spoken session about what to do with Boots. The psych team was being bleeped in, and the front-line must have been wielding the needle as we could no longer hear his protestations. I had no insight to offer — this had smacked me out of nowhere. I was frankly disappointed; I really would have thought Boots could do all this in computer simulation, virtual self-abuse. After all, as Dec had obviously gleaned, it wasn't about the real Janie for Boots; she was a byte-sized artifice for him; he'd probably have fainted if he'd ever seen her tits. Some people were just made to stay home and type.

'He's gone mad,' I said, knowing that doctors hate you to use the lingo flippantly since it took them so many years to master it.

'He certainly is experiencing some psychological disturbance. The burns are moderately severe although confined to his hands, and will take some time to heal. So we have to decide whether to keep him here or move him on to somewhere else where they'd be better equipped to treat him.'

It was pretty clear that I had expended my small productive value with the drive over, so he took Lucy and Dec off to make some phonecalls, as each said they could help. Perhaps they had to mitigate some phantom guilt. Lucy was probably so ashamed at her party's outcome that she'd need to go straight to OR and donate all her organs, effective immediately.

I think I'd started to fall asleep when they came back out.

'I did all this the last time too, with Janie; next time its someone else's turn,' she said, uncharacteristically surrendering the world into the well-meant molestations of some other eager acolyte.

Removing him to the clinical ward of a private mental hospital sounded wonderfully efficient — transference is a marvellous substitute, almost comes across as achievement. Lucy was excited that the place she suggested was the same place Janie had been and, as if it doubled and sanctioned the logic, Dec had suggested it too. They'd called Boots' sister in Wisconsin who agreed they should send him there.

'How did you get her number?'

'I have my Christmas card list on me.'

It was barely summer. I didn't even ask.

Cans of the soda no one likes, gritty cups of grey coffee and cigarettes we couldn't even taste — these entertained us until the main attraction. I don't normally smoke regular sticks, but it's obligatory in hospital if you aren't the patient, that and pacing. The paperwork done, the phonecalls made, the invalid was rolled out to a waiting mini-ambulance. Even in his horse-tranq sedation, he turned his eyes on me and said, 'That's not Janie. She killed Janie and took her for herself, she has eaten her. She is not Janie, she is not Janie.'

Lucy pressed my arm in unnecessary condolence as Dec shook his head and smiled at me.

We trooped back inside to be checked over in case of shock, but the only shock was on the face of the elderly bullkisser nurse when we walked in reeking of hash and beer and each other.

The journey back to Manhattan was a ghostly affair as the sceptre of the burned man whistled through the engine sounds. Lucy was itemising each step as if we'd missed it, and then made a near exact copy aloud of everything the doctor had said to us all, as if she'd been listening with special magic ears and had to translate for us mortals. Just when I'd almost phased her out, she said how glad she was that they were sending him to the same place as Janie.

'How good a place can it be, in that case?'

'Janie was fine just after she left.'

'Jesus. Suck on a fuckin' serum, girl, and see it like it is. If you buy a fresh bread in the morning and find it mould-ridden later that night, is that acceptable? No. Jesus, I wish I hadn't mentioned bread, I'm starving.'

Lucy saw another chance to save.

'We could swing by the beach,' she said. 'There might be some chocolate Rice Krispie squares left.'

'No, I'm sure they were all eaten even before we left.'

Dec can pull it and still sound so sincere.

We dropped Lucy off. It took five goes to escape her ideas.

'This whole thing is fucked,' he said.

'Not nearly enough for my pleasure, my dear; I'm off to find Italian Tony in the morning,' I responded, wondering how my thoughts got so aloud. 'See if he can defend himself, maybe find out the level on the drugs.'

'Don't, don't do that. It'll just get him excited and then he'll stab somebody and then someone will shoot someone else, and we'll all be sweeping up for months.'

'All the better,' I said. 'That way we can keep it mixing till some virgin pieces shape out. Conversation makes men anxious, someone's bound to break their pledge. Right now, with the burgers and beer, it's all too safe, it needs wrenching. I tell you, some party pig back there knows more than the rest.'

He parked the car in a tow zone where it was quiet, and looked at me for what seemed like forever before recovering a flask from its duct-tape under the dash.

'Me,' he said. 'I know more than the rest for a start, so you can't shake it like that or I'll be put away and you'll have a lifetime of writing letters and smuggling dope to me inside homemade gift items like calendars and cookies and things.'

He slammed a good half the flask. I smiled the one I know makes people nervous.

'I'm going to tell you something important,' he said, 'partly in the hope that you'll leave it all lie, partly because Jim won't answer my calls and it's driving me to milk, and partly because your insanity is so fucking infectious.'

He handed me the flask and began.

Gardener Jim (Dec explained, voice prone and eyes closed heavy) had a black market going on the slick, dealing in patients' medication and their weekly allowance of hospital dollars and real money, exchanging them for whatever favours he could meet: magazines and messages, drink and harder, tickets and clothes to escape in. Sometimes their affliction made them easier to con. One guy surrendered the bulk of his stipend for coffee, Jim doing nothing to calm his fears about them poisoning the stuff at the big house. Another paid him big money for handing strange epistles directly to God, but it became work when receipts were required from God in return.

Apparently Janie and Gardener Jim had no money games on the go, but when she was being acquitted, or whatever the term is, waiting for a friend to drive her back to the city, she'd gone down to the lake and said she had to ask a difficult favour of him. Not having much in the way of caring bones or scruples, but always open to a plan, he'd said, 'Name it, whatever, it's done.' To which she'd said she'd brief him closer to his function.

Knowing how the patients, whether ill or seeming cured, had heads full of multicamerous worlds where all sorts of things did and didn't translate into reality, he'd thought no more of it. A few weeks later, curiosity still on hold, he'd found a small tote bag sitting in his shed, with a note attached. He presumed it was a rather large package for God, and first opened the note in case the bag contained something too earthly to unfold into a tight space.

In the note, Janie explained that she had come there late in the afternoon, and would be dead by the time of his reading it. She reminded him of his promise of help. She said he was to find her body, take it to the sea, and sink it, so it could never rise to the ugly surface again. That's what she called all this, the ugly surface. The payment in the bag was coke enough for a Hollywood year. Jim's strange own-fashioned kind of ethical code was one he always stuck to, so there was no question now of going back, the thought of the drug money propelling his ethic on nicely.

He couldn't filch and transport the body alone, and, knowing Dec was indebted and that he had a past for that class of adventure, he'd asked him to co-crime for a straight-down split. He'd give Dec half the wherewithal once the job was done.

Jim had been well tooled up — wire-cutters, body bag, flashlight — and had managed to scope the layout during the service, even snip a wire in the gents while Dec guarded the door. But the midnight hour spooked him when it came to the application, and the one vital detail, the taking of the body, had wracked his nerves to shit.

So, when they'd hit the dumping juncture, Gardener Jim could not find enough red gut inside of him to relinquish the very same body which he had so not wanted tenure of an hour before. They'd had to pick a place empty of cars and eyes, some barren spot along the shore, but Jim, in his freak had refused all ideal suggestions, until Dec had said they might as well take the body home, lie it on the window-sill to keep out the draft. They'd driven up and down the coast for hours, near enough to where the bonfire was.

Jim had been constantly sobbing since his initial fear of hand-on-shoulder capture had worn off. He was a mess, couldn't do it, he was close to turning the whole venture in. Instead he'd left Dec to salt and pepper the task alone on a stone string of coast too thin to call a beach and only dirt track behind — left him with the body, a fifty, and the promise of the whole white stash, before driving back up the ghost road to the hospital to inveigle a handful of siesta-style drugs.

Dec and dead Janie were the only two people in the world. He'd sat alongside as she lay in a strew of seaweed edging the waves. Like a bridegroom wanting to see her face before embarking on the act that would tie them forever, he'd placed his hand on the shroud to trace its contours, touching through to her face, to how she might have looked when she needed this enough to ask the promise. Blind to the look of her, he'd pared back the gauze, believing that if he could stare her in the dead eye she could advance him to the deed. But the person was gone from the face. He'd then caught a glint of tiny gold at her neck, and, as if not to wake a sleeping child, had drawn out a claddagh on a thin gold chain, shining with more life than the brightest eyes. He knew the sign of friendship well, and in it could read how she lived past her end in the ways and rememberings of others. He took it from the wane of her, wore it for the strength.

I listened to Dec lost in Janie, and wished I had saved the joint as he described how he had tried to say a prayer, but didn't know any that meant anything. So he'd sung this song his Dad would roll out when under the sway of a late pint. He sang a line of it again there in the tow zone and I almost couldn't listen:

'The water is wide and I can't cross o'er, and neither have I wings to fly....'

The body bag weighted down with helpful stones, he'd wanted to stay forever with her living in the ocean as he'd walked shoulder deep out into the water, and placed her there as the tide turned back to the bigger sea. He'd shivered near the water's edge for the rest of the night and half that morning, and when she hadn't returned on the next full tide he had walked the dirt-track back to the road.

I handed him the flask of deliverance.

An old trucker man knew what shape suffering wore, and had driven him to a station; no questions, even of the mundane kind, were asked of him, nor was he looked at enough that the trucker man might one day have anything to tell.

He sucked it dry.

He couldn't keep the claddagh, knowing there were people who had earned a wider right, and, having scared Jim into finding her last home address, he'd mailed it to whichever friend stumbled on it first.

Only then did I know what Sammy was holding in Happy, and wanted it enough to turn time back to fetch it. I'd swap all the other papers, photographs and clothes, just for that little gold heart.

He'd made straight for the laundromat to wash the sea and the grief from his clothes that day, and on seeing me there he couldn't walk away, not now that he was connected. And the rest, as the man said, is known.

'And did you get the coke?'

'It felt like a brass cold nerve to demand it after that. It's still at the hospital with Jim.'

'Did you suggest that place for Boots or did Lucy?'

'Sort of both — we kind of clashed in a consensus with the doctor.'

'That was some keen bid there, let me tell you. You've a good reason now to cover stopping by your friend, a chance to make it handy with the payment.'

My habit was starved of its feed and I was beholden enough to mother it to saturation, to poke around there for big Janie, but Dec seemed less than keen on the junket and puzzled at my interest.

'What is it you want? A cut?'

'No, no cut. My appetites are more of an acquired taste.'

Drink settled and, conversation slowed, we realised it was morning.

'Anything else you need to tell me?' I asked, hoping he'd emptied his surprise sack for the night, my eyes closing, shuttering my bulging head.

'Yeah, you did have two salads, one as a starter and one with your lasagne. And I have a question for you, too.'

'Fire away.'

'Did you kill Janie?'

'I thought it was going to be a restaurant question.'

I called Josh the next morning and got the rest of the story.

After we had bolted in the car, it was all quiet but for dune stragglers asking what had gone on.

Wise in the aftermath, everyone was saying they just knew he was ripe for a fall, and lighting stress-relief cigarettes by the dozen as they catechised his manner and mildly reprimanded themselves for doing nothing, making up for that oversight by talking it over thoroughly.

Then they began to drift towards their own cars or back to the beach, where the music had been killed and the fun was over, sat on by a big bad move, rolling up their sleeping bags, leaving their unopened cans, touching the unused condoms in their pockets, and heading home, suddenly sober.

Stranded without transport, and with Sammy standing stupid alongside, Fat Molly had stood in the dark, holding the pavlova, tears running down her face, probably thinking what perfect revenge Janie had wreaked on her for being such a wench. Fat Molly was downed. She whipped a snarl at Sammy to find her a ride home.

Some time later, Josh and his brother, Adrian, sat a long distance from the remaining others, smoking, and as quiet a space as the night had seen.

'Do you know what sun dogs are, little brother?'

'Yeah, *The Deer Hunter* thing,' said Adrian, wondering why they weren't heading home. 'That thing where there's clear circles round the sun.'

'They call them sun dogs because it's like mad dogs chasing each other's tails around the sun. It's supposed to be a bad omen.'

'Did you ever see that?'

'No,' said Josh, 'but I did see moon dogs.'

'When was that?'

'Tonight,' said Josh, pointing up at what no one else but Boots had noticed — a white moon full overhead, a halo hanging round it from the mad-dog path.

'Guess the bad luck fell to Boots,' Adrian said, lying back to watch the ring around the moon.

'No, those are the lucky ones, the moon dogs are.'

'Don't see how.'

Josh asked me if I could see that, and I told him I didn't believe in luck, just action.

Two hours on from that, the rescue car hadn't returned (we were pacing the corridor and drinking plastic coffees at that point), so, origami-style, they had squeezed inside the car. Josh had switched funny to off, out of respect for the happening.

This time he had spoken without the benefit of conviction.

'I didn't know Boots knew her that well, I didn't know. I thought he'd do fine on the tranqs; the doctor said they'd make him drowsy so I thought that was the deal — no one said nothing about freaky.'

'Can people die from burns like that?' asked Fat Molly.

'I hope so,' said Josh.

'That's an awful thing to say!'

'Is it?'

He echoed the question to me and I told him that I thought death was kind, to the dead at least.

Janie

She surrounds herself with people, collects them like pebbles to keep herself safe from dreaming. But if you watch the friends for long enough, you can see that she stands alone. Her lip no longer firm, her skin blue-white, the young woman drags her tiny body and her heavy shoes down the avenues, drowsy from too much sleep, and goes into a café that will never close. Most days she eats breakfast, but half-sized, sparking comments from all. She will never admit to them her secret ritual, not knowing that they already know.

She goes with them as they potter about in the markets or cafés, and when they go to the conservatory where the symphonies are, listening to the music — strings, wood-wind, brass — or to hollow plays which they will pack with meaning, squashing in a poetry session or club, depending on the betterment they plan for that day.

But soon she tires of the adventures in the city, especially now that the play has left town without her, and goes home to her apartment to curl up on her large bed and wonder where the magic can be found.

She feels lost without the wake-up cup of tea from her father, without shopping trips to town with her mother and aunts. No one watches her eat dinner most nights now, no one takes her on a drive through the Wicklow mountains, no one turns off the hall light to mark the time for sleep. She has no book to bind to as when she was young, no novel to rescue her back to days of old where she could rest a few hours in parlour talk, with horsebacked men, and news of the regiment and of hats. There is no filthy strand to walk at night, no black suede coat to hold her if one should appear.

She is slowed, she is driftwood beached where once she was a sand-speck tossed in the wind.

Now she has no purpose to her days and weeks, no performance to attend, all structure pulled loose like an old spider's web. Life runs rampant, tumbles at the endless edges and over. Time is one vast blue, where once it was marked into mouthfuls the easier to take the bitter draught. No demarcations, she is everywhere, all control lost, save for a few small places where the day is pinned to certain tangible sites, like the start of the traffic, and the letter which arrives, cheque enclosed, without fail.

She is sitting in the livingroom to read the letter, one piece of normality to stabilise the day, thinking as she opens it that maybe it is time to return to them, to confess her life for the failure that it is, when, as if to nail time drastically to the unravelling fabric of life, the words strike her, fierce in their simple way. Barbarism begins at home they say.

Her parents (meaning her mother) have written that they are thinking of returning to the farmhouse that summer, and ask her whether she remembers it or not, throwing in some references to people and landmarks she is sure she never knew. Does she remember it? The question has her laughing a small but hideous laugh which turns into a cry that aches from the force of it, tears that are dry so deep are they drawn, the continuous moan gripped to her hard breathing.

And she knows she cannot go back.

This is what she always wished for, and now it can never be.

Next they tell her that her cousin just gave birth to a healthy baby boy, photograph on its way later, how lovely it is, first child from the younger generation....

She stumbles for the kitchen to fetch a pill to deaden the vein that throbs through her head. But there in the kitchen cupboard sits another cruel all-comer, a black new surprise to deeper brand the day, reinforcements, cankerful back-ups, loaded with harm. There sits a stack of children's cakes, yellow pink and white, sugar and cream in them enough to kill a horse.

She locks herself inside the kitchen with the key she jealously keeps, to play out the battle to the end. A picture of a baby boy swimming in front of her, she imagines her parents arriving at the farmhouse, and wandering down to walk her beach the next day where they speak to a local and ... perhaps she will only have one cake and then go to Happy for one margarita and then sleep one full night and awaken to a single new day full of hope ... speak to a local and ask whether the families who used to live here have all grown up and moved ... perhaps just another and then she will go ... perhaps...

She cannot stop; shaking she holds on for the ride. Twelve cakes eaten, the slide gathers momentum and her parents are entering the farmhouse again and the baby is growing and screaming red.

Chaos victorious, she is falling, pushed another few miles by the winds that gust to blow her further from safety. She fumbles her way through the stockpiles in the cupboard and the fridge, pushing the food in faster than she can swallow, and her parents walk the beach over and over, each time asking a different question, this time following the wolf-dog, this time combing the cave, this time watching out to sea. So hot now from the eating and the imagining, she strips down to an old nightshirt, leaving her clothes where they land on chairs and floor. Moving on to her flatmate's scant supplies, as her parents stand over a bundle in the sand, she eats fast through these also.

Too much pain to continue, belly tighter than a drum, she throws up into the bowls and plates from which she has taken the food, and, once the food is all consumed and all disgorged, she eats the vomited clods, and throws these up again also, this time not catching the issue but letting it fall where it will.

This time no peace comes crawling from the empty pit.

She is knocking her head against the kitchen counter, her white skin bleeding beneath; she can hear the sound but feels nothing. She takes up the carving knife and cuts her hair, she is nothing, she sheds handfuls over the floor and the table, leaving it where it lands, some sticking in the vomit, the rest on her shirt, the chairs and the floor. She can hear, a thousand miles in the distance, her flatmate arriving in, but the outer world is nothing but pale dreams, and no rescue drags her from this endless whirl.

She is humming and rocking as she cowers into a corner, drying vomit and cut hair down her arms, legs and shirt and on her feet. She sits on the floor between the cooker and wall and, one newly short hair at a time, she plucks random sections bald. Not stopping at her scalp, she pulls out every lash and balds each brow. For an hour she sits here, continues working round her head, plucking herself into a dead place.

Dear Me,

I will hide this letter from them, I have already told them too much. Do not let them take the dream away, do not let them cure your whole existence. When I stare into the water in the lake I feel the boat-boy is beside me. Only the gardener is there to stop me, but he will help me to get there in the end. I have a plan.

Love, Me

Aimee

*I*t was as little like a hospital as they could make it, which sort of gave the game away; they had frosted over the sickness with interesting décor and a pedigree cat. The whole hutch smacked of committees, moneyed women who came only on open day when all could acknowledge their magnanimous confession of practical uselessness.

We sloped in like some poor apology around four in the afternoon, hung concerned looks on our faces and wondered what Boots' real name was, as when claiming close association a first name is often beneficial. I was certain he'd said Sean in the notebook, but such places spunk off on euphemism so 'our friend' covered the job, and their allusions to 'the patient', in return, made me wonder if they'd only copped similar nominal success.

We were prepared by a buttoned-through nurse for a certain confusion (I presumed she meant his). He was heavily medicated, chemical redress for clawing at people and biting them after his hands were tied, an unfortunate but not unusual reaction, she said. He was unwell, she insisted with every second sentence, in case we thought it was a lifestyle choice or he'd been signed over to the arch-fiend in a sub-let deal gone sour.

I was ticcy as a windowed fly — supervised madness is

as fake as the nation gets, the old velvet-handcuff routine.

Boots offered no hellos so nor did we, seeking our protocol from a man gone to seed. He sat subdued in an armchair, none of the fury of the burning and the book, but apart from that and the Lysol smell, the day-and-a-half had done little for him. Dec and I perched on the edges of our comfy swallow-sofa like nervous blind-daters while he talked on in a holy-man tongue, an animal language that dripped from his mouth, touches of white at the edges, his struggle apparent against the sedation. His was a broken mind, any light glanced off it at all angles, making for a mess of messages which, even if rearranged word by word, would probably add up to only a different mess.

'How are you?' I ventured.

'Yes,' he replied (or rather, relocated), 'I am looking at a different play, a scene in a play with the sea, in a much of it is become my wifely person and due to troubles and roubles and the rent and all that, yes haven't got a red cent. But, of course, now I am referring to the Russian problem, from one table and to another table but, yes, and they all keep stretching and that's why there is the nature of the rushing thing, all too much really for the one name and her name is Janie which I may not be in the hand of things. Let alone all the other tests that have to be done about the gas and the other invisibles, her underwear, for example, and what with it being so cold. And several levels of possibly eight or even yes....'

An orderly walked in to take away a dangerous vase of flowers, shunting Boots back inside himself, where he spoke now only to the people we were deaf to, told the rest of the story to the dead if they would listen, mouth and pressure-gloved fingers moving with the local mandate of a medicine man, limbs still as logs, eyes deeper than the width of his head. He was slowed and confused, like a newly castrated dog; you'd almost prefer the wild version only you'd also like to safeguard your hide from untimely puncture. He was ended.

The nurse was ready with her kind expression when we returned; I tried to look nonchalant so that she'd put it away.

'Is he going to get better?' I asked as a matter of form, realising as I said it, that a better state than absolute insularity might not exist. She said something very nothing and looked to show us the over-polished hallway door when Dec explained that his friend James Whitby worked there. It hooked like a ten spot, and we were redirected out along the walkway to the lake.

We'd abandoned the length of the previous day to some difficult sleep, and during the upstate journey the fact that I was calmly basting disaster the better to taste it, and the equally cold fact that he'd served as handmaid to death, seemed to sit between us like an unpopular uncle. But now, since Boots had restored permission to gum-flap unspecific to decorum or theme, I asked Dec if he'd do the same for me in those straits, the same as he did for her, heaven forbid and all that.

'Would you?'

'I don't know. Probably. Until yesterday I would have said never again, but now I think I'd do it for anyone who asked. From this distance of days it feels as if I tucked her into bed and nothing more than that.'

'It's normal in India, you know.'

For this visit I'd garbed up in Janie clothes from in to out, my hair in her hat, and hoped Gardener Jim might think me her when he looked over from his moiling fallow. I hated him with every bone; he'd abandoned Janie in her hour, ripped her from rest and then defected when his thin will gave out. He was one great manful of hollow.

There, in plain view as we turned the corner path, was the lake, not more than a dirt puddle with delusions, the kind to induce a body to do the Shelley rather than the Wordsworth thing, and beside it a man standing with a garden rake and no loose anything to gather but air. He was smoking a cigarette, out of boredom as much as addiction it seemed. He could see us approaching but didn't break a move, continuously watching as we neared from so agonising a distance that, by the time we were twenty feet away, I wished I could remember a dance routine.

He was medium square set and freckled, with the style of eyes to typecast him a victim or a perv, dark red hair and red overalls to clash. His reception was no more correct than Boots' had been, a silent host, like a QVC port-a-guru, a Sammy on much-fatter drugs. Evincing no reaction of any colour, he led us back toward a shed. As we walked, I realised what sense it made that she would go to him for help. Serenity, though dull, can be the only place abundant enough in which to lose the worst of the worst within its creases.

The sound of our shoes on the gravel was thunderous in the void, but everything I thought to say, my tongue sent back to my head unsaid with a great big query over it. Since when did I do diplomacy? Curiouser and curiouser, as some manic-dep sister once said.

We sat drinking Dec's old ever-present with Gardener Jim in the janitor's den; it was dusty enough that if you sat too still you'd leave a portrait of yourself in silhouette.

'She knows,' Dec said, meaning me, which broke the silence all right, but then we all just sat around gazing at the shatter. There was slim chance of my promotion to some more trusted shelf in that hut, so, draining my tin mug, I said I'd go for a scratch around the grounds, and no one insisted I stay. And no one saw that I slipped for my road-ease the bundle of keys he'd tagged to a nail inside the door.

The grounds and the corridors all seemed strangely empty — maybe madness has a low season. It looked exactly how I always imagined purgatory would: dull lights and high-backed chairs, endurable if you were expecting to be checked out to heaven, yet obtuse enough to encourage you out to your hell. It was a polished-oak holding-pen, white-washed iron bars on the damask-curtained windows. Good thing Janie had the boat-boy to divert her, an extrinsic perfection to disappear off to when the coloured curtains began to bleed and the stillness of the lake was barred with spades.

Boat-boys. Pinkly wish things, giddysticks to stave into an oncoming life. Castles in the air are undeniably the bulwark for the times; build them higher than skies we do, all-times adobe with the muck from our livings and our final straws. But Janie went to live in hers, so they stamped her ass defective, purely on account of being over-ambitious in the domicile zone. Tough verdict, considering.

The corridors were wide and long and still I met no one of either mental persuasion. The clerical staff must have bunked off to their lunatic-free homes, while the nursing staff were probably pleated around some problem with their special faces showing. Or could be this duck trap was just fuckin' huge. It felt as if I was creeping in her path, which now narrowed, its boarders more precise, its direction clear.

The sign on the door read simply FILE ROOM, making me wonder what my sign would say.

The instant the fifth key opened it, I tapped the thrill that Dec had enthused about.

The room was dominated by a solid wall of letter-indexed drawers, big with files, paper bridges to span the abyss, K for Kelly sitting halfway along. The plastic pouches within were variously thin (as if for the pedestrian depressions of the daughter of an over-anxious multi-middle couple), or fat (for a lifelong compound complexity such that the whole family had long since turned visits into intent). I wondered if, being bulimic, Janie's file would be full or almost empty.

But she wasn't to be found there at all. Some stiffy-shirt bunch of underwriters must have whistled her notes up to the city, which I'd now have to track down, soon rivalling Dec on the forced-entry front. Then, saving me from catsuits and a life of further crime, I saw a special cabinet off to the side, marked 'Late Patients' in respectful leaky biro. I've never understood why they call dead people 'the late whoever'; it's like they're trying to kid themselves that the person isn't there because they missed the bus.

I began to flick through the deceased, enough to need to index, but Janet Kelly was easy to find, bound up in a plastic pouch in a black-crossed cardboard folder. Janie evidence, gathered and marked in a file named dead. You'd wonder if they'd made any effort. A few double-spaced sheaves of their own notes and some loose pages of patient contributions, or whatever name they give to offerings coerced from the ill.

I recognised her writing from the 'Dear me' letters, although it had shrunk under the pressure. She wrote tiny, tiny like those ants you think can crawl inside your skin.

The first Janied sheet of paper caught me up sharp because its title was prophetically amiss, and kind of funny outside the circumstances: KILLING YOURSELF IS JUST NOT POLITE, NOT THE DONE THING. A placatory essay, no doubt to gain some freedom like being allowed to close the bathroom door, written against their supportive scolding.

'Suicide is a very messy business altogether,' it read. 'Until they launch a speciality cleaning service that's content to sweep around the body and fluff the concluding pillow before the official finding, it will remain a logistical nightmare. And you wouldn't want to stain anything important, now, would you? Please, people have better things to be doing than getting down at your blood with a squeegee mop. The alternatives are rather attractive, but it's impossible to go down the same road twice, stargates get closed down. Once you have breathed salt water to your lungs, your legs will not gladly carry you there again, and as mentioned above, the open-artery thing is not a happy option.'

Maybe not so funny.

Next was a page almost obscured by the medical commentary that strangled the life from what she was trying to say, classified any meaning down to total subjugation, as the experts wrote comments in the margins, the safest place for their kind, in large looping letters in red.

'They tell me to have hope, but that is the one thing I have in abundance. This hope, when I let it, takes over all my functions, does my living for me and I only make sense as a helpless thing attached to it. Which is the parasite, which the host?' Her words peered through their critique. 'Move on, they say. But life is neither linear nor progressive, moving on is completely overrated, it's back we all need to go, back to happy. Advance, little Janie, to the first beginning, fall back into the boat-boy. This death by dreaming is a slow, slow end.'

Once again, a glance at the boat-boy and he's gone, one quick peep and the quarter falls. I listened out for the carpeted tread of anyone out to unhitch me from my information. Hearing none, I still moved to a new, visible space on the floor between the small filing cabinet and the desk, feeling safer as children do with cushions on their head.

The doctor notes were more clinical than concerned, day-by-timeclock-day accounts of diet and medication, then small pieces of her history, as if she were feeding herself to them carefully lest they choke on her. Until finally I found her horrible reality, written up like a drug detail, reduced from city-breaker cyclone into a gentle puff from an educated pen.

'Evidence of depression starting at puberty, raped and pregnant at age eighteen, no counselling received, unknown whether child was brought to term.'

Digging through various doctors' repetitions, the coveted matter strapped against the tedious, a base string of truth did out, of a kind to turn you on full time to mendacity.

On vacation with her parents in Portugal, Janie Kelly stood one night beside the shore, alone, looking out to sea. Out of a quiet town road a stranger came and asked her for a light, and then, without so much as a clumsy pass to threaten, he pinned her to the ground, the lit cigarette held an inch from her eye, and raped her soundlessly, then left, walking up the same road, smoking the cigarette.

She had wrapped it up in her head and told no one, in her head and in her belly. According to the notes, she refused all questions as to what occurred after, although a routine medical on arrival had shown evidence of childbirth, a proof she had battled with silence, giving them nothing more, as if her history stopped right there. Only she kept repeating that she stood on the shore, looking out to sea.

Behind the notes was slipped an envelope of drawings in wax crayons; the crayon upset me more than anything else, demeaned her in its childish connotation, a nix on the respect. Amongst the black and red scribbles and blocked-out pages was a picture of a boat with a man and a woman inside, and between them a baby. On the back of this page, written in her cloistered hand, untitled, unexplained by red notes, untouched by jargon, so conclusive, no mind-breakers needed:

'The Devil and Jesus sat with me in a boat. Jesus wept. He wept until his tears coursed as one with what ran from his nose and mouth. And dripping at the chin he made no attempt to wipe himself clean with his white shirt-sleeve, but stayed looking out to the shore. Jesus wore a Timex watch. He was 14.

The Devil wore a man-skirt and a bare-muscle chest, and smoked a brand of tar-thick cigarettes, the kind you can only smoke if you are born with black lungs. His head and his scar shone in the moonlight and the light from his cigarette.

The moon was full, a moon full of red and of the days and nights whose passing it marked. Jesus and the Devil and anyone else on the earth that night saw one bright moon, but I saw nine dark ones, all slotted one inside the other through time. Jesus knew I saw it this way and that is why he wept. He wept for the waste of me, as the Devil sat smiling with his too many teeth and his black eyes.

When his hand grabbed my hair it came away at the root. I thought that now I could maybe escape through the thousand tiny holes he made in my scalp.'

There was something odd about the page, and I realised with wonder that tears were falling onto it, large and wet and mine. There could be no leaving Janie behind, I was water-marked, bonded with her story, a part of the page it was told on. I knew where the boat-boy was to be found, a few lines further on from here.

I locked the summarised lives in their room behind me and followed the signs to the chapel, to ask God for a direction fix, seeing as all others had failed us.

It was a modern chapel of the ilk that comes with an acoustic priest and brown Jesus, sparse and carpeted snugly and smelling of wood and of over-breathed air.

I knelt at the altar-rail, my long khaki Janie skirt severe against the red velvet cushioning, and began to rhyme off a decade of the rosary, frothing prayer bubbles to keep everything protected, just like my sister and I used to do to prevent our father from climbing the stairs to our bedroom to break things. Just under my catching breath, counting off the verses with my sweating fingers for rosary beads.

'Hail Mary, full of grace, the Lord is with thee, blessed art thou amongst women and blessed is the fruit of thy womb, Jesus. Holy Mary, Mother of God, pray for us sinners, now and at the hour of our death, Amen ... Hail Mary, full of grace....'

And over and over until a truth began to dawn.

'... Pray for us sinners, now and at the hour of our death.'

And again it spooled around,

'... now and at the hour of our death.'

I had been dispatched to Central Park that night by Mary, Mother of God, to be with Janie at the hour of her death, but I bailed out on the escort at the final moment. I should have gone with her, gone with her through to the answer, should have asked the boat-boy to bring me to my mother in his boat. Was that God's plan? He's a meddling bastard at the best of times, at once invasive and elusive, a slippery fish. The accepted hypothesis is that God left New York City after being hit on the head with a brick during the Stonewall riots, but I like to think He flies in now and then to torch out a number with his rival, Joey Araris.

Of course, God is quite new and inexperienced — the world used to be run by a plethora of divine omnipotents, but downsizing hit the heavens (now heaven singular, except when its raining and they unbar old territories to reservoir the water) and one does the job of twenty. The Supreme Being gig almost went to a single mother but as she was vastly overqualified they awarded it instead to a thing called God, an amusing invention of some under-esteemed Israeli drag queen, who devised this disapproving Über-Father to give import to her lifestyle, house her doubt in a whole other person, get a little discord going to spice things up. So God is an elaborated wank fantasy for those troubled by creative enjoyment, but I rarely say it out loud, just in case He's tetchy about his humble origins.

These days God has lost the run of Himself entirely, He fucks with me when I sleep. Sometimes, in the middle of the night, I wake up rigid with fear and sweating like a rubber thigh, too afraid to close my eyes, too afraid to keep them open. If I fall back asleep, He commands his angels to take me away for all I have become. They throw me head-long into the dark gorge of history where I land back in medieval times as a prisoner gnawed alive by rats, or in the seventeenth century to be burned as the witch that I am, or in prohibition times where I drink endless lemonade. Sometimes when I'm wakeful, barely nappish, they send me back to the 1960s to be a Georgetown conservative and I think that's worst of all.

Two nights after Janie hung, when no action clamoured from the over-lit street to comfort me with normal, I became convinced that, on falling asleep, He would send me back to be Janie on the hour of her death. The externals I knew about, and I reckoned the inner living of it would mangle me to scrap, so I prayed with all my might; prayer after prayer came straining out of me to all the saints and dark angels and Buddha, that I would not be sent back to live her moment. I prayed for someone to save me from God.

I wonder if that claddagh could give me strength enough to be Janie for real, to meet the moment.

She smiled as she left Happy behind, all goodbyes, no see-you-laters or promises to call. She was instantly transformed once she hit the street, as if she'd been holding back inside, playing normal, now a thrill broke free and she moved along the road in expansive lurches, glancing busily about as if stuck on a highway without wheels rather than walking an almost empty street. The few people that passed would nearly return a smile at her exuberance, then finally look nervously away as she stared into their faces as if looking for a friend behind a heavy disguise. Her euphoria put the fear on them. Absolute bliss is rare enough to be grotesque.

She stumbled, laughing, over every piece of garbage and strewn person she came near, marching oblivious into cars which only missed by a breath, but strangely no one yelled or sounded their horn, so I slipped after her in the delay.

Pitching on forward, she pushed uptown forever. By 45th I was tiring badly, shoes cutting into my feet, but Janie sucked energy from the city, traffic, noise, wires and flashing neon, drawing fuel from the faces that she, smiling, passed. She dragged that dark, heavy coat on her back like an obstinate caveman returning with the spoils of a small hunt, as if its enormous weight were as only the tiniest fraction of what she was capable of carrying, what she carried, being invincible.

On one corner stood a huge and bearded man, seven foot and almost as broad as long, out of his mind on drugs or the city, and he swung his arms about, swimming to stand still, shouting that the day of judgement had arrived. As Janie passed him he loomed in her path and said: 'Young lady, the day is here, it is time young lady, it is time. He died that you may join him forever in the kingdom of Heaven.'

Judy May Murphy

For the last ten blocks I had kept only kitten steps behind her, so I pulled up short to watch her grab him by the hand in thanks.

'I know,' she reassured him. 'I got the messages.'

She seemed to quicken then, and I had to fall back a little so my legs could survive and my coarse breath not give me away. My feet were crippled from the mules, and the tightness of my dress meant I had to take three steps for her every two, and although my sweater was lighter than her coat I felt dragged backward against the contraflowing tide of needing to follow. With no hint as to her destination, with each block I thought that she had to stop soon.

When she got to Central Park, she jumped a side wall, and I watched as she ran at full speed across paths and patches of grass and small hills, with her arms outstretched to each side, like a child playing at glider planes. And laughing all the while.

Who could tell? At the time she just looked like a whole lot of freedom. I followed as best I could, shoes in hand, running now with everything I had. It felt as if my lungs were bleeding inside from the effort. Only something in my head kept me chasing.

When she was almost at the Ramble, I lost her. I stood at the fringes, still and listening for a while, no longer able to hear her running. I waited for a long while, twenty minutes at least, sitting on the ground, waiting for her to come out, sure she would emerge again.

Here would be much better for talking our first proper talk, about my mother and us and everything, just the two of us. It would be just the way you used to meet people when you were little, in a park with nothing to do but play, and you would say, 'Hello, what's your name?' And they would tell you and ask you yours, and it would all be quite simple really, just as it should be, and she would cry and hold me, and then maybe I would cry, too.

Just as it should be.

Except she wasn't coming out.

I now know she had that rope in her pocket while she spoke to her friends in the bar. She had been talking and laughing, and all the while with her weapon close at hand and the time of death not far off, fingering the strap which would stretch from this world to the next. A dead girl, laughing. I am careful of happiness now. I know that from now on I will always look at people who seem wrapped in enjoyment, seem to be normal glad, and look closely for bulges in their coat pockets or any sign behind their eyes that this might be the last time.

From Happy to eternity in around an hour. Any pizza man would be proud of such an achievement.

Finally, thinking I might be missing something, I went inside.

I can't describe the first few moments, I think all my brain got used up in surviving it and none was left for memory or sorting it through. At first, my first remembered moment, I got dizzy and the bile surged and then abated, and my head grew certain, its fogs gusted clear by the fastness of my breath. It was as though it was natural and she was growing into a butterfly inside her long black coat. Then, slowly, my shaking became less severe and my heart-rate calmed to just twice the usual and I found myself walking toward her.

Her feet were eight or so inches off the ground, so I dragged a rock over, and standing on it had to rise up on my toes to reach her head next to mine. Janie's taste was salt from tears, tears which had dried earlier into her face, preserving her sadness. I kissed her mouth, holding my lips against hers long enough for several breaths to pass between us. I soaked up her salt and breathed the last air from her dead body. I felt her hair against my cheek and the weight of her body in my hands as I pulled her slightly away from the tree, still hanging, the rope still tight round her neck. When she became too heavy I let her swing back to where she naturally rested, guiding her back with my arms lest she should hit against the bark. I wanted her to know no hurt again.

Just like my Mommy.

I stayed for maybe fifteen minutes, maybe longer, touching her face, arranging her hair behind her ears, away from her eyes, straightening her legs which hung twisted and turned in. I know I was talking all the while but can't recall what it was I said. It was a cold night so I placed my gloves on her hands to save them from the night chill, not quite managing to fit each finger into its correct place. I don't know why I stayed there instead of running for help. I suppose it didn't feel like an emergency; it felt the very opposite, as if no amount of flapping around would achieve anything. It was slow and simple.

When I first called around to Italian Tony's apartment, I think it was to tell him, but then I didn't, or couldn't, and it all went wrong, and then I really couldn't.

God knew all this already, so I left his place and headed back for the shed where Dec would by now be perfectly fugged for my comfort.

I saw my first sign of life in the corridor just outside, an old lady with pills in her dressing-gown pocket as all proper old ladies have. She looked a little cabbagey so I simply took the medication, and gave her back the bottle so they'd think she swallowed them. Might leave her slightly wobbly, the lack of them, might make her dance naked through the night. Maybe she's a dope fiend and I saved her, maybe I'm one and I just saved me.

'Thank you, nurse,' she said.

I asked her had she any money, knowing it would only go to Gardener Jim otherwise, but she started with this story about how she had millions in a Swiss bank.

'Which Swiss bank?' I asked her.

'The one in Buffalo,' she said.

I told her not to sign any cheques and escaped through the kitchens back to the gardens and the shed which the guys had now left, possibly to fetch the white.

Inside the shed, among the pulleys, chains and fuck knows what other marvellous accessories, whose uses took on sinister vibes considering their home, I found a length of rope. Slightly thinner than Janie's choice, but strong nonetheless. I put it in my bag, just because it pulled me closer, hung the keys where I'd found them, and headed down to the shore to where the two stood hopeless, having fallen deeply silent on my approach, or maybe it was one of Jim's slight pauses.

Gardener Jim was much better at goodbye; goodbye is allowed to be short.

I asked Dec to drop me off at Sammy's, said I wanted some cake but he knew I was lying. He didn't mention the new bag at his feet, which was kind of like lying too.

Doubtless ruminating on the question I'd asked of him earlier, Dec asked, 'Would you ever do that?'

'Killing yourself is not polite,' I told him. 'Not the done thing.'

Janie

*H*er hair is no longer tossed wild by the wind, but ruffled as tufts of small plants are. Powerless against the furious hold churning around her, she stands, breakable as driftwood, on one of the edges that litter New York. She is here on a holiday, she tells herself, a short visit only, and then they will come to collect her home. It has been a while since she left the big house with all its corridors and staff in white, and moved into a new apartment to wait for the coming.

Safe, at a small distance from the raging tides, she now walks her way up and down again; sometimes looking out to the horizon, the sky full of birds that roar overhead, she idles away her last few days here.

She smiles at the locals as they pass on the road, and they sometimes ask her how she is this fine soft day, or something very like.

Every now and then, a local woman holding her baby will pass, and Janie will smile and be pleased for them, feeling the small card in her pocket.

A few weeks before, while still at the big house, down by the lake the gardener said that a card had arrived for her, but that someone had tried to throw it away. She handed him as thanks the ten-dollar bill which had sat in the pocket of her robe since soon after she arrived. He handed her in return a small piece of card, the kind that comes with flowers.

It says, 'TO MY MOTHER'. She reads it again now, standing on this big city street, this card from her son.

Anyone passing might think it was the gentle rain, but Janie is now crying because soon the New York friends will all be dead, and there is nothing she can do to help that.

The next morning she finds the letter she has waited for. A letter to inform her of the boat-boy's coming:

The future is written. He is so close you could almost touch him. In one week you will know.

She cleans her room to leave it tidy for the next guests to arrive. She knows that they will understand that everyone must return to their own home some day, life's summers are always far too short, there and then swiftly gone.

One week to the day, she is looking at her birthday cake which just arrived outside the door. She has no desire to eat it, knowing she has ultimate control. Today she will be born.

She is ready for the endless day that follows this dark night, candy in her pocket, enough for them all for a thousand years. She has bought a new compass to guide them to eternity; he will be so pleased that she remembered. She has a strong rope for the rescue. She pats her pockets to reassure herself of her survival kit.

Outside the bar, end-of-summer-term goodbyes said, she hovers above the footpath as she heads home, the cold air waking her to the thrill. Cars cannot come near her, as they drive off to a place a few miles up the road; people cannot touch her as they go to work the land and the shops. Her heavy coat she leaves behind with each step. On uptown she rushes, finally free of the tide.

A tall, bearded angel has been cut from rock and sent to guide her. 'Young lady,' he says, 'the day is here', and she runs down the final stretch of footpath to the garden wall. She jumps the wall and runs the flowerbeds to where the loved one waits, making tea for them both.

She moves through the air like a bird, she becomes the aeroplane, she is her own breeze gusting to the other lands.

She pulls the rope over a top branch, her body soaked from wading to the source of her happiness. She stands on the lowest branch, rope in a noose around her thin neck, jigging up and down a little on the doorstep of it all.

Dear Me,

No need to worry anymore. Everything is going to be just fine. At last I am getting back to happy.

Love, Me

Judy May Murphy

The Friends

*D*ec had a 'gum or swig?' moment as he held on to see
Aimee safe into Sammy and Fat Molly's building. It struck
him how much she always swung through like in a movie, a
procession of cute little gestures and looks, actions to let slip
whatever her eyes and mouth held closed away. And what a
mouth, such tacks and screws and nails it spat, such cool
patterns her words left.

He settled on the gum, then decided he'd write an anony-
mous letter to the police with enough information that they
could maybe shut the Janie case tight, but not enough that
they could track him down. Next big decision — well, he
wasn't a movie man himself, so handing over the coke with
local rag cameras flashing, and then going to work at an
orphanage wasn't necessary. He'd sell the stuff — might be
enough to enrol for night classes in mechanical engineering.
The idea of that had always appealed, might even give him
reason to cut back on his more fluid social duties.

He then looked to the floor at where Aimee's feet and
coat had been, to reassure himself of the treasure bag.
Couldn't trust her an inch; it was fun.

Right on the floor beside the coke bag was a photograph
which he couldn't remember ever having seen there before. It
must have fallen from the glove compartment with the

notebook. He picked it up and, elbows resting on the steering wheel, held it in both hands and looked at it hard, trying to think why it seemed so familiar. The gum got swallowed as he suddenly realised the photo showed his old family home back in Ireland, a rambling wooden house by the sea.

It had been years since he'd even thought about the place, but now he could picture the conservatory where he and his sister used to play, the kitchen where his father read the paper, and, staring closer, he thought he could see someone standing by the side wall. Now who was that? Must be that retarded kid next door, the one they used to torture with soap slivers wrapped up like candy. His Dad or his sister must have put it there for him; he couldn't remember having seen it before.

That was a fine place, he thought, as he drove away; in fact, things never seemed quite right after they left.

He turned off for home, wondering what Aimee could possibly want with Sammy, hoping she wouldn't give the guy too hard a time; her mind was a scythe to his hay. It was funny how he felt she could see through him. As if he was a normal person. And that was OK, or what was it they used to say as kids? It was grand.

Lucy wasn't used to her own phone ringing, the deal always flowing the other way, and almost didn't pick up.

'Luce? Josh. They busted Italian Tony.'

'For drugs?'

'No, for dancing. Yes, for drugs, and I'm scared to shitting ribs they'll be at my place next. Can you come over and help me get rid of the pot smell? It's even in the curtains.'

'I'm kind of tired Josh, I want to just chill on my own for a while.'

'Oh, OK.'

He hung up and called his mom, asked would she come into the city to help with a weird smell he'd just noticed, probably dry rot. Called Lucy back to see if she was all right.

Fat Molly stood, half comfort-wrapped by the curtain, hating a salad she'd just shaved into a soup cup, growling at the traffic that rolled by her window. Not in the mood for Aimee or anything or anyone or especially Aimee. Everyone acted so fucking tough, so at ease, as if shadows didn't register in their eyes except if they actually existed. She left the window, dropping the salad which began to pick up carpet calories, and ran past Sammy and Aimee to her room.

They found her sobbing into her blind old teddy bear.

'What?' demanded Aimee, new to the sympathy thing. She presumed someone had insulted the meringue.

'I can't tell you,' she sobbed and then immediately did: 'I think I killed Janie. Remember I told you about the throwing up thing, when she cut off her hair? Well, I made her do it, I left out all these cream cakes and I knew she wouldn't be able to handle it. You see,' she continued as if explaining math to kids: 'If you left a vast amount of cake sitting with her name on it, Janie would lose it, fall apart like a snowflake when she couldn't check her need, you know? So, on the morning of the day she died, I thought if I left her a cake, then she'd have to go back to the hospital. I didn't....'

There was about two more minutes' worth but it was drowned in Fat Molly's weepy gasps. Aimee thought to maybe leave her in it, splashing around like the inept she was, but something, maybe if only a sore ear, made her deliver. Remembering what she'd seen in Janie's fridge, Aimee threw a thin little rescue line, like you would to a sinking enemy.

'If it was a yellow birthday cake, it didn't bother Janie much; she gave it to me because she knew I liked yellow. And birthdays.'

'And cake,' said Sammy helpfully.

'Yeah.'

Against the plan, Fat Molly started sobbing even louder. 'You see!' she wailed. 'I can't even kill someone I hate. You hear about six-year-old kids who manage to waste their siblings and classmates. I'm such a fucking failure.'

'Yeah,' said Aimee, without needing to gear up to any civility, 'but at least you did it — you pulled the trigger, so to speak. You proved it to yourself. You won.'

This was over Sammy's head, he was stuck a few sentences back.

'Did you say you hated Janie?' he shed the question simply. 'I thought you guys were best friends?'

'Women don't have best friends, only girls they keep closer tabs on.' Casting glib asides was like blinking to Aimee.

'Oh.'

Fat Molly wiped her eyes on the back of her hand, things were looking brighter. 'And at least I didn't steal the body,' she sniffed. 'I mean, I'm not some kind of sicko. And you know,' she brightened further, 'if you ask me, Janie could never have killed another person, she was just too weak, that's why she killed herself. You have to feel quite sorry for her, really.'

Fat Molly's sense of right and wrong was so completely subjective that her mind could be changed on the most serious of issues with hard ethical argument along the lines of, 'but I love you'. Virtue was a seasonal thing.

Aimee felt strange sitting there with her hand on someone else's shoulder for non-sexual and non-drunkard reasons, sitting there with so much to say that could cuff Fat Molly straight back into the forest of fear. But she had blunted her axe, perhaps with her own earlier tears; it did all feel a tad bizarre but not too bad, like sex with a wooden condom.

Sammy was confused again; he'd always lived life straight-line, and was gradually grasping that the rest of the world was curved. Perspective is a brain jam, a deceptive little whore, as, often, something presumed to be faraway and colossal is discovered to be closer by and tiny all the while. The geometry of life was fucking Sammy deeper up his outlook, as everything receded into the foreground, confusing him beyond his average despair.

Fat Molly reapplied her make-up and decided Aimee wasn't so bad after all. The hostess in her came alive and she nipped out to Happy for a bottle of vodka, gamely leaving her den full of live quarry, and her gone.

In case Sammy wasn't feeling like enough of a spare straw, Aimee (crowbarring him into opening up and admitting to what she had seen) detailed an article she'd read that day about the stolen picture and how it said that the woman in the stolen picture was the artist, Cindy Sherman. Except Cindy didn't resemble herself in the slightest (no, that would be too easy) — she'd transmute, with every picture, beyond recognition.

So, Sammy thought, if the look didn't tally with the person it really was, how could he have deluded himself that it looked like Janie Kelly, simply because he needed it to?

Through the mist he was squinting at a certainty, a realisation that an image couldn't cough up the poorest of truths, no matter what guise it arrived in to sucker you sweet. He'd bet his last line that not one could even scratch accurate, that it was beyond the best of any picture to deliver life back to him, to hand him his existence in some steely, discernible frame.

Aimee, too, was rethinking its importance, wondering how a picture could strive for anything at all when the mind's eye twists and wrenches everything to fuck. The complexity would lurk, the hidden web and snare behind the simple view.

They figured out how to make coffee and sat down at the kitchen table to drink it.

'You thinking of sticking around, or is fame a-panting back west?'

'I don't think I'll be going anywhere for a while. I'm handing myself over to the police.'

'On account of the picture?'

He wasn't surprised, he kind of expected her to know. 'I think I went a little nuts when I heard she died,' he handed her as explanation.

'You might want your defence team to phrase that more succinctly.' Her cynicism then dampened to a merely apathetic, 'Think about it, Sammy, look along the line, chaffing irons, warped screws, haemorrhoidal cops who'd rather be watching the game, any game, lawyers who start the expense clock if you so much as cough in the same city as them, buying a suit specially so you can stand in it while they tell you your mother isn't proud — is all this sounding OK? Think about it, seven odd years in a breeze-block room with a poten-tial smack habit your only viable ambition apart from learning how to read again from bleeding-heart college girls with glasses and kilts. That's a pretty big decision you got there.'

'Exactly,' he said. 'It's a decision. I don't want to hang out here like a spare piece of pie, wondering if and when they'll come, waiting for someone else to tell.'

'Maybe they'll count Hollywood as time already served.'

'Anyway, I don't think I'll be confessing to the real crime.'

'What, did you kill her with a cream cake too?'

The moth was pushing to light his own flame.

'I did kill Janie. She said if I left her, she'd kill herself.'

'For fuck's sake, Sammy, everyone says that, it's just another way of phrasing "please don't go".'

Just then Fat Molly phoned from Happy to say she'd met some people and would they like to join them. 'In a while,' Aimee said.

'I didn't take the body, though,' Sammy said when she'd hung up, 'but I wish I had, wish I'd thought of it first.' He was sure that, of anyone in the world, Aimee would have the answer to that puzzle, 'Do you know where her body is?'

'No, I don't.' Which is true when the vastness of the oceans is taken into account.

Maybe, thought Sammy, I did and didn't kill her; the truth and the untruth, the real and the unreal Janie — they don't exist anywhere. Maybe no one knew, not just him. Perhaps people were just standing in their ignorance with a more confident air.

Aimee

God, such a fuss and nothing different at the end of all that dancing. Same dead girl, same corpse making protein of the ocean. I didn't want the picture as much as I did the day before, I don't know why except sort of.

I asked him if I could see it anyway.

It was a bit of an anti-climax, but then most things are. If Janie chose to walk in the door that second we'd probably have been a little disappointed with that too.

'I used to love to sketch in charcoal,' Sammy was saying, twisting a pencil in his fingers like a fine cigar. 'They'd let me do it in class instead of the lessons. I was really good.'

We decided to repaint it. If he was going for the insanity plea it wouldn't make much difference, might even help. Sitting at the kitchen table with all the paints, knives, and memories of the last few days spread around us, we set to our de-composition. But where to start? The oil paints were wrong, said too much, too much of what didn't want saying.

'And what colour was Janie anyway?' I mused.

'Janie was whatever colour you painted her,' said Sammy.

Good fuck — could be some action waking in that dusty little head.

Without saying it aloud, it was like we suddenly understood that the Janie we now needed was a flagrant nothing, a screech-clean slate, an enormous void to breathe in. Maybe that's what she had been at the start.

Sammy found a half-parched tin of white emulsion from the cabinet below the kitchen sink. I scooped out a fistful and let it leak over the canvas, smearing it with my fingers, painting over the stolen image, breathing deep and fast as the picture gradually disappeared under my hand, stroked away. Until there she was. Nothing. The canvas was empty, and Sammy was smiling through wet eyes.

Going to wash my hands, I caught a look at myself in the bathroom mirror. I wasn't too surprised to find myself there. I think I'd like to dye my hair pink, that would be cute.

'I found some drugs in the bathroom, you wanna smoke?'

'That's my Asian cold and flu infusion.'

'We could smoke it anyway.' But neither of us had papers. 'By the way,' I laughed as I remembered, 'on your mobile phone the message says, "Sorry I'm not home right now."'

'Yeah?'

'Well it's a portable, so ... never mind.'

Sammy definitely lived in an easier place.

'Why were you guys together?' I asked, fixing some more coffee and planning the next move on the picture.

'Janie used to tell me stories. I don't really remember them, they all sounded kind of the same, about ... I don't know, trees and stuff.'

'Boys and girls and beaches?'

'Yeah, that kind of thing. I think maybe she wanted to be a children's writer or something. They weren't all that interesting but it kind of reminded me of when my parents used to tell me bedtime stories. I could never follow their

stories but it was kind of like a tune, especially if they told the
same one over and over. That was why I spent nights with
her. The days were about me thinking I should be dating
someone who was also into acting, you know, like um...'

'Bogart and Bacall?'

'Who?'

Yeah, he wouldn't have interrupted any dreaming. Some
men were rich or interesting lives you could step into,
Sammy was a fluffy white cloud.

'So, Sammy, what do you want to add to the picture?'

'I just want to kiss it goodbye.'

Perfect, he should kiss it with a red mouth to stick, to
mark it with goodbye so he could turn then to his house
with good leave taken. But purple and green paints would
not mix to red. Knocking through Fat Molly's make-up
shelf I could only find cruel, black reds, but such a doing
compelled a blood-red mouth, life rilling through, to lay
open the coincident smudge, the laden blush of it.

'We need a blood red,' I said.

Blood red, and he knew what was his to do. Taking up
the unwashed carving knife he steeled himself to the task,
placed the knife against his mouth and, with one hard slice,
rent open his bottom lip from side to side with a clean, deep
cut. His blood spilling from the gash, pouring down his chin
and dripping onto his hand, he bent over the creation and
kissed it full on the mystery of Janie, staining it the real red,
closing it in blood.

He sucked on his lip, swallowing down the tincture he'd
freed, tasting the white paint that now stuck to the uncut
parts of his mouth and skin around it.

We had it now, no graven Pygmalion image, but permission to continue on without her. New masters of our
own walk, no one sitting on our shoulders pointing us in
wrong directions.

The wrought void lay before us, a slight high steaming
from the paint fumes, tasting dry with the coffee, words
away for once. I looked in my bag for a Janie photo I'd
taken from the box to give to Sammy, but I must have left it
at home by mistake. We sat in silence, looking ahead. The
lip wound was still pumping like sex, though more quietly
than before, old sex.

Destiny, death, alcohol, all discounted now. Janie had
become everything just because she showed nothing; such a
monumental nothing comes full circle when pushed by a
need, it becomes the totality, a blank on which the world
will project its sordid need. Janie was the sublime. The
cancelled, empty canvas, the inexpressible, the unknowable
in the primed mind, the horror of the vastness of eternity,
the punishment of God's heaven. Janie was all and nothing
depending on how you were looking at a half-glass of wine
that day, she was a handy enough place to put your trouble.

I could ask him for the claddagh or get him wasted and
then steal it, or both. Just as I decided something complex
along the lines of faking a fit and sending him out for help,
he handed it to me.

'I'll see she gets it,' I said, which made him smile.

Might go down to Happy, meet these new people of Fat
Molly's. I feel connected to people right now, which is
strange seeing as how my borders are back, how the line
around me is drawn, not smudged. All the time I thought I

was steel, I was, in fact, graphite — firm in only one direction, in other ways flaky enough to rub off into a million words, shedding, wearing myself away.

'Later, Sammy.'

'It's Howard, really.'

'OK, Howard.'

'See you, Aimee.'

Yeah, it's Aimee really. First I'm going to drop into my apartment and call my sister, say 'hi' to her and the kids and the business-husband, and then my Dad to say whatever won't piss him off too badly. I might move back home for a while, just to work out what I really want to do. The tears thing starts with me once again as I walk down the road, holding my new, little golden heart.